SHADOWBOUND

KATHLENA L. CONTRERAS

Flying Tiger Press
flyingtigerpress.com

Cover by Streetlight Graphics
streetlightgraphics.com

ACKNOWLEDGEMENTS

This story wanted to write itself, but that doesn't mean it didn't have a lot of help to become what you read. First, for their enthusiasm, support, and excellent suggestions, Dave Poyer and Lenore Hart. They're both such great writers, and helped me make this a much better book. My husband, Bob, and my dad, who I can always count on to be in my corner. My critique partners Laura and Lara LaVonne, who were patient enough to go along with me while I found my way. Last but not least, to Ursula K. LeGuin and Victoria Strauss for making me ask, "What if?"

Prologue

"How much do you want for the girl?" A man's voice, low and compelling, spoke from the main room of the house.

Jen froze in the doorway of her room, then retreated. Familiar close darkness enfolded her, full of the scents of onions and apples and stone, the dry, earthy smell of potatoes, the moldy smell of cheese in its rind. Two backward steps and her calves bumped her cot. It creaked and scooted on the earthen floor. She jumped as if an unseen intruder had breathed on her neck. There was no one, but in this room, in the dark, she always felt there was.

The room was too small to hope to hide in—little more than a closet holding close its sacks and barrels and shelves, and her cot. Dug, stone by stone, out of the hulking mass of the City Wall, the room offered no exit other than the curtained doorway.

Jen cursed under her breath, rancid curses learned from years on the City streets. She did not know the voice, but the man must be the same she'd seen in the marketplace.

Surely her father would turn him out, would lie and say that all his daughters were grown and gone. Jen might be only a girl, but she brought in *money*. Every day she brought in coppers and ivories, and bags of fruit, sometimes even a fowl or a basket of eggs.

That was why she went to the marketplaces and the squares, to be valuable, so her father would never think of

selling her. To be sold like her sister—to become a possession, like a cookpot or a hen... The thought made her sick
and frantic.

She heard the man's quiet cultured voice, then her father's replies, crass and uncouth by comparison. Heard
numbers spoken, *fifteen, twenty-seven, thirty-three.*

Jen's heart thumped, quick like that of a hunted thing.
She held her breath and darted across the shadowed hallway to her brothers' room.

Rik was up, peering around a fold of his own door
curtain. Col was in bed, sleeping or pretending to sleep.
Jen grabbed Rik in passing, jerked him away from the
doorway.

"Who's that man?" Rik hissed, glaring as if she were
responsible for the intruder's presence. Rik was twelve and
thought himself nearly a man.

She had no time to waste on questions. She was still
dressed in the knee-length breeches and vest and oversized
shirt that let her pass for a boy on the city streets. No one
would notice another boy roaming the streets after dark.

"Boost me," she whispered, heading straight for the
tiny window on the opposite wall.

Rik folded his arms. "You know who he is." With his
dark blond hair sticking up in tufts and angles, he looked
like an irritated porcupine. "Tell me."

Rik would do nothing until she answered. He was a
boy, accustomed to getting what he wanted.

"I dunno who he is," she said. "I seen him at the back
of the crowd at market today, watching."

And she had sensed someone hunting her through the
labyrinthine streets all the way home. The tricks she'd
thrown in his way should've thrown him off the scent.
Obviously, they hadn't.

"What'd you do?" Rik demanded. "You did the big stuff, huh? Threw lights and fire. Disappeared. Somebody called you a street-corner witch, and you had to prove 'em wrong."

Col had one open eye above his blanket now, and it rolled from his brother to Jen. Ignoring Rik's accusations, she made a wiggling motion with her fingers, pretending to cast a spell, and the eye disappeared.

"I didn't. Only little stuff. Birds out of my sleeves. A mouse from under a man's hat."

And the usual, reading stones and bones and palms, twisting willow sticks into baby amulets. Nothing big, she knew better than that.

"You gonna boost me, or do I gotta drag a barrel over from my room?"

"No," Rik said with a jeering grin. "Just disappear. I seen you do it before."

"In here, you dizzard? It's too small! They'd just have to stick out their hands to find me!"

Rik only stared with that lopsided grin.

The blanket on Col's cot burst open like a seed pod. A thin boy emerged, with big brown eyes and curls as untidy as Jen's own. Without glancing at his older brother, Col hurried to her, bent on one knee and laced his fingers.

"Quick, Jen," he whispered. "Don't come back to-night."

She hugged her youngest brother quickly and planted a bare foot in his palms. "Not tonight," she agreed. "Maybe not for a couple days."

She grabbed the splintery window frame. Col strained, she heaved and worked head and shoulders out.

Col whispered, pushing at her, "I'll put the red stone by the door if it's safe—"

He stopped speaking. A hand caught hold of Jen's belt and pulled her back. Splinters raked her belly. The window frame rapped her head.

"Gently, gently," a deep voice said as she landed in a heap against the wall.

Her father stood over her, thin face bunched in fury, lank blond hair messier than usual. Behind him stood the man she'd seen in the marketplace, although then, from a distance, she'd only been able to make out fine clothes and dark hair. Now she saw that hair, interspersed with threads of iron grey, fell in thick waves to his shoulders, and that his face was stern and lined.

Storm-grey eyes took her in whole, gave her own image back: thin wiry frame that could pass as a boy's, an exuberance of short curls the color of well-steeped tea, eyes the same color. They gave her away, large in a small pale face. Sheepdog eyes, her older brothers had said, laughing.

Jen blinked and shook her head, found herself looking out of her own eyes again. Her father was cursing her, drawing back a hand to strike. Jen glared at him. His hand hung upraised, threatening, then fell and jammed into the waistband of his dirty breeches.

Once, he would've struck her for the look alone. Not now. Now, he only cursed again and spat a glob of phlegmy spittle that spattered on the dirt floor by her hand.

Rik made a sound that might've been an uneasy snicker. Their father whirled and descended upon him in a fury of slaps and curses.

Jen stiffened and drew breath for an angry shout, but the stranger spoke, as if only she were in the room. As if father and brothers were only a mummer's show.

"Go get your things, girl," he said quietly.

Jen went cold all over.

She couldn't have gotten up, but Col came and tugged at her. "C'mon, Jen. C'mon."

Somehow, she gained her feet. Her brothers' room was full of smells: unwashed clothes, her father's beery reek, a faint, smoky herbal scent that was new, that came from the stranger. Blank and numb, Jen let Col's tugging hand pull her around the men and out.

She threw a glance at the dark tallow lamp on a barrel and flame sprang awake in it, throwing more shadow than light in the stone closet that was her room. She did not like to look at the shadows, so she looked instead at the shelf with her few belongings. Not much, not much to take.

Shaking, her hands moved to pile things on her blanket. Her single change of clothes, the battered, carved box that held her stones and bones and the few small treasures that had come her way over the three years she'd worked the markets and squares. Col sniffled and touched them: a chunk of purple quartz, an enameled brooch in blue and green, a tiny face carved of ivory with closed eyes. Of all of them, she most treasured the last. She took it out.

The ivory face on its length of twine rested in her palm, small and serene, a talisman of protection. While she was awake, its eyes were closed and it slept in her treasure box. But at night, she took it out and put it around her neck. It opened its eyes then, guarding so she could sleep.

She put the face back into its box, bundled the box into the blanket; all she owned.

Col's eyes glittered in the light of the little lamp. Jen hesitated, biting her lip, then unwrapped the blanket again.

"Here." She held the ivory face out to him. "Give it to Ma for me. Tell her—" She stared down at the carving. "Tell her to wear it for— For good dreams. Promise."

"I promise," Col whispered.

He stared down at the little face, then snatched it, darting out of Jen's room like an escaping wild thing. The curtain swayed in his wake. After a moment, a hand appeared, long and fine, and moved the curtain aside. The stranger ducked under the doorframe, taller than she'd realized.

Crouched on her cot, clutching her small bundle of possessions to her, Jen looked up at him, too numb even for fear. He looked down on her too, distantly, like a cat.

At last, he held out his hand, clean, uncallused, graceful. "Come."

To her dismay, Jen saw one hand untangle itself from her bundle and settle in his. Cool and strong, his fingers closed around hers. He drew her to her feet and through the door curtain.

The house she'd lived in all the fifteen years of her life looked like the rooms on street painters' canvasses, scenes picked out in light and shadow. The main room opened in a dull orange glare of firelight. The rickety table and stools, the dirty straw on the floor, the crumbling daub of the walls all seemed suddenly dear.

But Jen's father sat wide-legged on one of the stools, hands braced on knees. He stared at her a moment, then turned away. Her mother sat near the fire with her sewing in her lap, bent low to see in the poor light. Her hands shook over jagged stitches. Jen wanted to go to her, to put her arms around her mother's neck as she hadn't done since she was small, but the stranger drew her on.

So had her mother borne her other children leaving. The two oldest boys vanished to do whatever boys did when they were grown: join the soldiery or the crew of a ship or a gang of highwaymen. One girl sold—the man had said for guild labor; the other, the prettiest, with her broad hips and hair like a spill of honey down her back, gone to be the wife of a householder—a great triumph.

Their mother had kissed that daughter goodbye. Jen, sold like a heifer at market, like Dee, her next-oldest sister, would get no kisses.

But Jen had something the rest did not, what she used to make money. She gave a tiny smile as the stranger pulled the latch and opened the door, bringing her out onto the street, into the night.

She could throw a light that would blind him. She could hide behind illusion. Rik knew because she'd showed him, and her older brothers, too, boasting in the face of their boys' arrogance. She would do those things, and this man would find his fine, cool fingers full of fire or spitting cat. Then she'd find a place to live where she could keep the money for herself. And perhaps, sleep without fear.

The man led on, a pillar of shadow, a brush of brocade robe against her arm. In the dark, her mind danced like the sun on water and magic glanced, gathering.

Suddenly, it seemed that sun sank into twilight. Something dimmed and stilled her thoughts.

Dreamlike, City streets unrolled before her: houses, lights and people, snorting horses, carriages clattering over stones. She seemed to drift among these things, though she could not say by what means. A gate rose before her, very tall, all curves and scrolls of wrought iron. Beyond it lay gardens, and a tall door carved with vines. She came to herself with a jolt.

The man was leading her across rugs in sea hues, across marble floors, cool under her bare dirty feet. Rich wood paneling and shimmering tapestries covered the walls; flames winked like watching eyes in lamps of brass and blown glass. Somehow she had slipped from the real world of stinking alleys and ragged clothes, and into some opulent Otherworld.

Another tall door opened and the stranger drew her into a single room larger than her whole house. Fear stirred like a sleeping animal, twitching, but she sank into the chair to which he guided her. He sat in the chair opposite and took her other hand.

She would have jerked away, but the impulse died like an ember beneath a smothering blanket. Her heart battered at her ribs, fighting to push its way up her throat, but a strange calm swaddled her. Distantly, she felt a chill sweat crawl across her skin.

The man's dark eyes seethed with lights that had no outside source. The rich rugs, the soft chair, the hissing lamp-flames, all faded. Only those eyes, flashing with uncanny lightning, and the sensation of his fingers encircling hers, remained.

The whirlpool of his will drew her down, engulfed her. Jen struggled once, too late, then drowned in a flood of images.

The images were from her own life, the thoughts her own. They streamed across the curtain of her mind like a magic lantern show, accompanied by the symphony of thoughts and emotions. But a gaze watched over her shoulder, a murmuring purl of thought not her own spilled into her mind. She tried to wrench her inner eye around, to confront the watcher, but could not. Her mind's eye, unlidded, stared helplessly at the swarming images.

Coppers dropped into a child's dirty, upheld hand; games of sticks and stones played with brothers and sisters; pears and poultry stolen in clamorous markets. These shifted to darker scenes: gangs of jeering toughs, shopkeepers wielding sticks. As if she were dragged down into deep water, the darkness grew. She heard drunken cursing. A woman screaming. Panicking, she fought that darkness, knowing what lay at the bottom, in the oozing muck that invaded her dreams. Inexorable, the unseen watcher still watched.

Abruptly, she ceased her struggles and tried to blind those invading eyes with the blaze of her own powers. She filled her thoughts with fire. Fire lit darkness, repelled what struck in the night. She refused to turn to the memory that hunched, slavering, in the basement of her mind. The watcher could never see it. She could never bear that.

Jen fell against the cushioned back of the chair, her breath coming as fast as her heartbeat. The man still held her, gaze and hands, then the air around him seemed to shimmer, like heat rising from an oven. She must tear her hands from his grasp. Must flee, now, while she still could.

The shimmer expanded to envelop her.

She would've screamed, would have bitten and clawed, but could only sit in the chair, shivering, while that terrible shimmer permeated her. Her skin tingled as if with the forerunners of a lightning strike. That tingle measured her, then sank through to her very core.

Within, something changed. A power enclosed the flame that was her soul. A mind infiltrated hers with the delicacy and inescapability of air.

Terror broke free at last. With a wrench of will and muscle, she flung herself to her feet—

—and found herself in another room. She froze in fright and confusion.

The man was there too. "You will stay here," he said, gesturing.

She turned as if he'd set a hand on her shoulder and turned her. Rugs of deepest blue patterned with blood-red covered a floor of polished wood. Drapes of the same colors fell from ceiling-height. Upholstered chairs and footstools, painted wardrobes and a high bed piled with pillows filled the space. In one corner, by the marble hearth, a copper tub sat steaming.

She couldn't breathe. Her hands and face felt cold, cold with the realization of her bondage, cold with fear of what awaited her.

"Wash," the man said. "Then dress and come downstairs. I'll be waiting."

The door clicked closed behind him. She sank down where she was, on the fine carpets of midnight and flame.

Chapter 1

Jen's washstand creaked as she worked pestle in mortar, pounding gallalan leaves for a fertility potion. A sharp, feral scent made her head spin. She wrinkled her nose. Dull, petty magic, little better than witch's charms, but simple enough she could do here, in her room. Her refuge, the one place in the house her master never came. Not since that first night five years ago, when he'd brought her here.

Jen.

She flinched at her master's voice, unable to escape the deep, compelling whisper within her head. No magic of hers could bar it. She'd tried. Just as she'd tried to break the binding that held her here.

Now, her heart fluttered in her throat, odd for nothing more dreadful than a summons.

Then she heard it, the difference: her name. In all the years she'd been with him, he had never called her that. Only *girl*, always, from that first night in her father's house.

Her hand shook, and pestle clinked against mortar. *Yes*, she replied.

Mind-voices couldn't quaver, but she dreaded what shade of emotion hers might carry.

Come, her master commanded. *I wish to speak with you.*

Straightening shirt sleeves, smoothing boy's breeches, she cast out her senses to find him, then rose to obey.

Even now, in her master's house, where all knew she wasn't a boy, she hadn't been able to bring herself to relinquish the disguise. The fine dresses in her wardrobe, the necklaces and earrings in her dressing table drawers gathered dust until some servant came in and took them away to replace them with what was currently in style. Her master said nothing of it, but always there were new dresses.

Jen hurried past the wardrobe, more ominous and suggestive today than it ever had been. Closing her door upon it, she paced the hall with its multitude of closed doors, past the staircase leading down to the parlor, the dining room, the kitchen. Another stairway, one that led up, lay at the end of the hallway, dimmer, narrower than the stair that led down. She'd stood at its foot many times, looking up, but had never climbed it. Had never been allowed to climb it.

There had been many such places in the house when she'd first come: doors that opened onto darkness, stairs that ended in midair, rooms that seemed lined with watching eyes. The gate that opened onto the outside world had frustrated every attempt at escape. No matter how high she had climbed, it was higher; no matter how tightly she squeezed between the bars, they closed tighter.

So had the house thwarted her. Even now, when her movements were much freer, she felt the house watching as she approached the stair at the end of the hall, felt its ponderous deliberation as she stopped at the bottom.

She put a booted foot on the lowest step. Air sighed past her, the house's scenting breath. She took one step, put a foot on the next and climbed on, up the coil of stairs.

Windows passed in amber circles of bullseye glass that angled shafts of honey-colored light on stairs or wall. Jen counted windows, wondering if the house would make her climb until she gave up. It didn't. She came to a landing a little wider than the door that gave onto it. Slowly, as if under water, she opened the door.

A small, round chamber met her gaze. Lining the walls were shelves crammed floor to ceiling with books, and tall point-arched windows whose diamond-paned casements had been flung open to the evening air. Rugs patterned in black and forest green lay beneath her feet. And in one of a pair of dark green upholstered chairs sat her master.

Jen bowed her head. "Lord."

His stern lips twitched in the merest flicker of a smile. He beckoned. She took a single step nearer, no more. At his gesture, she eased into the other chair. It tried to swallow her, drawing her down into its soft cushions. Repressing an impulse to start to her feet again, she pulled herself forward until she perched on the edge.

Her master watched her, then said, "You must call me Barras."

The hair on her neck prickled as if at a cold touch in the night. "Yes, Lord Barras," she said, a small elusion, a small insistence of distance. Again, his smile flickered, but he only turned to the low table crouched on bowed legs between them. A cut glass decanter of wine and two glasses waited there. *Two* glasses. Her heart sped.

Her master poured wine and slid one glass toward her, an unprecedented cordiality. The glass glinted with ruby and garnet. At last she leaned forward, took it up. The wine sloshed; Jen steadied her betraying hand.

"So, Arajenei," he said, "you wish to begin your masterwork."

Her heart jumped. First *Jen*, now *Arajenei*. The name her mother had given her at birth, and unused since.

"Yes."

He spoke of her masterwork as if she had spoken of it first. She hadn't, only brooded in her high bed at night, alone with the moon and stars and the sentient breathing of the house. As he had known her name, so it seemed he knew her dreams, as well. She fought the impulse to rub her arms.

"How old are you now?" he said.

Her heart beat faster, and she swallowed once. "Twenty."

"Already."

His face was the same as she had first seen five years ago. The lines between the brows, those bracketing the mouth were the same, neither more nor deeper, the iron grey threads in the thick wavy dark hair no more numerous. But his gaze, ordinarily distant, fell upon her now with new interest that made her shrivel within herself.

"Five years my apprentice, and now ready to fly?"

She'd never been able to read him, and could not tell now whether she heard mockery or challenge.

"Yes," she said again.

Unbidden, a thought slipped out: *ready to fly free*. Not a dream, but a hunger: freedom from the binding she could neither break nor escape. And with that freedom, safety.

He sipped wine. "There are all sorts of freedom," he said, with insight—or intrusion—that by now Jen only resented. "You are young. You'll find some bindings much more profound, much more difficult to break, than others."

"But—" She closed her mouth on the rest.

"But," her master prompted.

In the face of his gentleness, it burst forth in a rush, a noisome sticky stew long lidded and seething. "But why did you have to bind me? In the slums, I learned from the sorcerers and witches. I would've learned from you, too. But I can't bear—"

She gulped down words, gazed into her wineglass, still full. No. She wouldn't tell him that, the terrible dread of being so completely in another's power.

He made no argument. He never did, his silence an implacable wall to her vain flutter.

"What would you do?" he inquired then.

"I thought I might open a gateway to one of the Otherworlds." Her voice came out breathless.

When she'd read not long ago of the Otherworlds, Jen knew she'd found, at last, a means of escape. An Otherworld might take her beyond her master's reach. And if he thought the conjuring of a gateway to an Otherworld was no more than her masterwork—

His dark brows drew down. Jen stopped the thought, unwilling to reveal her scheme to his wizard's sensitivity.

He only made a dismissive gesture. "I should think there are challenges enough in this world. Should you fail, I have no wish to lose the time and training I've invested."

He said nothing of the money he'd paid. Never that.

"I won't fail."

Again, that smile like a candleflame. "Journeyman wizard, seeking your fortune."

He drained the remainder of his wine and rose. He paused by her chair, raised a hand as if to stroke her cheek. Her muscles wound tight, and she held her breath. For a moment, she felt the butterfly-wing tremor of his power upon her skin. The sensation faded, and his hand fell once more to his side.

"Let your hair grow, Jen," he said softly, stepped into shadow and disappeared.

She sat frozen in the devouring chair for a moment more, then gulped down her wine. He'd asked how old she was. Told her to grow her hair. And now called her *Jen*.

She closed her eyes and shivered.

お

Last night's meeting with her master lay heavy on her, like a bad dream. Jen found work she could do in her room, but every sound made her jerk her head up, listening like hunted thing. She cursed herself for hiding as she had when her master had first brought her to his house. She was no longer a child to cringe and cower. She pushed away from her worktable and paced, from door to window and back again.

She stopped, head tilted, breath held. Running foot-steps echoed through the house, and the call of a page boy. The sound of raised voices came from outside. Jen crossed to the window. She stood to one side and cracked open the casement so she could see the front gate.

The voices immediately became louder, angry, demanding. She couldn't make out words, and could see little more than the top of a carriage, the backs of four horses and the foreshortened figures of men dressed in blazing red.

Something out of the ordinary was going on. Something to do with her master's changed behavior? Jen bit her lip and hesitated, then came to a decision.

She stripped off her leather apron and hung it on a peg, rolled down her sleeves and donned a short jacket of black-trimmed burgundy. From another peg, she caught up a cap of black velvet and perched it on her curls. She stood, willed herself outside and was there.

Alannan, lord and ruler of the servants as their master was lord and ruler of the house, stood inside the gate, arguing with a man outside. Jen stepped up beside him. He started, halting mid-sentence. The man on the outside, dressed all in red with the Prince's insignia of a snarling boar on his breast, weighed down by gold braid, stood with his mouth open. When Jen looked at him, he shut it with a snap.

"What's going on here?" She put an authoritative ring in her voice, though without her master's instructions, she was hardly in any position of authority.

The man—a soldier, she presumed—scowled and opened his mouth again.

Alannan interjected smoothly, "This gentleman requests audience with our lord, who, as I have explained, is engaged at this moment. He brings gifts from the Prince, and a petition."

More curious than ever, Jen made a show of looking the soldier up and down. His face turned nearly as red as his uniform. She craned her neck, examining the fine red horses standing quietly before the red lacquered cart covered with red cloth.

"All of this?" she drawled. "The soldiers, too?"

Alannan put a well-tended hand over his mouth and coughed.

The soldier, redder than ever, demanded, "Who are you?"

She smiled her own version of her master's flickering candleflame smile. "I'm Jen. Apprentice to Lord Barras."

"You're only a boy!" The soldier laughed. So did the two on the driver's seat. The first said, sneering, "I'm charged to see the master. I have no use for the apprentice."

Jen gave him a cold, tiny smile no ordinary mortal would wish to see on a wizard's face. She was no wizard— yet. But the soldiers' laughter withered.

"Is that so," she replied. She might have said more, but more was often too much. She'd learned that, too, from her master.

The soldier at the gate shifted uneasily. The men behind him shifted on the seat of the cart. Even the four horses raised their heads and rolled their eyes.

"Yes, well, I-I-I," the soldier stammered, then closed his mouth and swallowed. "But my Prince..." he began again. Any other words he might have spoken seemed to dry on his tongue.

Jen pitied him, but, Prince's envoy or not, she'd have his respect.

"You seem to have this well in hand," Alannan murmured with a nod and took himself back to the house.

Jen transferred herself outside the gate, rematerializing by soldiers and cart. The soldier on the driver's seat drew his saber with an ominous hiss partway from the sheath. She glanced at him. He wet his lips and slid the blade back again.

"Give me a token," she said, turning to the first soldier again. "And your message. I'll take them to my master. I don't promise he'll accept either one."

He stood over her, bigger, stronger, armed, but she only folded her arms. At last he turned in a whirl of short cloak and busied himself at the cart. He returned, bearing a box of mother-of-pearl bound with brass and opened it. Within lay a necklace of silver with cabochon stones of moonstone and amethyst; Jen, who never wore jewelry, reached out a finger to touch it.

The soldier neither snatched away the box nor snapped it shut. "My Prince wishes the honor of an interview with your master. He has proposals he desires to put to him personally. My Prince sends this gift and others in the cart as tokens of goodwill."

Gently, Jen reached up and closed the box's lid on the lovely necklace, shutting it out of sight.

"I will tell my master," she said, and sent her thoughts searching the house for him.

"Wait." The soldier held out the box to her.

Surprised, not expecting someone would give such a thing into her hands, she nevertheless took it. Nodding once to the soldier, she sent herself inside again.

She materialized on the landing outside her master's private study, immersed in the sea-green light.

"Come," her master's voice said and she took a step through the door.

Books lay everywhere, stacked on the floor, on the unoccupied chair, covering the small bowlegged table, open on the windowsills. Her master perched on the edge of a chair, an open book on one knee.

His gaze flicked to the box she clutched, then back to her face. "Yes?"

Her heart beat foolishly fast. She drew breath and repeated the message, adding, "I said I would tell you. It seemed courteous. And they are, after all, from the Prince."

His candleflame smile came and went. "Courteous," he repeated. "Well, then tell them I have a surfeit of clients. Although I'm honored by the Prince's interest, I have other agreements to honor first. I can't possibly meet with the Prince at this time, with my humblest of apologies."

He'd loaded the word *humblest* with irony. Jen wondered if she should repeat it that way.

She took a single step nearer and held out the box. "I'm to give you this, lord, a token of the Prince's goodwill."

Her master waved the offering away, returning his attention to the book on his knee. "I don't want it."

She bowed her head and turned to go.

"Jen."

She stopped. That same prickle ran across her shoulders like the touch of a hand.

"Keep it for yourself."

"Thank you, lord." She made her escape, back to the gate, the soldiers, and the cart.

The first soldier paced. His compatriots sat fidgeting on the seat, one picking his nails with the point of his dagger, the other bunching the reins in his hands. They started and straightened when she reappeared.

Jen stood alone with the soldiers outside the gates to the gardens, her heart beating with more assurance than when she'd stood in her master's presence. She held the box a moment, then handed it back to the first soldier. He took it with some dismay.

"My master the Lord Barras is honored," she said. "But he cannot possibly accept the Prince's gifts if he is to refuse his proposals." She repeated the rest of the refusal, suitably flowery, even adding her own small embellishments. Slum-born as she was, she'd stood by during many a meeting between her master and honey-tongued merchants and lordlings, and so knew that speech could bear a great deal of empty finery.

The soldier nodded once when she'd finished and turned to climb onto the cart behind his men. At once he stopped, head tilted as if considering, then thrust the box back into her hands. She had to take it or let it fall to the ground, and she couldn't bear to do that.

"Take it," he said with a wink, man to man. "More politic that way, if you know what I mean."

He swung up then, leaving the box in her hands, having cheated her into accepting a gift she would rather have refused.

They turned the cart then and merged with the flow of sulkies and traps, phaetons and carriages, the other conveyances parting like grain before a scythe as the red-laquered cart with its red-clad soldiers and matched red team came among them.

Jen leaned against the gate and closed her eyes. Transference was no small magic, and she had transferred twice—no, thrice. The latch clicked, the gate quivered and swung soundlessly open, nearly depositing her on her backside. Stumbling, she caught herself, scowled at the gate in passing, and headed for the house.

A low box hedge bordering a path of washed stones led among scents of rose and jasmine, lilac and honeysuckle. Jen didn't linger to enjoy them this time, only plodded on to the house, the mother-of-pearl box with its gift weighing heavy in her hands. She carried it upstairs to her room and closed the door.

Necklaces and bracelets, earrings and brooches loaded the drawers of her dressing table. She'd thought to put the necklace in with the rest, but instead found herself holding it spread across her hands.

It was a man's necklace, ornament for a wizard or minister, long and heavy, the silver circles surrounding the stones stamped with starbursts. Still, it was beautiful. Jen faced the mirror of her dressing table and settled the necklace over her shoulders.

Behind her, the door opened. Jen ducked out of the necklace, sent it sliding across the dressing table with a liquid clash. At the door, a woman carrying linens stopped in surprise.

Tall and rawboned, hair coiled in a braid on her head—grey now, where it had once been an indeterminate brown—Marin, the housekeeper, dipped a curtsey. "Forgive me, lady, I didn't think to find you here. I figured you'd be working."

Jen hurried the necklace back into its box, but not before the woman's keen glance lighted on it.

"I—no," Jen said, stumbling a little. "The master had an errand for me."

Marin was a county woman who had, as far as Jen could tell, at least twenty children and innumerable grandchildren and who'd come to the City for reasons not entirely clear. Jen was certain she called her "lady" only to embarrass her.

But Marin had also mothered her mercilessly, plying her with treats and tales, bringing broken-winged birds for Jen to fuss over—something more helpless than Jen herself—and once a puppy, all black and white spots and speckles and round brown eyes the same color as Jen's own. She'd had to give the puppy to the gardener's daughter, though. The house's magic had driven the pup under the bed, a sanctuary from which he would emerge only if Jen were there.

"Did Master give you that necklace?" Marin said

"It's from the Prince."

Marin's eyes grew wide. "The Prince!" She looked Jen up and down.

"The Prince sent it to our master," Jen explained. "Master didn't want it, and said I could have it."

Marin opened her mouth in a silent *ah* and nodded in satisfaction. Jen wondered uncomfortably why.

"What does the Prince want with our master?" she asked instead.

Marin crossed to the bed and began tossing pillows into an armchair, preparing to change the sheets. She shrugged. "Same as any man wants, I'm guessing—Master's services."

"But he's the Prince." In her mind, the Prince must live on a hillside very near the monks' god, who was said to live on a mountaintop so high it reached into heaven. She couldn't imagine what need such a being could have of a wizard.

Marin flipped back the bedclothes and humphed. "And princes wouldn't be princes if not for wizards. No, don't underestimate Master."

"But he's the *Prince*!" she insisted.

Marin left off bundling up bedclothes. "And no matter where the power comes from, he's still the one in power, is that it? But there—don't you see?—he'll have more power if Master backs him up. The Prince'd be the terror of the peninsula cities, I guess, at least so folks say. But people talk, and you can't always believe everything you hear. Especially when it comes to princes and wizards, but I'm sure you already know that."

Jen didn't. Conversations on such topics spluttered to a halt when a wizard's apprentice came within earshot.

"So," she said, following Marin's reasoning. "Princes and wizards, one's about as strong as the other. Except that princes need wizards, but wizards don't need princes."

Marin barked a startled laugh. "Well, I suppose that's about the truth, as long as the wizard doesn't need the prince's gold and horses and fine sight-hounds. But don't go saying that sort of thing aloud, girl. Or wizard's apprentice or not, you might find yourself on the point of an assassin's blade."

Chapter 2

Princes need wizards, but wizards don't need princes.

The realization fired Jen's heart, a goal even more desirable than freedom from her master: freedom from anyone who might try to master her.

But had her master left her free to pursue her masterwork? Sometimes it seemed he had. Other times she doubted so. Of course, the simplest thing would simply be to ask, but if he then told her *no*—

But there was another, safer way to find out.

In her room, Jen extended wizard's senses. Her master was below. The house echoed with voices, the hurrying footsteps of servants, the opening and closing of doors. Servants bustled, one escorting some stranger, others hurrying to open doors and bring refreshment. This was her chance.

Jen slipped out of her room and down the hall. At the bottom of the twisting staircase that led to her master's study, she put one foot on the lowest step. Above, in the empty study at the top of the narrow stair, were the books she needed, books that would lead to the Otherworlds. She took a breath and began to climb.

At last, she reached the landing. The door swung open upon the room of black and green, on books and bookshelves and pointed-arch windows. There was the chair she'd sat in for the first time the night before, and the little table. This time there was no wine, only the table with its concentric pattern of inlay.

A queer combination of triumph and relief swelled in her chest. Jen savored the smells of leather and parchment, relished the glow of sunlight upon gold leaf and polished wood. Her master's will was the will of his house; it—and he—had allowed her to come.

She paced the walls, one after the other, trailing fingertips along the spines of books, stopping now and then to read a title in gold leaf. She paused to glance out a window between bookshelves, down on a wilderness of roofs and chimney pots. Strung laundry, distorted through the little diamond panes, caught the sun like flags waving in the wind. Jen paced on until she came to the end of the bookshelf. She stopped.

Where there should have been another window, between this bookshelf and the next, she found a door, one she hadn't seen before. Curiosity tickled her. Opening the door, she slipped inside.

Closed curtains glowed red and green around the edges, the same deep green as in the study outside, the same flame red as in her own chamber. The room itself lay in shadow. The undefined bulk of furniture lay before her; scents of lavender and cedar teased her nose. She stepped further into the room, toward the drawn curtains. She folded them back just enough to let a slice of sunlight illuminate the room.

Light flashed back from some reflective surface. Squinting, Jen stepped to the side, then saw a dressing table with a mirror. Upon it lay a box much like her own treasure box, carved and set with small colored stones. On another wall stood a washstand, with its basin and pitcher, tortoiseshell comb, and—

A shaving cup and brush. Straight razor, with a handle of swirling green malachite.

Jen's gaze froze on those things, then jerked around the room. A bed, piled with pillows, careened across her vision. A man's slipper, resting on its side. An armchair draped with a long coat and tunic. A book, open on the bedstand beside an empty wineglass.

Someone's bedchamber. With a cold splash of realization, she knew whose.

Her heart hammered. Her hand, trembling, lost the brocade fold of curtain. The curtains fell closed once more and shadows sprang up where color and form had been. Jen lunged for the door.

She hit with a thump that jarred her arms in their sockets. The door was closed. No, there *was* no door. Her hands scrabbled over solid panels of wood. The door had been here. She knew it had.

"Let me out," she rasped, breath whistling through her throat. "Let me out, house!"

She spun away from the doorless wall, back to the window. The rooftops had been far below when she'd looked out. It didn't matter.

She ducked behind the curtains. Sweat filmed her face and neck as she fumbled with the defiant window catch.

Jen, a voice said.

She flung herself flat against the wall. But the voice, her master's, had spoken only in her mind.

She pressed her hands to her chest as if to still her heart and answered, *Yes*.

Come to the drawing room, he said, and added, *Dress well*.

She had a flash of the dresses in her wardrobe and wondered if it was a thought of her own or one of her master's. A wizard could drop thoughts into a mind. Like the stones at the bottom of a still pool, one couldn't know the dropped stone from the ones there already.

Holding the image of the quiet pool, she answered, *Yes, lord,* and pushed through the curtains.

The door had returned. She dashed across the room, wrenched it open and fled.

When she burst through the door into her own room, Marin stood in front of the wardrobe.

She started and spun. "Gracious gods, girl, you scared me half to death. What's wrong with you?"

Jen closed the door, leaned back on it. "Master called." Her voice was breathless, but her hurry explained that. "I'm to dress." She made a face. "*Well.*"

Marin studied her with a shrewd eye. "And that's the cause of all the ruckus?"

"I wasn't expecting him to call," Jen said with perfect honesty.

"Then for once I knew before you did. That's why I'm here." Marin turned back to the wardrobe and sorted through the dresses there.

Jen frowned. "No, Marin."

"Oh, humor an old woman, will you?" she said, taking something out.

In honor of kindnesses done a frightened fifteen-year-old, and many done since, Jen only sighed when Marin removed a dress of dove grey whose sleeves and skirts were slashed with deepest purple.

In spite of herself, Jen paused, wanting to touch the velvet of that night-dark violet, admiring the rippling sheen of the grey satin. Then she snorted.

Marin lowered the dress, which she'd been displaying for best effect. She clicked her tongue. "Why in heavens not? Everyone in the house knows you're a girl. Not even a girl any longer—a young woman. Why not dress like one?"

Let your hair grow, Jen, her master had said. Bought and bound and brought to this house for—

No. She was an apprentice, nothing more. The dresses would stay safely in the wardrobe, and that brassy boy street magician Jen would become a powerful wizard. Never again would she be Arajenei, weak and vulnerable.

"Because," she said at last, and Marin raised her brows expectantly. "Because," she repeated, then said, grasping at pretexts, "no one would take me seriously."

Marin made a noise of disgust and hung the dress in the wardrobe again. "Master would."

Would he? Jen thought. Instead, she said, "What about when I'm my own master? Will the men of the City come to a skirt to turn bandits from their trade caravans or to read the signs for propitious business decisions?"

Marin blinked as if Jen had spoken of conjuring speaking sheep or flying mice. "I thought you and Master—"

"Marin," Jen broke in, closing her eyes. "Please."

"Then choose what you want, if you're going to be unreasonable."

Grateful for the change of subject, Jen donned a black and violet doublet, black ruff with thin green trimming, dark green hose and hat with a feather that brushed one shoulder. In the mirror, she looked garish, extravagant, like a young dragon. She gave Marin a jaunty grin. The housekeeper rolled her eyes and shook her head.

Adjusting the hat on her dark curls, Jen took her leave and went out, cantering down the elegant curve of steps like the boy she appeared to be. She entered the drawing room quietly, waded through shadow to the pool of light in the center of the room.

Two men sat in damask-covered chairs of deep colors. Between them a table of polished cherry wood held dyed glasses and a flagon of wine. Two or three days ago, Jen might have had to hold in a sigh as she took her place behind her master's chair, a place she'd spent countless long hours listening to the plots and problems of the City's lords and rich merchants. Today, she felt only gratitude that his lightning-sharp gaze was bent upon another.

Jen studied his companion, a bony, long-jawed man clad in a robe the yellow of the god's sunlight, the garb of a monk. The sunbursts stitched in gold thread marked him as more than common. But then, she wouldn't expect a common monk to come calling at this house.

"My apprentice," her master said, introducing Jen with a languid gesture.

She bowed her head but said nothing as the monk looked her over, from the feather in her hat to the pointed toes of her shoes.

Within the haven of his yellow sleeves, his hands folded and refolded. "Lord Barras. I'm sure you appreciate the delicacy of this situation."

"Of course," her master replied.

The monk's brows settled in a determined line. "I would prefer to keep the matter in strictest confidence."

"Indeed. If you find my apprentice objectionable, I'll bid you good evening."

Jen, having had years to learn to decipher such utterances, felt a burst of surprised gratification.

"I assure you, lord, I have no opinion of your apprentice's acceptability. That is," the monk stammered, "I'm sure he is more than acceptable, but please—"

"Then you should have no objection to my apprentice handling the matter."

The monk mouthed silently for a moment, then blurted, "But, lord! We come to you as our last resort. If an apprentice could do what any wizard could—" He closed his mouth on the blunder.

Jen bit the inside of her lip. She should have known better than to be gratified. Her master had trapped them both. The monk had admitted he'd sought the help of other wizards before seeking out Barras. And now Jen would be given some task those wizards had been unable to accomplish, sent to fail before she'd even begun, and find her masterwork snatched away for certain. Her hands, clasped behind her back, clenched.

"Do you mistrust my judgment?" Barras asked mildly.

The monk lifted one hand in a placatory gesture. "By no means, lord, but—the presence has resisted our every effort to banish it. It heeds neither prayers nor exorcisms, nor magic." His lips thinned. "It's some curse those foul women laid upon us."

Even without seeing his face, Jen knew her master's flickering smile came and went.

He said, "Then perhaps it will heed my apprentice's command of banishment."

Cold anger splashed her at the betrayal, no matter how subtle, of what she was—a woman. But the monk, looking only unconvinced, bowed his head and rose.

The monk took his leave, Jen in tow with her feather and her dragon colors. After descending the broad marble steps to the driveway and a waiting carriage, she expected to be dismissed to the footman's post, or perhaps, out of respect for her master, to a seat by the driver. She hesitated, uncertain, until the monk leaned forward from his seat inside and snapped, "Get in, boy! I'll not have all the City see you riding into the temple dressed like a popinjay."

Jen got in, not hesitating at all now, pretending no embarrassment that she'd hesitated before.

The carriage jolted, then rolled, crackling on gravel, then clattering over paving stones. In the diffuse glow of the carriage lights, the monk regarded her sullenly. Hands on thighs, elbows propped akimbo, she only gave a wry twist of a smile. The monk finally produced a tiny book from within the yellow folds of his robe and studied it in the too-dim light.

At last the carriage lurched to a stop. The monk alighted with the help of a yellow-garbed footman. Left to her own devices, Jen shrugged and followed the monk, who affected to have forgotten her.

Before them, showing dark and pale by turns in the thin moonlight, rose a flattened dome supported by pillars. From a central rotunda, colonnades radiated outward like the rays of the god's sun, glowing with light from countless lanterns. She saw the gleam of new marble, the bright glitter of fresh-cut granite, the unworn paving stones.

Somehow, it all seemed grimed with the same sullen bleakness that befouled the slums. Hate was here, and rage, and the greed that made man murder man for the coin in his purse or the shoes on his feet. A kindred darkness rose in her. Jen shook it away.

"This place is new. What was here first?" she said, the first words she had spoken in the presence of the monk.

He spun as if he had truly forgotten her. "The filthy grove of those night-worshipping sows. Sisters of the Moon." He said the name with a sneer. "The very ground was polluted with their offerings, the wind cold with their whispers. But the Sun gazed upon them and toppled their trees, drew off the vile waters of their well and cleansed away the defilement."

Jen didn't say that apparently, the Sun hadn't completed the job. "How long has the presence haunted you?"

He did not answer immediately. Under Jen's steady gaze, at last he said, "Perhaps from the beginning. Laborers muttered and ran off, having less fear of the stocks and the whip than of working here. Only when the Sun's light would not remain in the temple, and the brothers heard whisperings of lust and death and greed in the dark…" He set his long jaw and hunched bony shoulders, his dark gaze full of challenge.

She raised an eyebrow, debating whether to take up that challenge. Better, though, if she managed to prove herself capable of doing what she'd been sent to do. So she only said, "Take me there."

He turned and strode along the bright-lit colonnade toward a core of darkness. From adjoining colonnades, lamplight cast a wan glow into the central rotunda and gleamed on the gold leaf embedded in the tiles beneath her feet. The altar that stood at the center of the rotunda lay dark and cold. Her steps echoed and a light wind nudged the feather in her hat, flicking it against her neck. Near the altar, she stopped and turned, scenting.

The monk stood silhouetted at the end of the colonnade. Jen turned to face another brightly-lit colonnade. With her wizard's senses, she heard murmured prayers, smelled the sweat of dreamers. Down a third, she heard hissed arguments, mocking laughter, smelled the mildewed pages of uncared-for books. She paced on around the altar, until she faced a fourth colonnade.

At once, the night wind was back, breathing between columns, slapping at lamp flames. A mutter of old malice quelled even the most fervent prayers, exhaling a miasma of ancient, insidious power throughout the temple and into the streets beyond.

"It's here." Her voice resounded beneath the dome.

"Yes," the monk said, his voice tinged with surprise.

She started down the fourth colonnade, past the rattle and smells of the kitchen, past the splashing of the laundry and the baths, to the end where doors were smaller and lower, the lamps fewer and guttering. The monk stopped at the edge of the light, hands wringing within his sleeves.

Jen faced a door on which a yellow sun had been painted. Other marks marred it, fresh gouges not easily seen against the new wood. Iron, still grey and rough from the forge, banded and locked the door.

She looked at them all, sun and marks and iron, and laughed. The monk, still standing in the light, started.

"This is what your hireling sorcerers did?" she asked with a contemptuous flick of the fingers. "Iron and incantations and signs of binding on the door?"

The monk nodded.

"And the presence," Jen went on, "still fills this place, doesn't it?"

"It smothers the Sun's light." The monk's voice shook slightly, either with fear or anger. "At the closing of his Eye, the brothers light the flame in the altar. And each night it goes out, and leaves us in darkness."

Jen grunted and laid her hand flat on the door, over the iron lock. Magic welled up, a glittering warmth under her skin. The lock sprang open and after it, the door.

The monk took a step back. "You're—you're going in there? The others did not."

She shrugged. "Maybe that's why they failed," she said and stepped from reluctant light into the dark.

The light of her wizardry swarmed over her skin. She moved in an illuminating nimbus of her own creation, haloed in softly gleaming silver that showed a low, long stone room cluttered with splintered planks and broken tools, piles of shattered crockery. The damp smell of stone seemed to press the breath from her lungs. She pushed back. Shadows jumped and danced; dust rasped her throat with every step.

The back wall of the room was of a different sort of stone, older, rougher, crusted with dead lichen and brittle brown moss. The planks of the door in that wall were black with age, black as the iron that bound them. Jen stopped, put her hand on wood cold and heavy and smooth. The door wheezed open beneath her hand. A shallow stone stair led down, the steps cupped at their centers with the wear of ages. Air smelling of damp stone and earth touched her face. And something ancient watched, and breathed.

A quiver began in her middle. She damped it, took a long breath, and went down the stairs.

They were difficult; broad, and too shallow. She took them slowly, for fear of tripping; slowly, for fear alone. The presence she'd sensed in the rotunda enfolded her here as fully as the darkness. Like a small, bright fish, she swam through it, seeking its source.

The stairs ended at last in a round chamber that echoed the lofty rotunda above. But where the rotunda had been filled with air and light and an altar that climbed to the sun, this was filled with a stifling closeness, and centered on a well. The stone coping came barely to her knee. She came to the lip and looked down.

The well was like an eye of darkness. Again, the feather of her hat tickled her neck as air sucked past, down into the well.

Woman, a voice breathed in her mind, a voice as vast and deep and echoing as the hollow places beneath the earth.

She swallowed on a suddenly dry throat. "Yes."

Strong, the voice said.

"Yes." She waited, felt herself scented.

Not priestess, the voice said. *Not sorceress. Not witch.*

"No," Jen agreed. "I'm a wizard."

Another touch that dimmed her silver light a little. *Not wizard.*

"No," she said, concentrating hard on maintaining her light. "Not quite. But I've been sent to banish you."

No man can banish me.

In spite of the tremor betraying her, she gave a one-sided smile. "I'm not a man, remember?"

Not wizard, the voice said again.

She declined to argue. "Why do you put out the monks' light?"

Somewhere at the bottom of the well, the presence shifted, like the slow grinding of an earthquake. *They stole from me.*

"What did they steal?"

The voices that spoke to me, the voice said after a moment, reluctant to answer or not knowing how. *The gifts they brought me.*

"What gifts?"

Light. Life. Power.

Curious, she lowered herself to the stones of the floor, rested her elbows on the low coping. "Those monks won't give you any of that. I wouldn't be here if they would."

You come because I can give what you seek.

Jen hesitated. *Can you?* The question trembled on her lips. She swallowed it down.

She propped her chin on folded arms. "If only you'll stop putting out the monks' light, I'll leave you alone."

I will not be alone, the presence said.

The weight of its will came down on her like a rockslide. She could barely breathe. Her light dimmed to a bare glimmer. The rough coping stones bit at her elbows, and the cold of the stone floor seeped through her clothes.

You will stay with me.

She held herself from struggling, knowing it would do no good. "My master will come fetch me."

You are mine.

"No. I'm bound to him."

I will break that binding.

A grim laugh pushed out of her. "What, and be bound to you, here in the dark? If I'm to be bound, I prefer the binding I'm under."

Shadow binds you, it said, a sinuous whisper.

"No." Within, the memory of a long-ago night rose. She shoved it down. "I'll give you a choice. You have the strength to keep me here—while I live—or you can let me take you away."

Weight bore down on her, threatening to crush her. She bowed head against forearms. Water dripped somewhere, hollowly, and a smell of death rose from the well.

Abruptly the hold over her broke and the pale light of her power spilled out once more across the tiny chamber.

Bring me out, the voice said, passionless again.

Headache pounded behind her eyes, but she sent a careful tendril of thought down the well, toward the source of that hollow voice. She did not trust it, thought it might use guile to snare her where force couldn't. From the vantage of her inner eye, she saw the well empty of all but a moldy dampness and a consciousness as old as the stones themselves.

And one of the stones *was* that consciousness.

Jen explored its outward form: a stone the size of an ox. Its surface, a matte black shimmering with a strange iridescent sheen, floored the well.

She clambered to her feet, dusted off seat and sleeves and considered. She'd have to transfer it, set such protective wards as she could and trust they would hold. Or else return to her master in defeat.

The wards would hold. They would have to.

Extinguishing her light to conserve strength, she enwrapped the stone, a stretching that thinned her powers near breaking. Then she swallowed the stone whole in her thoughts.

She had transferred herself or small objects before, but never anything of this size and weight. Never anything that sucked energy from her as cold rock sucks the heat from living bones.

For that instant of transference, anger coursed like a freezing black river, pouring through her until it seemed her own. Memories of darkness, the whisper of voices, the implacable strength of earth filled her, threatened to turn her heart to rock, her blood to ice.

At once, the wards she had raised shimmered, veils of bright fire. Behind their protection, Jen shifted her awareness to the floor beside the well. There she disgorged the heavy thought that was the stone, and was left light and trembling as a candleflame.

Air feathered her face, chilling the sweat there. She still had to move the stone from this chamber, then from the temple to…elsewhere. Dragging a sleeve across her forehead, she took a breath and once more enfolded the stone.

Out of deference to the sensibilities of the monks, she could scarcely appear with a black rock the size of an ox wafting along ahead of her. The seeming she cast made it appear no larger than a pumpkin she could carry in her arms. Jen took up the stone and climbed the worn, shallow steps, from dank darkness to the musty, dusty dark above.

Her power consumed her, a burning that she must constantly feed with the strength of her will. She scarcely saw the monks gathered in the colonnade, crowded close around the door. In a rustle of yellow robes, they muttered and fell back from the wizardry that shone from her, from the dark ageless presence in the stone.

She walked into the twisting chaos of City streets, among people and beasts and noise, passing from lamplight to shadow. People who saw her also fell back, perhaps seeing a son of some rich family, a madman outrageously dressed, carrying in his arms through the City streets a stone.

Beasts saw more clearly. Horses snorted and shied away, dogs snarled and slunk off. Even the rats hissed and scampered into shadows as they would at nothing else. Jen saw all this, yet did not see, spending every spark of power on guarding herself from the stone she held.

At last she neared the river, a part of the City far from the monks' fine new temple and the estates of rich men. The houses here leaned over narrow, guttered streets. Stench rose from a trickle of water in the gutter. A man cursed, and a child wailed. Old fears walked in Jen's belly. She shut them out, thinking of the stone, of its silent, ancient watchfulness.

A wall rose ahead, and in it a gate, still stout but carved with the marks of idle blades. From some reserve, she dredged up more strength, reached out an unlocking thought. The gate groaned open, its hinges showering rust. As Jen stepped through into moonlight, a garden unfurled.

It looked just as she remembered it. Wisteria ramped over the surrounding wall; rose brambles barricaded the high foundations of a tall narrow house. At the center, a live oak overhung a small pool that reflected the night sky.

A little wilder, maybe, after so many years, but still as beautiful as when she'd fancied it a small Otherworld far removed from the ugliness of the slums. Even her brothers shouting outside the wall that long-ago day—*Jen! What's in there? Anything good?*—hadn't marred its magic, its impossible tranquillity. And nah, she'd told them—the big, boastful boys looking askance at her, a skinny child who could pass untouched through the spells that locked them out—nah, ain't nothin' there but broked glass an' weeds and spiders big as your fist. Ain't nothing you want.

That had been true, because they didn't care about the beauty. She wouldn't breach the spells for them then, and in all the years since, it seemed no one else had, either. Now, Jen set the stone down under the oak, stepped back, and let magic unravel into the enchanted stillness.

The stone's awareness expanded into its new surroundings. *This is my place*, it said at last, question and statement at once.

Jen nodded and ran a finger under her ruff. Sweat chilled her. "Can you feel the power here? It guards the place from—" She thought of the filth and poverty she'd forded to get here. "—from what lies all around."

No one is here.

Jen shrugged. "I've done all I can."

You will stay, the stone said.

"We've already talked about that."

There is much I can give you.

A swift calculation ran through her mind. "Do you know of the Otherworlds?"

The Otherworlds. The stone's voice whispered in her mind as if drifting far away. *The Fey travel freely, stepping from world to world as if across a threshold. They come speak to me, sometimes. Their magic knows no bounds. They fill me.*

"The Fey are gone. But if you'll tell me about the Otherworlds, I'll come speak to you."

Stay with me here. It is not dark. The presence might have been pleading, but Jen knew better.

"Remember, stone, you owe me. Don't try to hold me again. Leave me free, and I might be able to bring the Sisters of the Moon. I doubt they enjoyed being driven from their sacred well any more than you enjoyed being left alone."

Bring them, the stone commanded.

"Don't try to hold me here," she insisted.

The stone remained silent a moment. *You came to me,* it said at last, its vast deep voice echoing in the lightless places of her mind.

"But I won't come again if you don't agree. Understand?"

Once more, the stone fell silent. Jen waited, a small wind fingering her curls, plucking at the feather of her hat.

I do not hold you. Kinship does.

"I'm no kin of yours."

Perhaps, it said, but Jen could not tell if it agreed or disagreed.

A chill stalked up her spine, a sense that she bargained foolishly with a spirit more ancient than any wizard, more guileful, and maybe more powerful. She ought to walk away and leave the stone to its unkempt garden, and search elsewhere for lore of the Otherworlds. But in her heart she knew the stone would have knowledge she might find nowhere else.

As a wizard's apprentice, she knew how words could trick and twist.

"I'll come. I'll speak to you. I'll even look for your Sisters. But leave me free to go my own way."

Let it be so, the stone agreed.

"Done." She spat on her palm and slapped the cold black surface, sealing the bargain.

Triumph bubbled within her. She'd accomplished what neither monk nor master had expected her to, and maybe gained another tool for her quest for the Otherworlds. With a little swagger, she left the abandoned garden to the black stone and the moonlight.

Chapter 3

Jen wrapped her fingers around the wrought iron of her master's gate. The moon was well down after her long plod across the City. She closed her eyes, leaned her head against an ornamental coil of brass.

The gate sprang open of its own accord, dragging her with it. She scrambled to get her feet under her. A warning prickle swept her, then a transference spell plucked her up and deposited her in her master's study.

Her master closed his book, placed it on the table beside his wine. "Well?"

She wished only to sink down somewhere and sleep. Drawing at the last of her strength, she straightened.

"The presence the monks feared lived in a stone at the bottom of a well. I brought it out and took it away."

Her master regarded her out of storm-grey eyes. "In other words," he said at last, "you did exactly what any blacksmith's boy could do with a pry bar, block and tackle and a barrow."

"No blacksmith's boy could do what I did!" Jen cried.

"You were sent to banish the spirit. Instead, you picked it up and moved it, wholly disregarding my instructions."

"I didn't!" she gasped as if struck. She'd expected prearranged failure, but hadn't obliged by failing. "Is it disobedience to use wits rather than wizardry?"

She turned to leave without her master's dismissal. In turning, it seemed the room swung around once, a reeling of bookshelves and arched, small-paned windows. The floor canted and she toppled, but strong hands suddenly gripped her arms.

Her master held her upright, kept her from crumpling to the floor. He stood very close, frowning down from the height she had almost forgotten.

"What have you done, girl?" he demanded.

Jen's knees refused to hold her. His arm came around her and he swept her into a chair. Her treacherous knees buckled and the cushions swallowed her. She could do nothing but subside into them, muddled and mortified. A glass touched her lips. She sipped wine, saw her master holding the glass and raised shaking hands to take it.

"Be still," he commanded.

Her hands fell back into her lap.

The room's whirl and sway gradually abated. Her master half-knelt by her chair, still frowning.

"Rather more than a blacksmith's boy could do, I'll wager," he said.

Blood rushed to her face. "Yes," she said, sullen because she'd nearly fainted in his presence, wishing rather she had made it out of the room and tumbled down the stair.

He stood. "I want to know what you did. In detail."

She got halfway through the tale when he interrupted.

"You spoke to it?" He frowned more darkly than when she'd hung fainting in his hands.

"Yes. How else could I convince it?"

"You could have banished it, as you were sent to do."

This time Jen frowned, then immediately smoothed away the frown. "Banish it for the crime of simply being? Those monks took everything it valued. And locked it away."

His grey eyes narrowed. "Such spirits are dire and perilous things. You should never have spoken to it. Best you hadn't gone near it, as the others had the good sense not to."

It was on her tongue to say, *Then why did you send me to deal with it?* but she'd said more than enough already.

"I wish to know precisely what it said." His hand approached.

"No." Jen recoiled into the cushions and blocked his reaching hand. She had no wish for him to delve her thoughts and memories, to rifle through her mind as he'd done when he had first brought her here, and on infrequent occasions since.

His hand hovered, ready but not threatening. Not quite. "Why not?"

"I'll tell you," she said. "You don't have to take it."

Insight glimmered in his eyes, swift as a shaft of sunlight through storm clouds. He sat, offered the glass of wine again. She took it and sipped, grateful to have something to look into besides his wizard's eyes.

He took the glass. "Now," he said. "Tell me."

She closed her eyes, built around her again the darkness of the chamber beneath the earth, the burdensome sense of watching; repeating word for word the conversation she'd had with the stone. When she came to the stone's assertion that it could break her master's binding, her tongue passed over the words. Smoothly, as if they'd never been spoken. So, too, did she pass over her promise to come speak with the stone, only hurrying to the end of her adventure.

She opened her eyes. Fear fluttered at the back of her throat, fear that his wizard's eyes would see what she had withheld.

"You walked back here," he repeated when she'd finished.

Relief spilled over Jen. "It was all I could do."

"You might have bespoken me."

She blinked.

"But no," he went on. "You never ask for help, do you? Therein lies your failure—your unwillingness to admit your limitations."

The words went through her like fire. "You sent me to fail, so you could say I'm not ready for my masterwork! To make me think I have no choice but—" She bit the words back.

"But what, Jen?"

So gentle, those words. So dangerous. She only shook her head hard.

He rose, stood looking down on her again, hands clasped behind his back. With his dark hair, in his long coat of dark brocade, he seemed a pillar of shadow. "You believe I scheme to undermine you?"

Exhaustion made her reckless. "Yes!"

"Then let it be so."

Jen sucked in a shocked breath, but no words would come. She mouthed, speechless, the promise of the Otherworlds snatched away at the utterance of those few short words. He, in turn, looked down at her with a gaze like a wind ruffling still, deep waters. She buried her thoughts with what battered strength she still had.

He turned away in a swirl of coat skirts. "Go to bed, Jen," he with a sigh.

She struggled free of the green cushions and worked her way to her feet. The room remained still and steady. She took one step, then another. Concentrating only on her feet, on reaching the door.

Her hand was on the latch when he said, "And no work tomorrow."

Her wizard's ear heard a note of tension or emotion in his voice. She slipped a glance back. He stood before his chair, beside the low table with its half-empty glass of wine. A peculiar tightness compressed his mouth.

Her throat closed. Jen swallowed and whispered, "Yes, lord."

Her fingers fumbled at the latch and she escaped out the door.

Chapter 4

In her dream, Jen crouched unmoving on cold stone, as watchful as the silence all around. Darkness pressed around her, hollow with the drip of water. The darkness changed, became closer, drier, stitched with smells: earth, dusty mold, onions, apples.

That palpable watchfulness, the sense of presence faded, leaving her alone. She should have felt relief, but instead felt greater fear than before, a fear that made her shake helplessly, that squeezed the breath in her throat.

Nearby, a sullen glow filled a tall rectangle in the darkness. Her eyes fixed on it as if it were the doorway to hell and horrors might come pouring forth. A shadow appeared and her breath stopped as if throttled.

Even in the dream, she knew what was to come.

Head and shoulders, the bulk of a body showed, outlined in dull red. She couldn't move, couldn't flee—there was nowhere to which she could flee. In the dark, surrounded by stone, she was trapped, and that shadow came toward her until there was nothing else, only the bulk that made the shadow, the rasp of breath.

A man's weight came down, crushing. She cried out, and a hand clapped over her face. She struggled then, but the darkness was seeping inward, covering her eyes, stilling her limbs, filling every hollow with pain and horror and betrayal. From her core, she called up fire and light—

Jen shot upright in bed, gasping. Light streamed aurora-like from her skin, etching the rumpled covers of her bed, the dressing table, the washstand, the wardrobes against the walls. A sharp odor of wizard's fire hung in the air. Her fingertips tingled and burned as if she'd launched fire, but there was no sign of blast or burn.

Her breath went out in a rush. The darkness was only the ordinary nighttime dark of her room.

Her room. Here. In her master's house. Not the place in memory, where the—the thing that had happened still spewed forth in dreams.

She pushed the covers aside, swung her legs over the edge of the bed and lowered her head into shaking hands. Light from her fingers pushed through her closed lids, dispelling the dark there. It could do nothing for the memory of darkness, though, could never burn bright enough or pierce deeply enough to drive it out.

Abruptly, she slid off the bed and crossed to the dressing table. Pale dawn light pressed against the windowpanes, showed hints of blue and red at the edges of the curtains. Not enough light. Not nearly enough.

Every lamp in the room blazed at her thought, changing the light from stark jumping silver to soft gold. Water sloshed onto the marble of the washstand as she poured it into the basin; water soaked the front of her nightshirt as she splashed her face.

She looked into the mirror, saw the pale face there bordered by a scrollwork of dark curls. Saw, too, the thin wet fabric of her nightshirt plastered to her breasts as her curls were plastered to her face. She whirled away from the glass to one of the wardrobes, dragged out a robe of burgundy brocade and hugged it around her.

The house did not trouble her as she ghosted along the hall and down stairs. At times, Jen could almost swear it slept, as it seemed to now. At this moment it was no more than a great, fine house whose master and servants yet slept, in which only a wakeful apprentice padded barefoot down stairs and through still kitchens.

Cisterns like big stone tubs hid in the lowest basement, where granite foundations crouched on bedrock. Much like the chamber of the stone—cool, dark, slightly dank— but the smells of soap and lavender brought the upper world of life and bustle here. Washtub and clothes drying frame, wicker baskets of laundry, the pressing board with its iron cluttered the clean-swept stone floor. All familiar and homey, but Jen hesitated in the doorway until she noticed the smell of onions from some storeroom nearby. Calling to life every lamp in the basement, she hurried into the low chamber containing the cisterns.

She made a bath in the washtub, warming the water with a touch. The soap she used was the same the maids used on the laundry. It stung, but she scrubbed, wishing she could rasp her body across the washboard as the maids did the dirty clothes, hating the betraying swell of her breasts, the open vulnerability of her womanhood. She stopped and gazed at what she could see of herself above the soapy water: a body still thin, though not as thin as five years ago, flat-muscled with the wiry strength a wizard's power demanded.

Jen remembered her master's strong hands when he'd supported her. That kind of strength she did not have. This woman's body never would. She drew up her knees and pressed her face to them.

"You're in my washtub," a woman's voice said.

Jen wrenched around. Wynne, dressed in her maid's plain skirt, shawl pinned primly over her bodice, stood in the doorway, hands on hips, frowning. Her hair, too, was covered, yet defied modesty. Like mahogany sheathed in copper, it peeked flirtingly from beneath the folded linen cap.

"Dammit, Wynne, y' scared me half t' death," Jen said in the flat accents of the street.

"If you let someone sneak up on you, that's your doing, not mine." Wynne came and stood over her, arms crossed. She was a little younger than Jen, and totally unintimidated by her. "What happened to you? You're all red. Did some spell go wrong? Better not've messed up my washtub." She ran a finger along the inside of the tub, sniffed it and gave a single short nod. "Seems all right," she pronounced and went on with scarcely a drawn breath, "I don't know what you're doing down here when you can have a bath in that fancy copper tub in your own room. Now get out, I have work to do."

She usually enjoyed Wynne's impertinence. Now, she felt...well, *naked*. Dripping and embarrassed, Jen unfolded herself. "Nobody was awake yet to bring the tub and water."

Wynne tossed her a towel from the basket. "God's mother. Here! D'you think I'll laugh to discover there's a girl's body underneath those boy's clothes you wear?"

Jen toweled off quickly and wrapped the heavy robe around her again.

"It's just as well you're here," Wynne said, filling a bucket from the cistern. "I'm going out tonight, and I need a charm." She gave a little quirk of a smile. "You know the kind. Heat this, will you?" she asked abruptly, heaving up the bucket and dumping it into the drained tub.

Jen reached out and dipped a finger in the water. Heat flowed through her.

"Heat the water," she mocked. "Make a baby begone charm. What am I, your pet wizard?"

"No, you're my escort."

"Who says?"

"Oh." Wynne shrugged. "If you want to stay *here*, I suppose one of the boys can go."

It was a dice game: raise you a copper, I'll see your copper and raise you two.

"I suppose so," Jen said with malicious nonchalance.

Wynne's bucket thumped against the rim of the tub. "Jen! You can't do this to me!"

"Why? Because then one of the boys really will escort you?"

She caught a flash of herself drenched with a bucket of water. Jen grinned and waggled a finger. Wynne glared at her, then turned and flung the water into the tub instead.

Jen laughed. "All right. Where're you going?"

Wynne's scowl disappeared. "To see my sister." She giggled. "But I'm sure I can find my way if you have to go do your own errands."

Jen gave a quirk of a complicit smile, but thought of the stone, and of promises—hers to it, and its to her. "Yes," she said. "I think so. When do we go?"

"About lamplighter's bell, when I've finished my work. You'll have my charm done by then, won't you?"

"Yeah." Jen leaned against the doorframe and sighed. "Except I'm not supposed to work today."

"Huh." Wynne tipped another bucketful into the tub. "How do you manage to make that sound bad?"

"Believe me, it is. Come up to my room when you're done." She scowled up at the ceiling as if she could see her master. "I'll have your charm ready."

お

Sunlight, red as the patterns in the rug, had faded when a knock came at the door.

Uninvited, Wynne swung open the door and asked, "Ready?"

Jen nodded, then with petty defiance, used a spell of transference to send them both outside. Up the twilit street, some gentleman's house blazed with lights. Sounds of voices and laughter and music floated like bright bubbles on the air, the gaiety of a party that would last the night long.

Jen dangled a charm of knotted string before the younger woman's face. "Best have your fun before midnight. You might leave a maid and return a mother otherwise."

With the skill of a cutpurse, Wynne snatched the charm, dropped it over her head and tucked it into her bodice. She whisked off her linen cap. The freed tumble of red-brown hair fell past her shoulders.

Stuffing the cap into the basket under her arm, she shook her head. "Poo! What am I, an enchanted princess?"

Two merchants with their long straight robes and little belt purses paused, staring.

Jen took the basket, caught the younger woman's elbow and bustled her up the street, past manors and gated grounds. "Wynne! Watch your manners!"

She widened blue eyes. "You'll never tell on me, Jen. Did you see those old money-grubbers? They stared like I wore a string of gold coins around my neck."

"I promise you our master doesn't have to be told everything he knows."

Wynne sniffed. "You be afraid of him for both of us, then. I'm not." She flounced along the street, past shops crowded shoulder-to-shoulder. "He's only a man."

Three young men on horseback rode by and she kicked up her skirts. The men grinned and called out immodest suggestions. Wynne dipped a teasing curtsey, raising her skirts higher than necessary to keep them from the dirty cobbles. Jen pretended to be engrossed by the wares displayed in the candy-maker's window.

"If it weren't for you, Jen, I'd be pregnant ten times over," Wynne sighed when the swishing tails of the horses had disappeared in the crowd. She hooked her arm through Jen's. "Why do you pretend to be a boy? It's ever so much more pleasant to be a woman."

Jaw set, staring straight ahead, Jen said nothing. Wynne's arm tightened on her own.

"*That's* why—" She stopped, turned Jen to her. "Did the master—he didn't *do* anything to you?" Wynne's blue eyes regarded her with seriousness and sympathy Jen hadn't seen before.

Jen shivered. "Never!" she said, low and fierce, clutching the basket to her side so hard the wicker creaked. "Never yet," she whispered.

Wynne gusted a breath. "That's good. It'd be a shame, for all he's tall and so handsome, for an older fellow."

Handsome? Jen had never thought of her master that way, but he was, wasn't he? How strange that he could be so, that she could think so.

Wynne set them to walking again. Shopkeepers, taking in their wares for the night, called to one another, and people hurried past with laden baskets and bulging sacks.

"Not that I'd ever dally with a wizard, you know," Wynne went on. "And the thought that he could turn me into a rat terrier if I looked at another man could put a damper on things."

In spite of herself, Jen laughed.

Wynne swept her with an appraising glance. "But for you, he'd be just per—"

"No." The fragile laughter fled.

"You won't always be an apprentice, if that's the problem."

"It isn't." But it was, though not in the way Wynne meant. Jen frowned, thinking of her master's pronouncement of doom: *Then let it be so.*

Not every apprentice gained mastery in his craft, and with it, freedom. Some remained servants all their days. Others…

Others ran away. Jen had tried. Her master had bent his will to bringing her home, and like a dog dragged by its collar, she'd come. First the gate had opened and clanged shut again behind her, then the vine-carved door of the house. Nowadays, she knew the length of her tether.

Around them, the shops had given way to tall, narrow houses with scarcely room for a cat to slink between. Jen stopped. "This isn't your sister's neighborhood."

Toying with the charm around her neck, Wynne smiled. "Mmmm. Didn't you say you had errands to run?"

"Midnight," Jen said. "Or it's both our hides."

Wynne took the basket and strolled up the street, humming.

Jen turned the other way, down a street that wound its tortuous way between shops and through marketplaces, from there to the houses of craftsmen, then laborers.

The dim, quiet streets gave way again to noise and activity, but it wasn't the merry laughter of a gentleman's party. Here, voices shouted and cursed as often as laughed and sang. Burning rubbish lit the street and the sagging façades; the stench of sewage and rotting garbage hung in the air with the smoke. She passed among the brawling men and drunken women with the ease of old familiarity.

At last, she came to a square where entertainments held sway. A ragged singer strummed a lute that looked better cared-for than he did himself. A lovely young girl danced barefoot, her skirt lifted high enough to show shapely calves. A pale, emaciated young man stripped down to his smallclothes twisted himself into painful shapes. A street magician pulled coins from children's ears and doves from women's bodices.

Jen watched him awhile, then nodded. He was good, especially since nearly all his tricks were sleight-of-hand. She resisted the temptation to send a flock of birds made of flame singing over the crowd—one of her old tricks— and worked her way among the pungent press of un- washed bodies.

At the edge of the square, away from the crowd and some of the noise, she found what she sought. A woman sat throwing bones on a blanket.

To the people here, she would appear old, with moon- white hair and unseeing eyes also as white as the moon. Jen's wizard's sight showed her otherwise. Beneath the il- lusion the woman had woven, keen dark eyes darted eve- rywhere, taking in everything. Also beneath lay a hard, lined face, coarse black hair drawn back into an elaborate witch-knot at the nape.

A pregnant young woman knelt on the blanket before the older one, watching the cast of the bones.

Jen slouched against a soot-blackened wall and pre- tended interest in the contortionist, who was unwinding from one position and knotting himself into another. Someone made an obscene comment about the sorts of things he might be able to do and was rewarded by a storm of laughter. Jen did not laugh. If there were drink enough, and the mood grew foul enough, there would be those in the crowd who'd demand to see what the heckler had suggested. The contortionist looked in no condition to refuse.

At last the young woman on the soothsayer's blanket rose and departed. The older woman gathered up her bones.

"Well, daughter," she said with a flick of those sharp dark eyes that Jen saw and the others in the square did not. "What do you want? I don't think you need the likes of me to tell your fortune."

Jen shot a glance over her shoulder to see if anyone had heard, then drew a veil of indifference around them, magic that would send the curious elsewhere. "One is always blind to one's own future, they say."

"They say true enough," the soothsayer agreed. "But I'm sure you already know that."

Jen shrugged. "My own future is what I make of it. But what weighs on me, Sister, is a promise I made."

"Ah!" The woman rocked back, bracing big, businesslike hands on her thighs. "You know what I am! Yes, child, I was a Sister of the Moon. You see how low we've fallen since the monks' god took our sacred grove for his temple—telling fortunes to the rabble in filthy streets."

"I went to that temple. A beautiful place with its glittering columns and bright new marble. But the god's light wouldn't stay lit, to the monks' distress."

The woman chuckled. "I daresay not! Those monks never thought to ask what slept in our sacred well before they drove us off and shut it up. What will they do when it wakes?"

"I think they're discovering that."

The smile left the soothsayer's face, and she grew still. "What do you know of it?"

"I know something old, very old, waited in the bottom of that well. It was angry."

The woman's fingers moved in a swift sign. A bone or two fell to the blanket. "By the bright-faced Mother! It spoke to you?"

"Yes." Jen sensed a disturbance within the woman like thrashing fishes in a moonlit pond.

"Fools!" the woman spat. "Mere women tended that spirit, so they think no more of it than a hex for cramps. And now they've waked it. Will their greedy god protect them from it?"

"They thought to banish it."

"No more than you can banish the earth beneath your feet." The Sister snorted. "Why do they think a wizard the likes of Ruien put it there? Generations of Sisters tended the Well, and the thing in it did no harm. Now..." She gestured around her, at the filth, the worn-out storefronts, the hooting, jeering crowd. "You see what its will does."

Jen looked, and saw only the usual face of the slums, no better or worse than before. "That spirit isn't so bad, just lonely. It let me take it away."

More bones escaped the thick, strong fingers. "Out of the Well? Out of the water?"

"The well was dry."

"Dry!" Her eyes, dark and wary, studied Jen. "What are you? What power do you have?"

Again, Jen shrugged. "I only made it a promise, and it consented to come with me."

"What promise?" The woman's voice trembled with eagerness, or fear.

"To come speak to it. To seek its Sisters, and bring them."

The Sister scrambled to her feet. "Not me!" She gave a high, saw-edged laugh. Her eyes glinted, red and wild with firelight. "I've done my duty by that spirit. All the years of my youth, spent in the Mother's Grove, tending the Well of Knowledge. If that spirit has bespoken you, I won't come between!"

In a sudden flutter of tattered black robes, the soothsayer raised her arms, perhaps to push Jen away, to cast a spell, to turn and run.

Jen reached out a thought, a wisp of wizardry. As if snared by an invisible rope, the woman froze.

With a twist of an unpleasant smile, Jen crooked a finger, beckoning. "But I told the stone I'd bring its Sisters."

The Sister took a staggering step. Terror filled her eyes, spilled from her mouth in a high, thin wail that carried even over the noise of the square. Terror of her, Jen. Of her compelling power—

Aghast, Jen dropped the compulsion. The Sister stared at her for one horrified instant, then fled, abandoning bones and blanket.

Jen looked around the square, at the crude, coarse men, the degraded women, the neglected children. Shuddering, she turned her back on them all, on the stench and noise and jumping, jeering firelight, and escaped into a dark slot of a street.

She retraced her steps back inside the City Wall, along ever narrower and more crooked streets. Whores, stockinged ankles showing and bodice-laces half-undone, clustered in ungated archways, calling out to the men who passed. One or two even teased Jen, boy that she appeared to be. Peddlers sang in cracked voices, selling rags or bits of string or broken knives.

These houses weren't the ramshackle huts and hovels of the slums, but once-fashionable mansions left to rot and ruin. High-water marks on the walls and the sweetish stink of rotting wood and moldy plaster told of past floods; no doubt the reason why the rich had moved their estates to higher ground. Here, the only option had been to build levels above the flood-prone ground floors. Second and third stories shouldered across the street, blocking the sky and turning the street into a dank, moss-furred canyon.

Jen kept as close to the walls as possible. A perpetual rill of sewage down the gutter made the center of the street no place to lose one's footing. The reek combined queasily with the smells of cooking, rancid grease and smoke. At last, the traffic dwindled, the noise fell behind.

Old houses loomed on both sides, shutting out all but a narrow strip of starlit sky. A gate of thick planks, closed, banded with rusting iron and carved with graffiti, rose on the left. Jen touched the gate's massive iron bolt.

A spark of magic leapt from her fingertips, burrowed its way through iron blistered with rust. The bolt rattled, then shot back with a screech. The gate groaned open, dragging across paving stones. She slipped through.

The garden glimmered in starlight. Behind the ramble and riot of long-untended greenery, the house rose: tall stone foundation, three stories, steep, tiled roof. Darkened windows looked down, as unreflective as a corpse's eyes. Yet awareness glided stealthy as river-fog along the ground, touching her as lightly.

Jen crossed to the stone, lying in shadow beneath the black blot of the live oak that bent over the pool at its roots.

Its voice, deep and hollow as the sigh of wind in night-dark caverns, breathed into her mind.

You have come.

"Yes," Jen said. "As I promised."

You come alone. Where are my Sisters?

She hesitated, thinking of the Sister who'd defied her, and what she'd done. "Scattered," she finally answered. "Telling fortunes to poor people for eggs and coppers."

They will not come, it said, either seeing into her heart or having a great deal more knowledge of human nature than Jen would have expected.

"No," she admitted with some trepidation.

But you are here. Its voice curled around her like warm, enfolding darkness.

"For the moment." She squared her shoulders and raised her chin. "I've come for the payment you owe me."

The stone remained silent a long moment, as if searching memory unfathomably deep. At last, it said, *You wish to know of the Otherworlds.*

"Yes. I want to open a gateway."

Great magic. Very old magic. Can one so young wield magic so old?

"That's for me to know."

Great magic requires deep power. Old magic needs vast knowledge.

"Can you help me, or not?" Jen demanded. The stone sounded like an old witchwife, possessed of more theatrics and riddlery than magic.

Much I can do for you. Do you ask what you most desire?

The need that swelled was one so old, so well worn, she'd ceased to wish for it long ago: to be safe.

Jen folded her arms tight. This passage to the Otherworlds would surely lead to that safety. Of course, there were risks; she wasn't fool enough to think otherwise. But freedom, power... Didn't they make invulnerability?

"The Otherworlds will do," she answered at last.

Very well, the stone said with its usual impassivity. *Touch me.*

She frowned, uneasy. "Why?"

Do you fear me, wizard-woman?

"Don't flatter me. You know I'm not a wizard yet."

The stone went on as if she hadn't spoken. *Do you fear me, you who held me in your mind, who carried me in your arms with your power?*

Jen was wizard enough to know bravado served no useful purpose in magic.

"I know you're more powerful than I am," she said. "And anything more powerful can be a threat."

Powerful, O yes. As your power aided me, mine can aid you. And I have left you free, as I promised.

Magic did not allow the breaking of promises, for false words had a way of becoming the truth. The stone, certainly, was a magical being. But whether it was bound by the same rules, Jen didn't know.

"Yes," she said slowly while thinking very fast indeed. "But I can hear what you say. Why do you need me to touch you?"

I wish to show you. I cannot show you if you do not touch me.

She took a hesitant step. Even at night, her wizard's eyes saw the stone's strange dark iridescent sheen, like water on pitch. Jen reached out, hesitated, then barely touched her fingertips to the stone's rough cool surface.

Nothing happened. She let out a breath.

Have no fear. The stone's deep voice seemed to chuckle with underground waters.

Chill darkness seeped up her fingers to her arm, trickled along nerves, through veins. She struggled to pull away but found her fingers frozen to the stone. The fire of her power glowed in the depths of her mind. She dove for it, fumbled to shape it—

Images swam into her mind. Green land. Open fields. Tall bright forests of gold and green. A man and woman, both very slender, with silver hair that hung to their waists bound back by bands of silver and gold.

Fey, she whispered, or the stone whispered into her mind—she couldn't tell. The woman raised her hand and sketched a sign that shimmered upon the air. The world seemed to waver like colors painted upon a silk scarf, then rippled as if blown by the wind. Entwined with the colors of the world, the Fey man and woman stepped forward as if through a sheer rainbow curtain. It settled once more into place behind them.

The world became what it was, but the Fey were gone.

Hope or joy or triumph swelled in Jen's chest, a feeling almost too large to contain. The stone had just showed her a gate to the Otherworlds.

Jen's wizardly training engaged. She memorized the sign, the power that radiated forth. Unlike sorcerers or witches, wizards seldom used signs or devices. Like the Fey, a wizards's magic was his very being, as much a part of him as bones or thoughts. And like thoughts, that magic expanded into the world to manifest the wizard's will.

Thus if the Fey woman had to make a sign to direct and concentrate magic, the powers invoked must be immense, perhaps drawing on other magicks that must be called and combined.

"What other magicks?" Jen whispered.

The image the stone showed faded, leaving only the stone itself like a sleeping beast beneath its tree.

I am old, the stone said. *I watch. I have seen many things. But I do not know all.*

"But do you know *this* thing?"

I know more. Stay and I will show you.

Pretext or not, Jen was tempted. After a moment, she let her fingers slide from the stone's coarse surface. She glanced up at the sky. The quarter moon climbed high toward midnight.

Bitterness suddenly ran like thin fire through her veins, leaving a queer, foul taste in her mouth. She was tired of creeping about, of stealing moments of her own life from the master who owned her.

"I have to go."

Come speak with me again, the stone said, as it had the last time she'd left it.

She knew better than to bind herself with promises this time. "Maybe," she said, slippery as wizards can be.

You will come.

Jen caught no sense of warning or promise in the words, and was wise enough not to reply. She left the stone and closed the gate behind her, carrying in her heart the Fey woman's sign like a secret key.

Chapter 5

Jen carried the stone's vision locked in the jewelbox of her heart. Her master might forbid her masterwork, but now she had other means to her end.

There were preparations to be made. She couldn't open a gateway to the Otherworlds dressed in silk and brocade. She needed sturdy clothes. No one had ever questioned her when she bundled the dresses in her wardrobe into a basket and carried them off, returning later with garments more to her preference. No one questioned her this morning, though Marin had frowned and tutted at the basket laden with rich velvets and shimmering satins.

The flesh between Jen's shoulder blades tingled as she cantered down the stairs, crossed the marble expanse of the foyer, and walked out the front door. She smoothed the back of her neck, ignoring the watching prickle.

She stepped through the gate. A chaise drawn by a handsome bay rolled one way. Jen went the other, and soon streets rattling with carriage wheels gave way to maids bustling and pages running from shop to shop.

The clothier's shop was dim and quiet after the light and clamor of the street. Garments lay everywhere: fur-lined and embroidered cloaks, tunics of silk and linen. A beribboned dress of green silk brocade arrayed a mannequin. Jen scorned not only the dress, but the gentlemen's clothes as well.

"Well," the shopkeeper said from behind his counter. "It's the wizard's young apprentice."

His face was lined with old sorrows, but they seemed to have filled him with gentleness rather than bitterness. He looked about her master's age (though Jen suspected her master was a great deal older than he looked), and had always treated her with a kindness that had coaxed from her a certain cautious trust.

"Jen, sir." She set her basket on the floor.

"Jen. Of course. I haven't forgotten." The clothier smiled, a flash of white teeth in dark beard. "Jen who brings me dresses demonstrating taste superior to that of the doublets and jackets and tunics he takes away."

It was the closest he'd ever come to a question. Jen tensed and threw wizard's senses wide, seeking hidden meanings. She found only wry amusement at the affectations of the young, and a certain curiosity about the lady whose dresses were sacrificed to those affectations.

She shrugged and smiled.

"So what frippery will you have today, young master?"

"No frippery, sir, but travelling clothes."

His brows shot up. "Travelling clothes, is it? Going to seek your fortune?"

Jen opened her mouth to reply, but the clothier waved the words away.

"Never mind. I recognize that grim set of jaw and preoccupied look in the eye. It's a grand, brave thing to leave behind the safety and comfort of home to seek a new life."

Doubt fluttered like a moth under her breastbone. Jen nodded politely, trying to swat it away, but it hovered insistently.

"Well then," the clothier said, "I reckon I ought to give you a parting gift. Wait here." He turned and disappeared behind the curtain.

He returned a moment later and beckoned. Jen approached, and he reached out and took her hand. She held herself from flinching, but he only placed something upon her palm. Old magic hummed on her skin. He released her hand, and she looked to see what it was.

She held a knife no longer than her hand, its hilt bound with tarnished silver, its blade sheathed the same. A breath went out of her, for though ill-kept, it was clearly very old and perhaps precious. Curling fingers around the small hilt, she drew it from its sheath to find a blade not of metal, but of translucent black stone—obsidian, perhaps.

"A strange thing, isn't it?" he said. "I found it, naturally enough, in a heap of clothes brought in. It seemed worthless, but I couldn't bear to throw it away. It's much too curious. I thought," he added almost shyly, "you might be able to tell what it's all about."

Jen looked into eyes of a color somewhere between brown and green, sensed his curiosity. Closing her own eyes, she sent her awareness into the blade cupped in her hands, feeling carefully along the threads of magic that bound it. They were ancient, convoluted, tracing patterns she could neither name nor translate. At her wizardly touch, that magic quivered, prowled to the surface like a hibernating beast awakened.

Cut... The word breathed into her mind, sluggish in response to her prodding. *Cut the cloth...* Faintly, the words whispered, almost beyond her ability to perceive. *Cut the cloth of mortality, walk the ways of infinity.* It seemed there might be more, too faint or too alien for her to discern.

"What does that mean?" the clothier asked.

Jen opened her eyes to meet his, and realized she'd spoken aloud.

"I don't know," she said. "The magic is old. Very strange, like nothing I've encountered before."

"Well," he sighed, "I meant it only as a keepsake, anyway. Something to remind you, perhaps, of happier days when the road ahead grows rough."

Jen almost laughed, but knew he wouldn't understand.

お

"Heyo, little lady," a man's voice called from her master's garden. "Whatcha got there?"

Jen, the basket of clothes and her secret gift tucked under one arm, felt a spurt of furtive guilt go through her.

She swung her gaze unerringly upon the man who called to her. Ordinary mortal eyes would've been dazzled by the sun's low light slanting coppery through the leaves of the trees, but she saw him where he knelt among her master's roses: a brown man with leathery face and hands, sleeves rolled up to his elbows, silver-capped tooth winking in his grin. Tar, the gardener. He could know nothing of the knife, but was only teasing as he always did about the clothing she brought home.

"Heyo!" she called back as she would have to any neighbor in the ramshackle snarl of huts and hovels outside the City Wall. "I've got a dress." She watched in delight as Tar's mouth dropped open, then added, "For Wynne!"

An indignant look was his only reply. Jen laughed and ran up the marble steps and into the house.

"Mistress Jen."

Halfway up the stairs, she looked down. Alannan, her master's steward, stood at the foot, tall and impeccable and unruffled as ever.

"Master has a guest," he said, somehow managing to make his voice carry up the stairs without the indignity of raising it. "I believe he sent Mistress Marin looking for you."

The basket on her hip rested as heavy on her conscience as a load of loot. Jen wanted to get these clothes upstairs and out of sight. The clothes, and the knife.

"You needn't bother with that," Alannan said, gesturing at the basket. "One of the maids will take care of it."

She soothed her squirmy conscience once more. With a flourish of the street magician she'd once been, she sent the basket away, to the back of her wardrobe.

"No need," she said, trying to sound careless. "Thanks, Alannan," she said, then descended the stairs again, toward the evening's servitude.

The drawing room door opened, then closed behind her. Jen took her place as usual behind her master's chair and found she knew his guest tonight: a man named Palimur.

Palimur was a wizard; he knew what she was (and was not, and that she was not a boy), and he *looked* at her. What he was looking *for*, she often speculated—uncomfortably. Thus Jen had to affect not to see him, staring at some empty spot in space, ignoring the heat of the wizard's gaze on her skin.

Tonight was no different. From a table of polished cherry, Jen took a tray bearing globe-shaped glasses of liqueur and offered one to Palimur.

Palimur was a square man: square-faced, square-built, with large square hands like those of a bricklayer. His hair, a dull color somewhere between blond and brown, was gathered back in a clip of worked gold, but his eyes were almost amber, like a feral dog's.

Jen met them defiantly. Palimur's lips twitched and he took a glass. Jen offered the remaining glass to her master, then went to stand behind his chair as always.

"You really ought to meet with the Prince, Barras," Palimur said as if resuming a discussion interrupted by her entrance. "He's a generous man. He'll make your efforts well worthwhile."

Her master sat back and sipped liqueur. "I don't doubt that. However, as I've told you before, I have no interest in becoming embroiled in politics." He gestured with his glass. "Much too messy."

"You needn't worry about the politics. Gods above and below, Barras, all he wants is to be able to say you're in his employ. If he can do that, the threat will fall away like rotten cloth."

"Flattery."

"Not flattery," Palimur retorted, "but truth. Do you have any idea in what esteem your name is held?"

Her master's smile said, *Of course I know.* "Nevertheless, if I so much as have my apprentice make a good-luck charm for the Prince, I'll find myself tainted with accusations of meddling."

"Meddling! When the very City is at risk?" Palimur leaned forward. "If that's meddling, I can't think of anyone, merchant or minister, who won't kneel down to you in thanks."

Barras shook his head. "I have no desire for that kind of thanks. And I've given my answer," he said amiably.

"Without letting me explain the situation," the other wizard said. "The other cities of the peninsula are growing more aggressive."

"I am not so sequestered that I'm not aware of such things."

"Then you must know that the oligarchs of Castinay have been amassing troops, and the Merinome family of Gile has sent assassins—two so far. Terna's assembly has approved alliances with our enemies. If there's war," Palimur said, "what opinion will the beleaguered have of your principles?"

"If there is war," Barras retorted, "it will be because our Prince has succumbed to an outsized greed. These last years he's behaved like one possessed, like a farmboy snared by some witch's charm."

Jen blinked once at the terse opinion. Her master was, of course, given to terse opinions, but Jen thought it greatly daring to be so candid when speaking to the Prince's wizard.

Palimur only grinned, showing teeth as big and square as the rest of him. "The Prince does have his little ambitions, doesn't he? But so do we all." His gaze flicked to Jen and away again. "All but you, I suppose, eh?"

Jen wondered at that glance. Collusion, or calculation?

"Indeed," her master said.

"Think of it, if you will," the other wizard said, "as defending the City. In the end, that's what it comes to."

Barras' lips thinned. "And where do I draw the line between our Prince's aggressions and those of our neighbors? I will not take one man's part against another. I'll set spells of protection or of warning, do auguries and seeings, but if someone is interested in attacking another, even if that someone is the Prince, he'll do it on his own strength with no help from me. Wizardry is susceptible enough to suspicion and resentment. We don't need to fuel the fears of ordinary folk."

Jen had had five years to learn the intricacies of her master's code of wizardry. That code had always seemed to be overly scrupulous, a luxury indulged in by a wealthy and powerful man. Had he ever been poor and powerless, to know how self-indulgent such scruples were?

Don't use your powers for harm, he'd told her. Fair enough, most of the time. There were times, though, when one used what one had to survive. And then there were people who understood only fear and hurt.

"Ordinary folk have nothing to do with it," Palimur was saying.

"Except in how it affects their lives." Barras paused, then added, "Or brings their deaths."

Palimur opened his mouth to speak, but Jen's master waved the argument away.

"No," he said. "Don't try to convince me. I've seen too many wars over too many years to be swayed. You've come asking for help. Very well, I'll help you—in books, if you like. In knowledge. I don't fancy myself an arbiter of men's lives that I can tell you or your patron what to do. But don't expect more than that."

Palimur heaved a sigh. "The Prince won't be happy."

"Then he might learn to be more circumspect," Barras said dryly.

"You might consider the same, my friend."

Jen held her breath in the face of what sounded very much like a threat. Her master cocked a dark brow. "I'll do well enough. I generally do."

The conversation turned to other topics, the sorts of things two wizards will discuss, the things two men will discuss.

Then her master said, "Jen, bring down the Malmidion. Can you find it?"

Startled out of distraction, she said, "Yes, lord," and strode quickly from the room. She felt Palimur's gaze until she pulled the drawing room doors shut behind her. Surely her master was aware of it as well. Perhaps that was why he'd sent her out. But then why call on her to attend him in the first place?

No matter. She was going up to the study. That alone made her take the steps two at a time. She would have her gate to the Otherworlds, forbidden or not.

As she opened the door, the study lamps flared to life, flickered a little, then settled into steady gold flame that glimmered on leather-bound spines in mahogany and maroon and midnight. The air smelled of leather and old parchment and a smoky herbal scent, the same she'd noticed clinging to her master that long-ago night in her brothers' room.

Since that night, he'd taught her to read, and write, and cipher; had taught her the names of the stars, shown her the planets and the moon through a telescope. He'd taught her to read compass and clock, had her pluck apart small dead animals to see how they were made. The latter she had done unsqueamishly. She'd skinned and dressed more small creatures than she cared to remember, readying them for the pot. She had been rather more squeamish, however, when he'd presented her with a criminal's hand. Only when she'd seen the grimed and bitten nails, as her father's nails had been grimed and bitten, had Jen set scalpel to cold flesh.

She was no longer quite so ignorant, quite so rough. Now, she could pace the study walls, trailing fingertips along the spines of books, stopping now and then to read the titles in gold leaf while she pondered how to go about her search.

The sign the Fey woman had made in last night's vision still burned in her mind. She linked a seeking spell to it, sent the spell sniffing through the books like a faithful, tireless dog. Only then did she turn her attention to seeking the book for which she'd been sent.

The *Malmidion* was a massive thing, almost too big to carry. Whether she would indeed find it was another question. Like the house, the book possessed a consciousness; it hid or revealed pages or passages, even itself, according to whims of its own. It had even been said to leave a place that displeased it, only to reappear elsewhere.

She scanned the shelves, but didn't see the book.

"Malmidion!" she called. "My master is asking for you. He wishes to consult your wisdom."

Her master had said the book could be temperamental, even sulky, if it did not wish to be disturbed. It might make her look awhile, so she'd be properly grateful when she found it.

Dutifully, she looked, giving the seeking spell time to sniff out what she sought on her own behalf.

She didn't know what she would do if her clandestine quest proved fruitless. Nor did she relish the thought of having to tell her master—in Palimur's presence—she'd been unable to fulfill so simple a task as retrieving a book.

"Malmidion." Anxiety tinged her voice. "Won't you let me find you?"

A book bumped suddenly out of place with a squeak of leather against wood. Jen turned and saw, there on the bottom shelf, the *Malmidion*.

A breath gusted out of her. "Thank you."

Taking the *Malmidion* in her arms, she found it warm to the touch. Her spell had found the very book her master had asked for. Surprised and not a little confounded, she hugged the great book to her and let her seeking spell unravel.

She carried the book downstairs, desiring to search it and wondering how she would manage to do so before having to relinquish it. She glanced down the hall toward her room and hesitated. Then, rather than descending, she turned that way. It would take only a moment, she told herself, to find the page the spell had marked, and just a moment more to read it.

She sent a thread of power ahead to open the door and slipped into her room. Lamps winked on. She dropped the book on the bed with a *whump!* of compressing feathers. Settling cross-legged before it, she flipped the book open and began riffling through. The lingering warmth of the pages drew her fingers on. She smoothed the warmest with the flat of her hand and gazed down on the very figure the Fey woman had drawn.

With shaking fingers, she traced it on the page and gave a trembling laugh.

"Thank you, Malmidion," she whispered.

Elbows on knees, she bent to read, eyes racing over the calligraphy and archaic spelling, taking in all she could while she had the chance—

Jen. Her master's voice spoke in her mind. *Were you able to find it?*

She bit off a curse. *Yes, lord*, she thought back. *I'm coming.*

To the book, she whispered, "Malmidion. Will you let me read these pages again?"

Like the house, the book had no voice, and so gave no reply. It came up light in her arms, though, and she took that as a good sign. She heaved a sigh and headed downstairs.

Jen bore the great book to the drawing room. With each step, it grew heavier. Her master stood and came to her, lifted the book from her arms and carried it to a tall narrow table. Palimur stepped up beside him, not as tall but broader, his court clothes slashed with bullion and bold colors beside her master's straight and sober garb.

"The pages are warm." Her master glanced over his shoulder at her. "Did you use a seeking spell?"

"Yes, lord," Jen said on a dry mouth.

He looked for a moment as if he might chide or question her, but with a glance at Palimur, simply turned back to the book. Palimur took the opportunity to turn his burning-glass gaze on her as well. Jen, puzzling over her master's restraint, avoided his eye. Palimur gave his slight, square smile and turned back as well, watching Barras flip through the stiff pages.

At last, her master said, "Here it is. The spell of the Shadow-Way. I'll warn you, though, it isn't lightly used or easily mastered."

"This is a treasure, Barras. Even my old master, Illin, had nothing like it. What are you doing hoarding such things while putting findings and bindings on merchant ships?"

Barras only gave his candleflame smile.

Palimur bent over the book again. "May I borrow this?"

"Of course," her master said.

Jen drew an audible breath of protest. Both men turned to look.

"Jen?" There was nothing in her master's tone: no warning, no reproof, no surprise.

She stammered for a moment, then blurted, "It's so precious..." She trailed off.

"It will be safe enough," he said.

Palimur chuckled. "What sorts of things do you have

your apprentice girl studying? You'd best watch out. She might be less cautious than you!"

"She knows what she's doing," her master said, unsmiling.

The words turned this way and that, changing shape, changing meaning. She ducked her head.

"Go on, Jen," her master said. "Take the Malmidion to Lord Palimur's carriage."

She steeled herself to walk between them, to take the book and carry it from the room, to start it on its journey far beyond her reach.

"He knew," she murmured to the book as she carried it down the hallway to the front door, her footsteps on the marble floor echoing. "But how? How did he know about the sign?"

The book, having no voice, did not reply.

お

The *Malmidion* haunted her. Jen dwelled on it before she fell asleep. The pang of its loss pierced her when she awakened. To come so close, only to have the knowledge she needed snatched away! What could she do?

Nothing. Nothing but wait, and watch, and listen. After all, each day she spent with her master taught her more lore, greater power. A path to her escape might be found through means other than the Malmidion. She must find patience until it was.

So now Jen shifted on the high stool in her master's basement workshop. Her master stood close behind her.

The dressed stone of the surrounding walls gave off its own clear, shadowless light, giving the impression, if one didn't look up, of the light of an overcast day. She didn't look up. She disliked windowless rooms and stone walls, so she tried not to look at those walls or think of them. It helped to have a difficult spell to occupy her mind.

She willed her breathing slow and even, commanded her hands to remain dry and steady. Between those small, thin hands lay a green-enameled copper bowl full of dew. The dew, collected under moonlight, was precious, used again and again for perhaps more years than she'd been alive.

"Slowly, Jen." She felt the heat of her master's body close behind her. "Gently. Magic of Seeing is fragile magic."

She locked her gaze, her thoughts, on the bowl of water. Not on his nearness.

"Water pervades all," he murmured. "The moon sails silently above. What darkness moonlight can't pierce, water will seep into. With this bowl, you will be able to see into the most distant tower, into the deepest dungeon."

His voice was rhythmic, a cadence that lured her to sink into it. It was great magic—greater, perhaps, than she had done before—and she scraped the bedrock of her power.

And see into the heart of a wizard's house, perhaps? If this kind of seeing was so powerful, she might yet be able to reach the Malmidion.

Her master's fingers stole over her shoulder. She twitched, but kept from flinching.

"No, Jen," he said. "Borrow from me if you must."

Power coursed through his touch, a tingle as alien as the stone's cold grip had been. Her focus broke entirely. The water in the bowl quivered in concentric rings, then spattered in all directions in a rain of glowing white.

Jen spat a succinct curse and her master's touch vanished from her shoulder. Locking her hands around the now-empty bowl, she restrained the urge to throw it against the glowing stone walls.

"Still unwilling to admit your limitations," he said behind her.

She whirled. *Unwilling to let you invade me!* she almost snapped. "I'm tired, lord," she said instead.

The candleflame smile did not appear. "And distracted."

Jen dropped her gaze. "Maybe, lord."

"Distracted," he insisted.

The impulse to shrug like a sullen fifteen-year-old came and went. "Yes."

He paused for a long, excruciating moment, then said, "What distracts you?"

"I can do Seeings by fire," she said, unwilling to speak a lie his wizard's ear would detect. "I can See in crystal."

"Any sorcerer can See by fire," he replied, "and a skilled witch by crystal. They each have limitations. A Seeing by moonwater is the clearest form. And the subtlest."

Jen made no argument. Patience suddenly seemed futile. Her life stretched ahead, year after year of working wizardry ever more difficult, magic that devoured her days while never bringing her closer to freedom.

She thought of the sturdy traveling clothes tucked away at the back of the wardrobe and burst out, "What must I do?" She drew in a sip of breath and would have taken back the words if she could.

"Look at me, Jen." His voice was like a hand beneath her chin, raising her face. "Do what you must," he said at last, and she didn't know if it was answer to her thoughts, or to something else he'd seen.

She mouthed the words, *what I must*. A part of her reached out to him. But he'd bought and bound her and crossed every attempt at escape.

Her gaze fell once more. "Yes, lord."

She did not know if he meant her to hear his sigh. "Go on, then. Rest. You'll have some long nights gathering more dew for that Seeing bowl."

He stepped back, freeing her to slip off the stool without treading on his toes. She edged between him and the worktable, the tall shelves stacked with glassware and stoppered jars and vials. With a measured pace, she fled before he had a chance to change his mind.

Chapter 6

Soothsayers spoke of omens. What was Jen to make of hers? Her masterwork first given, then taken away. The Malmidion, the same. She'd received a vision of escape, and then the knife, a gift of embarkment.

She sat down at her worktable and swept aside charms of good fortune and of beauty; a glass to see through sorcerers' seemings when inspecting horses at auction. Her master's Seeing bowl she moved more carefully, though it was far too late for such care.

Setting the obsidian knife on her worktable, she rummaged a coil of silver wire from a bin on the floor and began to fashion a chain.

She was stringing the knife onto the finished chain when a tap came at the door.

Jen hastily dropped the knife on its new chain over her head, tucked it into her shirt and sent the door swinging open. Marin stood outside.

"Well," she said, pretending as if no such thing as the knife existed. "Come in."

Marin carried in a tray. "You didn't come down for dinner, so I thought you might like a bite to eat."

The knife lay against her heart, a guilty secret. "Thanks, Marin."

The older woman set the tray by Jen's elbow, then hesitated. Finally, she cleared a space at the end of Jen's worktable and half-sat. The table creaked and shifted on its old legs. Jen ducked her head and uncovered a dish.

"What preys upon you so, child?" Marin finally asked.

The house enfolded them, an attentive entity of wood and stone.

"I'm bound," Jen answered. "Isn't that enough?"

Marin snorted. "Nonsense. Look how much freedom you have, your own responsibilities—"

"Freedom!" she cried. "How can you say that?"

Marin caught Jen's clenched hands in hers. "What's happened, love?"

"Nothing that hasn't been happening for the last five years," Jen said. She turned her hands over, gripping Marin's practical ones with thin, strong fingers. "Do you know what it's like to have been bought, Marin?"

Marin freed one hand and ran it across Jen's curls. "Oh, child. Can you never forgive that?"

Holding tight to Marin's hand, Jen shook her head. Past the empty Seeing bowl, a watery view through the window showed the world in tones of copper and blue; the light of sunset caught like sparks in the tiny bubbles embedded in the glass.

"You may've heard me tell of my husband, Harret," Marin finally began. "We had a farm at the edge of the hill country. There were many good years, and children. And a few bad years, too."

Jen slowly turned back again.

"Harret was sick a long time," Marin went on. "But we kept the farm going. Then he died. The man we were buying the place from, the man we'd been paying faithfully for years, wanted the rest of his money. All of it." She shook her head. "Years ago, a man would never have done such a thing to his neighbor's widow, slaking his greed on her misfortune. But things changed sometime, like a curse that turns loose the worst in people's hearts.

"It was impossible, of course, even with what all of us, me and the children, could raise. I couldn't let him have the land back, lose everything we'd worked for, leave the children landless paupers." She sighed. "I went to the debtor's block. There was an auction—" Marin's eyes held no tears; they were either dammed within or cried long since. "I went to a lordling first, then to Master as payment for some spell or other. And here I am," she said in the manner of a woman relating her market-day adventures. "But my children own the land, and it'll never be taken from them now."

"I'm sorry, Marin," Jen said.

The older woman smoothed her curls again. "For what, love? For me? But you shouldn't be. I'm happy here—how could I not be? I live in a fine house, see my children and grandchildren often, and Master's good to me. As he is to you. You must know all he does, all he has done for you. Can't you see that?"

She didn't dare see it. What if she came to believe it? Long ago she'd learned people serve themselves. Forget that once, and you'd be meat on a trencher served to those stronger or more ruthless.

Abruptly, Jen stood and folded her arms tight. "I'm twenty. No boy man so old remains an apprentice."

"But Jen," Marin whispered from where she still sat on the table. "You're a young woman."

"A woman," Jen repeated, tasting the words like acid. "Wizard-woman," she said, as the stone had. She had thought it flattery then. Now, it seemed mockery. "What good is that? What good will it ever be?"

Marin reached out and disentangled one of Jen's hands, stroking it as if soothing a small, frightened creature. "Maybe that's what Master is trying to teach you."

In spite of the comforting touch of a woman who had soothed many distraught children, Jen couldn't tell her that she might as well have touched a sore tooth with the tip of a needle.

お

Jen walked night-bound streets, among houses of decreasing size and increasing squalor. The task of replacing the moonwater for her master's seeing bowl filled her nights, blessing and burden at once. Blessing, because it gave her the freedom to go where she wished as long as she returned with the precious dew. Burden, because she had little time or energy to devise her escape.

Now that she saw again the crumbling wattle-and-daub huts of her old neighborhood, the tiny weed-choked yards, it seemed mistrust had goaded her as long as she remembered. The old throat-gripping dread seized her, the clench in her middle that made sure she stayed alert to each voice and every movement. Why had she come here? Never once had she wished to return. Even now she wanted nothing more than to leave again, but something, a wizard's power and confidence, wouldn't let her.

How small the houses were! Smaller than her master's guest-parlor. The roofs weren't much higher than a man's head, the doors so low a tall man would have to duck through. They hadn't seemed so small when she'd lived in one, nor so decrepit, nor so sordid. The realization of their wretchedness shocked her, as if she'd looked into a mirror and seen not herself, but some stranger.

She walked slowly from house to house, searching the ramshackle hovels for the one that looked the most familiar of all.

At last, she found it. There on the side was the tiny unglazed window through which she had tried to escape; there, the tumbledown wall of stones that half-surrounded the yard. On the door, just visible to her wizard's eye, were the signs of peace and prosperity Jen had scratched after her powers had come. Her family had been lucky to have two shrivelled potatoes and a sprouted onion in those days, before she'd taken her magic to the streets. But she knew the signs, and even at the age of twelve, could make them work. Not well enough, though. Perhaps even as they were now, her powers wouldn't have been enough.

Her feet crunched in shards of broken crockery. The front door of the house she'd lived in for the first fifteen years of her life opened, and a strange woman with a lean angry face came out.

She scowled past the flicker of the rude tallow lamp in her hand. "Whatcha want?" she demanded in street accents Jen knew in her bones. "Gwan now, there's nothin' here for ya."

"What 'appened to the folks who useta live here?" Jen asked in the same manner. "Man and wife, two boys?"

The woman's mouth opened for a reply. Down the cramped alleys, a scream ripped the night air. Jen spun, and the door behind her slammed. The next instant, a fiery shape that howled like a tormented spirit burst from a darkened slot between houses.

Between one blink and the next, she realized it was a dog, coat ablaze, running from inescapable pain and terror. In shock and fury, Jen snuffed the flame with a thought. The dog felt the added assault of magic and cowered down on the dirt of the street, still twisting and screaming. Jen took a single step toward it just as two boys burst from the same alleyway.

"Hey, where'd it go?" one said, laughing.

People opened their doors and peered out. The other boy, looking around, stumbled to a stop and shuffled a step or two backwards.

"There it is!" the first said. Then, indignant, "Who put it out?"

Jen stepped forward. "I did."

The first one, she saw now in the spill of light through one of the open doors, was actually a young man, tall, rangy, with a bristle of dark blond hair. He headed for the still-cringing dog. It leapt up and darted for Jen, perhaps recognizing her as its rescuer. The other, a youth with a messy mop of brown curls, only stood staring.

Something, the hair perhaps, tugged at memory. The trembling dog leaned against her leg, sticky and fire-hot. The foul smell of agony and terror and charred hair and flesh rose. Jen absently reached down and stroked the dog's head, avoiding the burns on its neck and back. The trembling against her leg quieted as her spells of soothing, both of fear and of pain, took hold.

"That's our dog." Bristle-Hair began a menacing amble toward her. "Better give it back."

Jen looked down at the dog, and the dog looked up at her. "He says not," she replied with a slow, one-sided smile that held nothing at all of good humor.

The rattle of another slamming door startled her, but she didn't flinch.

"Well, ain't that sweet." Bristle-Hair grinned and slid a knife from his belt. "The kid's a real sorcerer. Talks to dogs and all."

The curly-haired fellow took a step forward. "Jen?" he said suddenly. "That you?"

By moonlight, she could scarcely make out his face. Still, she resisted the temptation to call light, an old instinct to hoard the advantage of surprise.

Bristle-Hair let the knife droop.

The curly-haired boy took another step forward. "It's me. Col."

Jen's light blazed into the air around her, a shimmering silver across the filthy street, over the hovels crouched like hunchbacked beggars all around. Someone gave a frightened cry and more doors banged shut. Jen did not turn. The two boys squinted, suddenly fearful in the uncanny light. Col was still Col, with large brown eyes and curls much like her own. He had their father's narrow nose and chin.

"Rik," she said, addressing the taller of the two. He might have been their father, except for his youth. And his hair, coarse and spiky where their father's had been lank.

He grinned. "Still remember me, huh? Never thought to see you back."

The dog whimpered. The stink of its singed coat and burnt flesh went to her head like rage, but Jen held calm with a will.

Rik's stained leather vest gapped open, showing his thin chest. On it dangled the little ivory face she'd given Col on the night she'd been sold. The one she'd asked Col to give to their mother.

Her calm slipped another notch.

Rik looked her up and down. "You workin' for that pelf what bought you?"

"Yes."

"Listen, Jen," Col said. "That dog. I told him—"

"Shut up, Col." Then Rik said to Jen, "Didn't think you'd still be dressing like that."

"Didn't think you'd take to torturing animals," Jen shot back. "Ma know you do that?" she asked, instinctively falling into the old mode of speech.

Rik shrugged and stuck his knife through his belt once more. "Ma's dead."

The blankness and unsurprise she felt shocked her. But emotion flared through one of her brothers, or both; she caught an image of flying fists, of her mother lying in a ragged, bloody heap on the floor. Jen's fingers curled where they caressed the dog's ear.

"You mean our father finally beat her to death," she said, changing accents, speaking as she spoke now in her master's house.

Col scuffed his foot in the dirt and fiddled with the hem of his shirt, but Rik said, "Nah. Baby killed her."

Jen smiled her cold wizard's smile and resumed stroking the dog. "You shouldn't lie, Rik. It lets bad things in."

His hand lashed out so quickly she didn't have time to block it. He caught the front of her tunic and jerked her toward him. His breath reeked when he shoved his face into hers.

"Ma's dead. Whatcha gonna do about it now?"

She felt like a spark borne upward on a hot wind. "Maybe what I ought to do about this dog."

Rik shook her, two hard jerks that snapped her head back and forth. "Think you'll come back now with your fancy talk and your ears that hear lies? Think you can stir up trouble, huh? Maybe with your rich master you can. But I'll give you a taste of trouble before you go."

Sparks seemed to dance at the edge of her vision now, pricked at her fingertips.

"Don't, Rik. Don't," Col pleaded, plucking at his brother.

Rik ignored him, shoving her back and back. Night dimmed suddenly into deeper shadow, and her back struck a wall. A rain of crumbling daub showered her head. Through the linen of her tunic, he grabbed her breast.

"You still a girl under there after garbing like a boy so long?" He showed teeth like a dog. Like their father. "Maybe I oughta make sure."

The old, familiar darkness plunged down again. Wizard's fire burst free. With a crackling hiss, it slapped Rik away, sent him skidding over the dirt of the street. Jen stepped away from the wall, feeding fire that did nothing to light the darkness within her.

She'd banished the worst of it, but the dog's pain remained, a seething, invisible cloud. This she drew off, funneled it into Rik. It danced around her brother's prone form, a writhing fire.

He screamed as the dog had, flailing.

"Here's your fun," Jen said. "Enjoy it. No? Too much fun all at once?"

Hands grabbed her. Jen jerked around, but it was only Col, eyes huge, lips shaping the word, *No, no.*

At once she doused her flame. Rik fell slack onto the dirt like a broken toy. People had reappeared at their doors. They stood openmouthed, hovering like rats at the entrances of their burrows. Col pulled her to him, wrapped skinny arms around her. Against his rough wool shirt, she lost sight of the people.

By the time she extricated herself, the people had disappeared into their holes again. She wondered what courage or what fear let Col hold her, blazing as she had blazed. She stepped toward Rik, now propped on one elbow. Eyes wide, he tried to hitch away. Jen stepped on a corner of his vest.

She found her hands clenched into fists, but didn't dare loosen them. Simply breathing for a moment, she fought the queer lightheadedness that threatened to whirl away her control. "What else do you do, besides torture dogs? Do you beat him?"

Rik shook his head in bewilderment. "Who?"

"Col. Do you beat him?"

"Nah. Not me. Do I, Col?" Rik tried to squirm free.

Jen straddled him, standing on the other corner of his vest. "I told you lying lets in bad things. Are you lying to me again?"

"Jen, don't," Col pleaded.

Rik wriggled. She stepped up a little higher on his vest. "Tell me, Rik, yes or no. But tell me true, else I'll take the truth from you. You know I can do that, don't you?"

Rik fell back, breathing hard. His eyes slowly filled with fear that welled upward like black water. "Yeah," he said. "I knock 'im sometimes. When he needs it."

"A fine young man you've grown to be," Jen said. "You torture animals, beat your brother, and threaten to violate your own sister. Do you have a woman yet, any children? Though it shames me to say it, you're my brother. I'd be no better than you if I did what's in my heart to do." She paused, considering. "Still, I think I should do something."

Col laid a tentative hand on her shoulder and said her name again. She paid him no heed.

To Rik, she spoke in the voice that made her words truth. "What pain you give, you'll suffer in equal measure. If you ever once touch in cruelty any child you have, you'll never sire another." Elbow on knee, she leaned down, whispering, "And I promise you, Rik. Never, *never* will you father a daughter."

She let the magic go. The curse settled like a stain into her brother's pores. It would doom him to a lifetime of suffering blows, rather than accepting the echoed pain of returning them, but she did not care.

He flinched when she reached for him, and yelped when she jerked the little ivory face loose from his neck.

Holding it in her fist, she said, "This was for *Mother*." She stepped away, then turned to Col. "Will you come with me?"

Col gazed at them each in equal fear. Behind her came the scrape of Rik dragging himself—away, or to his feet. She did not look to see. Jen wanted to plead with Col. But after what he'd seen her do, after the sort of life he'd led, he would hear only threat in her words.

Col nodded once to Jen. "Let's go."

"You little—" Rik began.

Jen turned and silenced him with a look. "Fare thee well, brother. Remember what I said." With Col and the dog beside her, she left him clambering to his feet, but kept wizard's senses tuned behind.

Chapter 7

The dog was badly burned, and Col… He was so thin and filthy Jen wondered when he'd last eaten or slept under a roof. She'd asked, but he only shrugged in reply.

She led boy and dog back into the City through the Boneyard Gate. The guards on duty shared some drink from a little leathern flask and bent over a game of dice. Jen sent a wisp of magic toward the dice. One man gave a crow of triumph, the others groans of disappointment. All shuffled closer to the little tin lantern illuminating the winning throw, and Jen, Col and the dog passed unchallenged through the gate.

An unfamiliar feeling of strength carried her striding through the streets. "I'll get you food and clothes," she told Col. "Somewhere decent to sleep—"

She deflated. How? How would she do that, and still keep him from her master?

She realized she'd stopped. The dog lay down on the cobbles, still and quiet as animals will be when they're sorely hurt. Col pulled at his fingers like the timid, nervous child he'd once been.

Gathering herself once more, Jen finally said, "I can get you something to eat, at least. And the dog—"

She could keep the burns from festering, coax the skin to knit and hair to re-grow, banish the ropy sheen of scars. But magic could only go so far in such matters before it did more harm than good.

Why can't I do more! she wanted to rage. As long as her

master held her in his power, she could do little enough.

She shoved her hands through her hair and pushed out a breath. "Come on. Let's find someplace you both can rest."

At Col's feet, the dog wagged a thin tail, one of the few parts that still bore hair. Jen knelt and renewed the spell to ease his pain, then looked around

The houses around them were small but tidy, with swept stoops and polished stair rails. Painted gates opened onto small yards. A dog yammered at them from one, a rooster gave a half-hearted crow somewhere.

Jen walked on, reaching wizard's senses past the gates. At last she stopped, touched open a gate and led brother and dog into a tiny yard littered with weeds. A gap-toothed trellis leaned under the weight of a dead vine. A shed stood against one wall. The boards were unpainted and splintery, but the roof was sound and the occasional coo of a pigeon within suggested that it might be dry.

She eased magic into the shed's warped door so it opened easily and without the screech of old hinges.

"Wait here," Jen said. "I'll get food." And something to put on the dog's burns. "I'll work a spell that'll keep harm away until I can find you someplace safe to stay."

She left them behind, wondering how well she'd be able to keep that promise.

お

A sound of footsteps came, the rustle of clothing. Jen fought to wake, but sleep pushed her down, a silencing hand on her face. She struggled, panicking—

"What in the name of the gods high and low are you doing there dressed like that?" a voice demanded.

Jen jerked upright. Her eyes flared open and sparks spat at her fingertips. A bed canopy and curtains stitched with red and blue paisley patterns showed in bright morning light, all the familiar surroundings of her room. Last thing she remembered, dim predawn light had bathed it after she'd left Col and the dog as safe and comfortable as she could manage.

Now Marin, scowling, stood fists on hips in the doorway.

Jen let go the magic and rubbed her eyes. "Uh."

Marin shook her head and tutted, placed a tray on the little table before the windows. "Get those things off. You look like a street urchin."

"I am a street urchin," Jen muttered, but peeled out of jerkin and tunic and breeches.

"I'll have the tub brought up," Marin said. "You stink like a pig-skinner. Might as well leave the clothes on the bed, since the linens will have to be washed, too."

"Sorry," Jen said and meant it, shrugging into a robe.

Marin eyed her. "You've got a guilty look about you."

Jen looked up sharply.

The older woman nodded. "You don't raise as many children as I have without knowing a guilty look when you see one. What've you been up to, girl?"

Jen thought of Col and Rik and the dog, but said only, "Keeping promises."

"Promises, is it? Well, it can't be all bad, then. Though Master may not see it that way."

Jen only made a noncommittal noise. "I only went out as the master ordered."

"Hmph. And I suppose the dirt and the rips, not to mention the burnt-hair stink, have perfectly reasonable explanations."

Jen shrugged and smiled, then cleaned up as Marin bid.

Jen had a great deal to do, and must do it without attracting unwelcome attention. She had two strays to protect and care for, brother and dog, both starved and one whose wounds would take many days of salves and healing magic to mend. She bent her mind to practicalities, moving from rich hallways to the plain corridors of the servants' territory.

Kitchen smells led her on: baking bread, simmering soup. Jen opened the kitchen door and stepped through, into the bedlam that reigned with the preparation of the meal—the clatter of pans, the bubbling of pots, and over in one corner, a flurry of feathers where a scullion plucked a goose for dinner. Over the racket came the scratchy voice of Elmanel, the cook, standing like the Lord of Storms in the midst of it all.

He pointed at a pot boiling over, and the seething froth of broth and herbs subsided at once. A boy carrying a tray was about to trip over a spill of potatoes rolling across the stone floor. The boy yelped as if pinched and jumped to the side.

Elmanel was only a kitchen witch, but here in his domain, that small, precise power answered him like a well-trained dog. His sandy hair was bound up in a tangle of witch-knots to keep the cakes from falling, the butter from scorching.

"Fasten that head t' your shoulders, Candy," Elmanel called in his broad, down-river accent to the potato-spilling scullion. "Ral won't be doin' no choppin' or scrubbin' laid up in bed with a broken neck."

Jen snickered. Healing a broken neck might strain even her master's abilities.

Elmanel turned to where she stood prudently out of the way. "Aye, Jenna. You're needin' somethin'?"

She felt a squeeze of fondness at the nickname. Elmanel had looked her up and down when they'd first met, and said, "Jen? Seems a boy's name to me." With that, Jen knew that *he* knew she was no boy at all, just as she knew Elmanel for a witch, each without being told.

She edged into the kitchen, meeting the cook where he breasted the confusion like an otter swimming through choppy waters. "I'm going out for the master. Can I take a bite with me?"

He shot her a curious, pale-eyed glance. Jen buried all thoughts of last night; of her brother and the dog, pushed aside the sudden prickle of conscience over the curse she'd laid. No witch could see thoughts, but here, in her master's house, there was someone who could.

Elmanel turned and called out, "Kitty, love, off to the pantry with you and bundle up Miss Jenna a bite."

A woman with a thick braid of oatmeal-colored hair and an enormous bosom shelving out over her substantial torso ducked her head and turned to do his bidding.

"A little more than last night, if that's all right," Jen murmured, hoping not to short her own meal while she fed Col and the dog, but having no intention of revealing such a plan.

The cook shouted after Kitty as she disappeared into the dimness of the pantry. "Double it!"

Wincing, Jen hoped the house had better things to do than listen to goings-on in the kitchen.

Elmanel turned back. "There. That'll be ready in a snap." He studied her. "Master's got you doin' double duty these days, don't he?"

She shrugged, grateful to be on safe ground. "I ruined

his Seeing bowl, so I have to gather more dew to fill it."

"Well," Elmanel said, "I won't be sayin' Master's too hard on you, 'cos I don't think that. But maybe you sometimes take the hard way 'round, if you know what I mean. Just to say you ought to be rememberin' there's often help at hand, for those who'll ask."

Unexpectedly, a desire to unburden her worries gripped her. Jen clamped her jaw and swallowed words until they made a knot in her throat.

Elmanel turned to call instructions to the undercook. Jen used the well-timed distraction to breathe deep, prying loose the tightness in her throat and chest.

Kitty returned, and he handed her the bundled napkin she brought. "Here y'are, Miss. There's more where that come from whenever you need it."

Much against habit, she touched his shoulder lightly and said, "Thank you, Lel," using her own nickname for him.

He winked, then scowled. "Now out with you. I've work to be doin'."

Thus dismissed, Jen carried the food and her secrets away from the house, where they'd be safe.

お

Fishbone Square already seethed with people, with noise, hours before nightfall this night of the New Moon. People danced and sang, filled the air with the sounds of drums and flutes and reedhorns to lure the Mother from her seclusion. Scores of feet danced upon the patterned pavers that gave the square its name. And Jen, standing with the dog at the edge of this dismaying churn, doubted the wisdom of agreeing last night to meet her brother here.

Nevertheless, she said to the dog, "Stay close, Burn." She used the name she'd given when she spoke words of soothing and of healing magic.

Wagging his skinny tail, Burn looked up and panted, happier after trimmings from a roast and the stiffened mold of porridge she'd given him.

They dodged swaying packs of young men singing loud and bawdy songs, squeezed between gossiping housewives, threaded around long chains of children playing Crack-the-Whip. They passed booths and trestle tables lining the square, selling everything imaginable: leather goods, pottery, honey, music boxes. Women sold bread and pastries from trays, sausages and soup from steaming carts; men hawked jugs of home-brewed gin; a troupe of mummers performed to laughter and applause.

Jen stopped and sent out a finding. The spell skipped and darted through the crowd, undismayed by the noise and kaleidoscopic motion. Bumped and jostled by passersby, Jen turned her cold wizard's smile upon a would-be pickpocket. The woman blanched, pulled her forelock and slipped into the crowd with a single, fearful backward glance. The spark and tug of Jen's spell led her along its thin, invisible line to her brother.

She found him by the toymaker's booth. The toymaker himself scowled at the scruffy young man who eyed his wares with such admiration, while Col kept his hands clasped behind his back like a child warned by his mother not to touch.

Jen touched his shoulder. "Col."

He started and whirled as if caught at some mischief. "Oh. Jen," he said on the outrush of a relieved breath.

"Come on." She caught his arm and pulled him away. Two little girls immediately crowded up to take his place.

Bags and barrels and boxes clustered in a corner of the square. Jen, with Col beside her, settled on a scrunching, squeaking sack of grain, against a rough brick wall. Burn snuffled around a bit, then folded himself at their feet. Passersby would have seen two brothers, elder and younger, with brown curls and eyes and pale skin. Yet the elder brother was actually the younger, and the younger brother, a sister.

Handing Col a skin of drink, Jen untied the napkin Elmanel had given her and produced brown bread, cheese, dried apples and crisp honeycakes. The skin, when she uncapped it, was full of the last of last year's cider, all the better for age.

"This bread ain't even squashed." Col tore off a hunk and stuffed it into his mouth.

"Our cook is a kitchen witch," Jen explained. "A squashed loaf would shame him for days."

Our cook, she'd said. As if Elmanel were a part of her household, rather than she and Elmanel being a part of her master's household. She shivered, appalled that her thoughts could so easily turn traitor.

Col broke off cheese and sent it after the bread. Intent and drooling, Burn watched. Col broke off another morsel and gave it to Burn.

"Have you been getting along all right?" she asked, watching Burn snap up the cheese with the speed and efficiency of a miser snatching a coin.

Col nodded and swilled cider. His arms were so thin, his shirt and breeches filthy, ragged.

"I should be able to get clothes for you," she said.

He wiped his mouth and offered her the skin. "Nah. Duds I can get."

She took a sip and shook her head. She knew where he'd get them. As a child, she'd gotten clothes that way herself, stripping drunks too far gone to protest, though she'd drawn the line at bullying younger children for what they wore.

"And where will you sleep, Col?" she said. "Rooftops are fine this time of year, but what about when winter comes? Rich men's guards have no mercy for a street kid found in some merchant's stable. That spell I laid on you can only do so much."

Col shrugged. "It's the same Out-Wall." He shot her a quick glance. "Why you think I stayed with Rik?"

Jen scowled. "Why were you still in the slums? I'd think with what my master paid—" Wetting her lips, she forced the words out. "He had to've paid good money for me."

She'd never quite determined how much. Hadn't really wanted to know. But somehow, she'd always sensed it had been a great deal.

"Da drank and gambled it away," Col answered, staring into the motley flutter of the square.

A flash intruded, wizard's sight so strong it obscured the real world around her: their father tossing gold coins in the air, then catching them again. *Lookit what that little witch of mine brung*, he boasted. *I oughta breed me some more!* Then, a roar of drunken laughter—

She locked her mind to Col's memory, fraught with such strong emotion she could see it without a touch. Her brother must've seen her wince, for he covered her hand with his own. Deliberately, she pulled her fingers from beneath his, but she squeezed his hand before picking up a slice of dried apple.

By the sausage cart, a dog darted in and stole a steam-

ing link from a young boy. The child wailed and his mother chased shrieking after the dog. Burn pricked up his ears,
but didn't move from his spot by Jen's foot.

"Jen." Col hesitated. "What'd that pelf—your master—what'd he want you for? For work, like Dee?"

"Dee," she murmured.

She hadn't thought about her next-older sister for a
long time, a girl so quiet and self-effacing, she'd been almost invisible. Jen frowned. But Dee hadn't always been
that way. When had the teasing older sister changed to a
shrinking drab?

That memory spawned another, more visceral: Jen's
sick, cold fear of the thin-lipped, smiling man who'd come
jingling a bag in their father's face, telling him how the girl
would do good, honest labor for the guild. Jen, eleven
years old and already possessed of the beginnings of wizard's insight, had felt something else from the man. Images, intentions that made her shake and clutch her sister
with horror and shame.

"He buy you for a servant, too?" Col asked again with
surprising persistence.

"I'm his apprentice."

The knowledge of the inner fire her master had set
free burned off, for the moment, every fear and resentment. When she used that power, she flew near the sun
like a dragon, light sparking and flashing from her wings.

"But Jen, why'd he pay all that jingle for you? I seen
boys go apprentice to masons and such, and their masters
never paid nothing for them."

She started to her feet, and Burn scrambled out of the
way. "I don't *know*, Col. Don't you think my mind would
be ever so much easier if I did? I don't want to talk about
this anymore."

"Sorry, Jen." The hand holding a bite of honeycake drooped, reminding her so much of the nervous child he'd been that she at once sat down beside him again.

"Don't be." She nudged him with an elbow. She slumped back against the wall, picking at a knot in the sacking. "It's just that—nothing I try works. Just when I think I've found a way to get free, the door slams on me again."

Col licked his fingers. "Well," he said, "maybe you're tryin' the wrong key."

Maybe so, but she'd tried every key she could find.

お

The dog was nowhere to be found. Jen, bearing his breakfast, had called him in the ordinary fashion, then Called him, the way a wizard can call to him any living thing. Four days now she'd called, and four days he'd come. Until today. She stood outside her master's gates, stretching wizard's senses to search the streets all around for any sign of the dog.

Over the rooftops and treetops, the distant, sword-crowned spire of Cormilone's Fortress glinted gold in the still-hidden rays of the rising sun. A milk wagon with its load of chilled jugs clinked up to the servant's entrance at Master Carin's house two streets away. Three of Sir Erlann's mastiffs stood wagging before their kennels, watching for the back door to open and produce the man who brought their breakfasts.

But no Burn.

Jen chewed her lip, then with a sigh, set upon the cobbles a cracked bowl full of table scraps. Hoping only that the dog had felt well enough after the few days of care she'd given him to go off exploring, she stepped inside and let the gate clash softly shut behind her.

Col, in some ways, was the lesser worry, for they could arrange meeting places. Still, she cringed with shame that she had to smuggle food to her brother.

She opened the front door and shook her head. The situation couldn't go on indefinitely.

Jen climbed the grand staircase to the second floor. One of the maids, hurrying downstairs with an overflowing basket of laundry, covered a yawn and dipped a curtsey. Jen gave her a preoccupied nod.

How long until her master relented and allowed her to pursue her masterwork again? *If ever*, came the spiteful thought, and then the whisper: *Why does he keep me?* Jen crushed that thought as she would a cockroach.

Without willing it, she found herself at the bottom of another stairway. The stairs, wreathed in dimness, twisted upward. At the top lay the study with her master's books.

A quiver began in her stomach, a tension of want and need so powerful it seemed to possess a life of its own. It tugged at her foot, raised it, placed it upon the first step. The other foot followed. Her feet took a second tread, then a third, one after another. At last, she reached the landing. The study door stood before her, closed.

The house had tricked her this way before, let her think she'd reached her goal only to find that what she sought did not, after all, lie beyond the door she'd opened. She hung poised, unable to touch the latch, unable leave it untouched.

The latch clicked.

Jen jumped as if the floor had sprouted needles. The door swung silently inward on the study, its rugs and chairs and books—

And her master.

As a child, she'd stolen for the family, for ordinarily stealing wouldn't cost little children their hands. Once—only once—she'd been caught. At this moment, outside the forbidden study, she felt just as she had then.

"Lord," she managed.

He stood splendid in embroidered silk the color of the edge of night, his still-damp hair curling darkly over his shoulders. Jen distractingly wondered if he used wizardry to transfer tub and water to his room.

"Jen," he said with a nod and a smile that lasted rather longer than the usual candleflame gleam. "Come in."

She stood still, trying to unravel whether or not trouble lay ahead. After what seemed like far too long, she bowed her head and stepped inside. He led the way to the chairs, gesturing for her to join him.

"You're up and about early this morning," he said in the manner of a man opening a friendly conversation.

Jen fixed her attention on lowering herself into the chair, banishing all thoughts of brother and dog. "Oh…" She floundered for a truth that wouldn't betray her. "I'm still up. From last night. Collecting dew."

"Ah. And how does the dew-collecting progress?"

Inspiration seized her, how she could help Col far better than just smuggling food.

She puckered her lips. "Not well. The City isn't generous with dew in the summer. But I know witches who sell such things, if you'd give me the coin for it."

"The dew might, perhaps, be dear."

She hesitated, then decided he was sparring with her, for no doubt he had money enough for cisterns of moonwater. But *she* knew how to barter. In this, she was the master. "I'll be months collecting, and you'll be without your Seeing bowl."

"How will you be certain of the verity of what you buy?"

"I know who to go to."

He stroked his cheek with a forefinger. He might be a better haggler than she'd thought.

"Another wizard would be more trustworthy," he said.

"More expensive." This was good. "But of course, you're right."

The forefinger stilled. "Then again, I am aware of certain reliable witches."

"But reputations can lie. There's an old man who taught me—"

"Are you sure I know them merely by reputation?"

Jen stopped with her mouth hanging open. "But you don't know anyone Out-Wall!" she blurted.

The smile that curved his lips lingered, no quickly suppressed flash of amusement. "Then how did I come to hear of a certain talented young street magician, oh, some five years ago?"

She snapped her mouth shut.

The smile gleamed in his eyes, as well. "I believe I trust the dew you collect a great deal more than anything I might buy."

Dumbfounded, Jen watched her masterful bargaining folded up as nimbly as an offended peddler's stall.

"You may have more success," he went on, "in the countryside, although perhaps you've already anticipated that suggestion. You've been rather well supplied for your expeditions."

Her heart stopped. But no, it was her breath that stopped, for she could hear her heartbeat thunder in her ears. A lie was an impossible recourse for a wizard—or almost-wizard—and her master stalked her with the craft of a fox.

She switched tactics. "Yes." She added, as casually as possible, "There's a hurt dog I've been feeding."

He made a thoughtful noise. "The gardener mentioned having seen a dog hanging about." His smile flickered. "A *bald* dog."

"Burned." Jen tried to keep the disgust and outrage from her voice.

"And you're caring for it."

She studied him, searching for clues to his disposition on the matter. She could find none.

"Yes, but…" He waited, and she finally went on, "He wasn't there this morning. He's still not well. I'm—" She'd been about to say, *I'm worried about him*, but swallowed that admission.

"A stray dog wouldn't be a welcome addition to the neighborhood. There are those who would be displeased with me for allowing it. Even a wizard has no wish to feud with his neighbors."

Her throat went suddenly dry. "He's hurt," she said again, but now her voice held a pleading note she despised. "I can't let him go like that."

"Can't you?" her master said. Between bookcases, a door in the shadows opened.

She couldn't help it—she jumped again. Through the door, she saw red and green draperies, the foot of a bed, a man's slipper lying on its side by a footstool.

Something tapped on the floor's polished oak planks and something moved inside the room. A dog—a *bald* dog—trotted from her master's bedchamber, nails clicking on the floor, to sit by his knee.

"Burn!" She reached for the dog.

Burn panted mildly, amber-brown eyes fixed on nothing in particular. Jen's hand dropped. Touching his mind, she found it filled with green meadows and sunlight and shady trees.

"You've bound him," she whispered, returning to herself. Burn seemed quite easy about the whole thing, but something desperate struggled in Jen's chest.

"Should I have left him to be shot, or poisoned?"

"He wasn't doing anything!" Jen reached again for the dog.

At her master's gesture, Burn got to his feet and came to her. She slid off the chair and put her arms around him.

"You know no animal will willingly enter a wizard's house," he said. "But that doesn't mean he won't trespass upon one of my neighbors. He is a dog. He can't help doing what is in his nature to do."

She laid her cheek on Burn's neck, where the skin was still red and hot and naked. "I was feeding him. He wouldn't have bothered Master Tyne's peacocks. You didn't have to bind him." The word *bind* came out laden with bitterness and loathing.

Her master leaned forward suddenly. "Not to save his life? Not to save the lives of those foolish creatures he might kill or maim, not out of malice or intent, but simply in obeying impulses he can't control?"

Jen recoiled from his intensity, sensing undercurrents beyond her understanding. She shook her head, first in disagreement, then in doubt. In the circle of her arms, Burn panted, gazing into the green distance of that paradise in his mind.

"You're no longer a street magician, Jen, casting illusions and making love charms for a copper or two." He still leaned forward. "You possess a wizard's power. That gives you responsibilities. Each of your actions carries consequences, and you must learn to weigh and judge those consequences."

She knew that. She didn't need him to tell her, as if she were still a child.

"What consequences does healing a burned dog have?" she asked, trying to control the angry shaking of her voice.

He studied her a moment longer, then leaned back again. "None, perhaps, for you. For the dog, and for Master Tyne's frivolous peacocks... The costs may be rather greater."

On the black and green rugs, she crouched as she had on her cot all those years ago.

He stood. "The dog is your responsibility. Free him if you see fit."

She stroked Burn's head, stopping short of the burns on his neck. Suddenly, freeing him seemed the greater cruelty, a realization that upended every conviction she held. She hated the idea of imprisoning Burn in the house, of binding him, but was that worse than leaving him to the mercy of some neighbor's over-zealous groundskeeper?

"Lord," she said.

Her master, though he'd started for the door, turned. She found she could only raise her gaze as high as the deeply-turned cuffs of his sleeves. They were of silk moiré, buttons of darkest amethyst winking upon them. She feared more for Burn than she did her master's opinion of her.

"What do you think I should do?"

"I would keep him here, bound, until he is sufficiently healed to return whence you found him." He paused, then added, "But I wouldn't think you'd need me to tell you that."

He turned and left then.

Chapter 8

Jen hadn't been able to protect the dog. Her master had shown yesterday how easily he could take what she cared for, how helpless she was to prevent it. And Col? She shuddered. She had no wish to think of it.

She reached into the pile of hay and shook at what lay hidden beneath. "Wake up, Col," she whispered.

Her brother wrenched up, flailing, testament enough of what his wakings had been. Jen had already cast a spell of silence, that neither drowsing horses nor snoring stable-boy would hear them.

Col rubbed a hand down his face and shook off hay. "How'd you find me?"

Jen grabbed his arm and pulled, not bothering to answer the obvious. "Come on."

"Where?" He clambered to his feet, raining hay. "Whassamatter, Jen?"

She took a fistful of sleeve, tugged him out of some cabman's stable. In their stalls, horses shifted and whuffed. Col padded along behind her through straw and the dim, horse-smelling warmth. The stable door, a shabby affair of cross-nailed boards, opened silently and shut again as silently behind them. This early, even the milk wagon didn't make its rounds, and only the soft tap of their shoes and the nails of Burn's trotting feet broke the street's stillness. The smell of bread baking wisped across the still air.

"Jen—"

"We're going away," she said, answering the question he'd asked in the stable.

He stopped, planted fists on hips. "Away *where?* You said you can't run. You can't get away. What happened?"

The dog's ears pricked with interest, so different from the vague, distant look all day yesterday and all last night.

"My master found Burn," she said. "He bound him and brought him into the house."

Col didn't move, but his stillness was that of a hunted thing.

"I don't see how he could've known—" She closed her mouth, suddenly closer to tears than she could re-member having been for years. "He won't find you. I won't let him."

She took a breath, then another, seeing in her mind's eye once more the Fey man and woman with their pale skin, their hair like twin falls of bright water. Again, the woman's graceful, long-fingered hand marked a glimmer-ing sign upon the air. Then all the world turned wavery, dreamlike, a thin curtain the Fey could part and step through…

To where? Jen wondered, then fiercely answered her-self, *Anywhere.*

Her brother set his hands on her shoulders. "You tried, Jen. You done the best you could."

She shook her head. "No. There's one more thing I can do." She trailed her fingers along Burn's head. Col was a gangly shadow topped by a tangle of wild curls. "If it works, we'll all be well away from here." She turned, and Col hurried after her.

"Whatya gonna do? Whatya mean, *if it works?*" He trot-ted on one side, Burn on the other. Col caught her arm. "Jen."

She rounded on him. "He's kept me bound all these years. And now Burn—" She didn't say that it had been a binding of her own making that the dog had lain under this last day and night. "Just stay back, and keep Burn with you. I'm going to conjure—a way out." She didn't need to see his face to know of his dread, his confusion. She added, "To someplace better, where we'll be safe. Where you have enough to eat, and a dog can sniff after rabbits and foxes in tall grass. If you'll come."

"Outta *here?*" He gestured vaguely. Though they stood in the midst of tidy row houses, she knew he meant the 'here' he knew: the filth and degradation of the slums. "'Course I'm gonna come," he went on. "'Sides, I ain't gonna let you go nowhere all alone."

She couldn't reply. Gratitude chased relief in a warm rush and she quickly turned, striding down the street once more. She led the way around a corner, to a narrow alley the nightsoil man and the gleaners used to carry the stinking muck and refuse away from the bright clean houses.

Blind back walls ran along both sides of the lane. Above those walls, bordered by a fringe of trees, a strip of indigo sky showed a few stars yet wakeful.

"Stay here," she said.

At the mouth of the alleyway, Col sank down and hooked an arm around the dog. She nodded once to him and walked a short distance further, putting some space between them. She didn't know what the magic would do, and didn't wish to put her brother and the dog in any danger before she had it under control.

She took a long breath, settled herself and opened her heart to her power.

Like water from a spring, it flowed upward, carrying her before it. Jen did not know what powers the Fey woman had called upon; she could know only the same intent, to go from *Here* to *There*.

As when she had lifted the stone from its prison, she plumbed and stretched and focused her power, sent all the magic she could muster down along her arm and into her fingers. It hissed through her flesh like some fiery liquor, hot and glorious. Her hand rose as if beckoning.

Jen sketched the symbol on the dim air of the alley, a hook, a loop with a short flag at the top. There at the level of her eyes, the sign hovered, silver fire against the dusky walls and air. A vibration like distant thunder came, a sensation so faint and low it might as easily have been imagination. Dizziness passed over her. She put a steadying hand to the wall and felt in the stones a subtle insubstantiality.

The sign she'd drawn grew brighter, its lines widening and merging. She squinted, turned her face aside. Oddly, it cast no light. The walls, Col and the dog down at the end of the alley, remained lit only by the slow-growing dawn.

And yet…something changed. Something she could feel with wizard's senses, the first thin threads of storm-winds. But those winds lay only in the metaphysical realm; the leaves of nearby trees fluttered no more than the increasing glare of the sign lit the alleyway.

The sign was a searing clot of light now, hungry, searching. Like some tentacled thing out of the sea, it sent whipping feelers out into the air, the trees, the stones. Into her.

"Back," Jen said, sparing enough power to fend away brother and dog.

Still, she fed the sign, channeling a stream that poured from the bright core of herself. Insatiable, it blazed brighter still, a young sun shining in the air an arm's length away.

Something quivered at her breast, as if a small living creature nestled over her heart. She grasped at it, and through the fabric of her tunic, her fingers closed over a slim object bound to the chain around her neck: the obsidian knife. She peeled away a sliver of consciousness to probe that strangeness—

Like a flare of light, a mind swept across hers, a new element in the midst of the magic she'd loosed. Jen's concentration shattered, but the sign still hovered in the air before her. It sucked power like blood from a wound, faster, draining her dry. Col shook at her, shouting over the soundless din.

"Go!" she shouted, but couldn't hear her own voice. "Get away!"

The knife quivered so fiercely it numbed the skin upon which it rested. Caught like a dry leaf in a surge and swirl, she suddenly saw her danger.

Shoving her brother away with mere body's strength, she fought the relentless current. The world narrowed to the sign that threatened to empty her of everything: power, mind, will, life. Its blaze blinded, its soundless roar deafened. She clung to the slender, humming shape of the knife as if it were the last solid thing in the world.

Weight fell upon her shoulders. Some new force wrenched at her mind, slammed between her and the sign that had become a sun, choked off the flow of power streaming from her. Still the sign, insatiable, groped for light, heat, the strength of stone, anything. She could not flee, could not conjure ward or fending spells, could not even look away. Gripping the knife, she could only stand in the tug of powers greater than her own.

The sign's pull ebbed. Its blaze fluttered, diminishing, then turned to an angry pulsing as it clawed for her power.

Jen felt no dismay, no fear or desperation. Within lay only a vast emptiness, of power, thought, emotion. The sign was a streak of coruscating silver without meaning, a dwindling, phosphorescent glimmer against the shadows. At last, it shrank to nothing, as blank and void as she.

Jen stared uncomprehendingly at the empty air. Walls rose on either side. The sky arced above like a strip of blued steel. Her every bone and joint hurt, as if she'd strained against some tremendous force. She found herself on her knees on the cold, uneven cobbles of an alleyway. Thoughts chased one another like blown leaves through her mind. She'd intended to do something, or make something… All grew jumbled and muddled then.

Weights lay on each shoulder. The weights moved, shifted, a grip that raised her to her feet. Then hands spun her, or the world itself spun, and she found her master before her.

Still, she felt nothing, unable even to wonder where he had come from. His hair stuck out in spikes and wisps, he was dressed in a long, loose nightrobe, and his eyes stormed with lights. Her wizardry, open, trembling in the dawn air, touched an emotion.

Fear. Raw, unchecked fear.

In her confusion, she thought it her own. After another long moment, it came to her that it was her master's.

Without a word, he whisked them both out of the alley.

They rematerialized somewhere dim and close. The sky and the trees were gone, but her master was still there, still gripping her shoulders. His fear and anger buffeted her, but his voice was low, controlled.

"What did you do, Jen?"

She looked around, trying to understand where she was, how she'd come there. She knew only that he'd asked her a question, and she must answer it.

"I made the sign."

"What sign? Where did you see it?"

They stood in a cluttered, stone-walled room. A low ceiling barely cleared her master's head.

"The sign the Fey woman made. I saw it in a vision." Jen answered scrupulously, each question in turn.

Her head hurt. The place in which she stood smelled of something...something frightening. It smelled cold. Earthy.

"Where did you see this vision?" he asked.

She knew this place, yet did not know it. A stone room, dark, low, small, like a dream she'd had, or a memory. The only light came through the door, a muddy orange glow. Fear set a noose around her neck.

"I saw it—in the dark." Breath rasped in her throat.

"When?" His voice was harsh.

Her master was a shadow against the dull light of the door. Fear gripped so hard she couldn't speak, could only stand staring up at him.

"When?" he said again. His fingers moved to her arms, closed tighter.

Stone walls. Shadow against dull light. A man seizing her.

She screamed and struck his hands away. Lightnings leapt from her fingertips, lanced toward him. He brushed away the bolts like stray sparks and reached for her again.

"Jen—"

"Don't touch me, filthy bastard!" she screamed and wreathed herself 'round with fire and lightning. Those lights flashed stark on his face, on the stones that hemmed her in. She cursed him, calling him the foulest names she knew.

He stood between her and the door. The room was too small, too small, and she couldn't get past him.

He took a slow step toward her. "I won't hurt you, Jen." His voice was that of a man speaking to a savage animal. "I'll never hurt you."

She flung up her hands, edged along the wall, cursing him, meaning those curses to stick. He stepped in front of her, blocking her. She threw gouts of fire at him, hot blue fires, clinging green fires. Against his power, the fires burst and spattered and snuffed out.

"Jen," he said softly, both with his voice and in her mind. "Be still. You have nothing to fear."

Her gaze jerked over the walls of the cramped stone room, to the gaping rectangle of the door, to the man's shadow looming over her, reaching.

"*Don't touch me!*" she screamed again.

Abruptly, as it had once before, instinct took over. Dissolving her being into a stray thought, her power carried her away.

お

Jen came back to herself in a little alcove between walls. She sat, head bent to drawn-up knees. Something warm breathed against her side. She made a strangled sound and tried to shrink away before she realized it was only a dog. Only Burn. He scrambled away. When Jen subsided again, he came back, snuffled in her hair and nuzzled her ear. She let go her knees to wrap her arms around him. Burn whined and licked what he could find of her face.

At last, she released him and straightened. Walls en-

closed her, ending in a small open space: a courtyard, perhaps, or a street dead-ending at the back wall of a house.
The air stank of privies and smoke and grease. Voices
came, echoing and distorted: a baby's wail, the shouting of
children. A blank void of terror weighed on Jen's heart;
there in her little alcove, she shivered and tried to remember how she'd come there, what she had to fear. Like a
child walking backwards, she searched memories in re-
verse.

Last had been Burn leaning against her after snuffling
her thoroughly; before that she'd been running, dodging
along streets and alleys, through yards and over walls as
she had done when she was young, running from bullies.
She'd used wizardry to transfer herself into the street
from...

The blankness and terror began there.

Stroking Burn, Jen frowned and made herself remember. There had been darkness, and stone walls, and a man's
shadow. She shrank from the image, touched the shape of
the knife beneath her shirt, groped once more after the
frayed thread of memory.

Another piece fell suddenly into place. She'd gone into
an alley to make the sign the Fey woman had made in the
vision. Something had gone wrong, though. The sign
hadn't worked, or the conjuring had brought into being a
monster, a memory—

Jen shook off the hand of fear that stole down her
neck. That was where the dream started. The darkness, the
stone walls, the shadow. A man's hands on her, heavy and
overpowering—

She raised her face, gripped her knees to anchor herself. She'd poured all her strength into the sign's making,
so that she could take Burn away, and Col—

Abruptly, she stood. She reeled and steadied herself against the wall. Burn scrambled to his feet as well and wagged his tail uncertainly. Jen peered down the alley. Where was her brother? He'd been tugging at her, shouting. Jen lurched toward the open space ahead.

Blank walls of crusted stone bounded the streets, making a maze of them. She turned corners at random. Old splintery gates and occasional open archways pierced the walls. Through these she saw tall narrow houses and small yards tolerating a few straggly vegetables, a dirty little boy with a leaky bucket. She followed the street to its end, turned another corner and knew where she was.

She walked slowly toward the ancient gate with its graffiti and rusty hinges and iron strapping and hesitated, torn between finding her brother, or answers. She chewed her lip, then touched the gate open. As always, it groaned, but seemed to shower less rust than before. Burn whined, then barked, a high-pitched yap of anxiety. Jen patted his head.

"Wait here for me. I won't be long." She stepped through, into the stone's wild garden.

You have come, the stone said when Jen stood before it in the shade of the live oak.

The first glimmerings of anger came, a sense she'd been fooled. Or betrayed. "What you showed me was wrong. I made that sign like the Fey woman did, but the magic went wrong. Something happened, and I can't even remember what it was."

Show me, the stone said.

Jen hesitated again. The sense of betrayal was strong, but she couldn't say who or what had betrayed her. "No."

You must show me, the stone said.

"No. I'll tell you." And she did.

When she'd finished, the stone said what stones usually say: that is, nothing. Jen cursed and turned to leave.

The wizard broke your power, it said suddenly.

Jen half-turned. "What do you mean?"

Great power is needed to open a way to the Otherworlds. You have power. I have felt it. The wizard felt it too, and came, and stopped it.

"Something was wrong before that. After I made the sign, everything turns strange, like a dream. I've never done magic that takes my wits like that."

Perhaps the magic did not take your wits. Perhaps the wizard did.

Jen frowned. "He's never..." She fell silent. Her master had bound her, looked into her thoughts, but had never done anything like that. *Had* he?

If he had, she'd have no way of knowing. The very thought twisted her stomach.

I cannot know what was done, the stone said, its vast hollow voice breaking into her thoughts, *unless you touch me. Only then can I see.*

Of course, it was right. But that dark place in her memory remained, where the dream squatted, its black eyes and broken claws and dirty tusks gleaming.

"No. I need to remember everything first. After that, maybe I'll come back."

Yes. Come back, and I will—

"You'll what?"

She took a step toward the stone, then stopped, feeling as if she'd gone into a room and forgotten what she'd come to do. The sudden beat of a single thought, an overwhelming desire, pushed the stone, pushed all else from her mind. *Home*, rang ceaselessly in her mind, *go home, come home, come.*

Her feet carried her across the grass, through the gate. A dog sat outside. *Go home, come home, come.* The compulsion drove her, sent her swiftly along streets, around corners, past shops, across squares.

At last, she stood before another gate, one of fanciful curlicues in iron and brass. It opened. She walked paths of raked gravel to the front door of a house, which also opened.

"Mistress Marin! She's here!"

Jen blinked back into awareness. A maid stood and stared. The young woman picked up her starched skirts and dashed toward the kitchens.

"Mistress!" she called again, voice echoing in the high front hall.

Jen, blinking and bewildered, squeezed her eyes closed. That shut out her master's front hall, but couldn't shut out her trouble. Her master wasn't here—yet. She didn't expect to enjoy the respite for long.

She snapped her eyes open at the tap of footsteps. Marin came hurrying down the hall with the maid in tow.

"Lady," she said, red-faced and a little breathless, "Come on, let's get some tea into you, maybe a slice of bread." She circled Jen's waist and urged her along, speaking softly all the while as if to a frightened child.

This wasn't at all what Jen had expected. She let herself be guided, waiting for whatever would happen. Marin only steered her to the orangery.

Jen lowered herself into one of the chairs by a little painted wood table. The maid who'd gaped in the entry hall now lingered by the door, still staring. Marin sent the girl off for tea, then fussed over Jen, spread a napkin in her lap, brought out silverware. The maid returned. Marin shooed her away again, set out the tea things and sat.

"Well," she said. "Where are you?"

Eyeing her, Jen answered, "In the orangery."

"How'd you get here?"

Jen opened her mouth to say, *My master Called me*, but said instead, "I walked."

Marin nodded. "You don't seem confused to me."

"Confused," Jen repeated, slightly questioning, because she was, indeed, confused.

"Master said you worked a great spell this morning, and that it near turned you inside out. He said to see to you when you came home."

Jen nodded slowly, still only able to remember clearly the calling up of her power. From then on, all drifted hazy until the moment she found herself near the stone's garden with Burn—

"Burn—" She started forward in her chair, to rise. Oh gods. And *Col!*

Marin put a hand on her arm. "The gardener will take care of the dog."

Jen settled back, but still fidgeted. What about poor Col? No one would take care of him.

Her actions—and her predicament—loomed large and awful. She dropped her head in her hands. Trying to work a spell blind like that had been incredibly stupid under any circumstances. And now—and now—

Her master would bind her more tightly than before. There'd be no hope of escape, no help for Col, nothing. Wretchedness pushed tears up, making the backs of her eyes ache and burn.

A hand touched her hair. Marin said, "Drink your tea, child, and eat a little. Things look brighter when you're fed and rested."

Jen said into her hands, "I've made a terrible mistake, Marin." Her voice shook shamefully, but she couldn't hold back the words. "I don't know what my master will do to me now."

"Well, if you already know it was a mistake, there likely isn't much point in him doing anything."

Jen raised her head. Marin gave her a sympathetic smile, but Jen couldn't tell her how unlikely her optimism was.

"Now, eat a little fruit and cheese," Marin said.

Jen made herself a nibble at small green plum. Marin nodded, then walked to the door, spoke briefly with someone outside. She returned and chattered of inconsequential things while feeding Jen as she would an invalid, arranging bits of cheese and dried apple on the plate, offering slices of a sweet bread flecked with poppy seeds and lemon peel.

Jen had worked enough spells to know she had to feed her body afterward or pay the price for days. But it was hard, knowing what was surely to come.

Finally, it did come. The door opened, and her master entered. At the sight of his stern face, the slice of bread turned to chalk in her mouth.

For a moment, Jen forgot to chew, and when she swallowed, the bread traced a painful lump all the way down her throat, then sat like a stone in her stomach. Marin patted her hand, but Jen scarcely noticed.

He came closer and a darkness seemed to form between them, rising like a foul fog from the bright tiles of the orangery. In it lurked the dream-memory—the stone walls, the man's shadow, choking terror—

Jen battled it into its burrow at the back of her mind. She placed herself in the room with its tall windows, took herself out of the darkness. She found herself on her feet, the chair upset behind her. She did not remember knocking the chair over, hadn't heard it clatter to the floor. Her master had stopped several paces from the table. Marin's hand rubbed up and down between her shoulder blades, comforting.

Bending to right the chair, Jen muttered, "I'm sorry."

Marin took a second teacup from the tray. She filled it and said, "Call if you need anything else, lord."

Jen made a move, quickly repressed, to retain her. Marin took Jen's hand and squeezed it, then left her to face her master.

The door closed, and fear rushed in. It seemed to be not for what would happen to her, but of her master himself. It took all her will to stand still as he came near and seated himself.

"Will it be necessary to lay a calming spell on you?" he asked.

Jen fumbled into her chair. "No, lord." She knew he could sense her fear. The knowledge humiliated her; she had not shown such fear since she was a child.

"I wouldn't relish warding off your defenses," he added dryly.

Shocked, Jen said again, "No, lord."

Even as she said it, though, an image flickered into her mind, of her own wizard's fire leaping at a man. She had thrown fire at Rik not so long ago. Maybe that was why the image seemed so immediate. But that still didn't seem right.

Her master said at last, inevitably, "I'd like to know what happened this morning."

She tried to speak but no words came. Clearing her throat, she tried again. "So would I, lord."

His dark brows arched up. "Indeed." He studied her, then slowly extended a hand across the table. "You make the link. Start where you will. I'll follow."

Her mouth dry, Jen stared at that hand, at the fine, graceful fingers.

So had he offered his hand when he'd taken her from her father's house, and not willing it, she had reached up and taken it. So too did her fingers steal from her lap to the table, then creep across the table to rest at last in his. Where her will ended and his began, she still couldn't tell.

His fingers curled around hers. "Begin," he said.

He'd taught her the mind-magic, a wizard's way of delving into a mind like an explorer of hidden places beneath the earth. Strong emotions and impulsive thoughts lay at the surface, often accessible even without a touch. To see secrets, a wizard must use his power like a beacon, illuminating darkened crannies, picking out thoughts and memories like gems encased in stone.

So had her master looked into her mind when he'd first brought her, gazing into the depths of her soul with the pitiless light of his power. Now he let her use that light, let her illuminate what she chose.

She was aware of him there in her mind, sensed the faint purl and murmur of his thoughts. She did not show her master the vision the stone had given, nor her rebellious plans. Those were clear enough, she reasoned, from her actions.

Before her mind's eye, the scene played out again, its clarity degenerating into confusion. Once more she felt the grip of her master's fingers on her shoulders as he spun her to face him—

Abruptly, he released her hand. Jen blinked into the present again, thoughts yet whirling. Almost, almost she had it. A memory of ragged, unreasoning fear… She reached out as if to snatch it back, but it was gone, lost.

"I brought you here, to the basement, to a room in which little harm could be done should the magic you'd raised linger," her master explained.

Jen returned her upraised hand to her lap.

He continued, "In your confusion, you fled."

She waited for him to ask where she'd gone, but he did not. The second grace he'd done her, this unexpected, gentle compassion. Dread gnawed at her stomach. She hadn't earned it.

"Why should I have been confused?" she asked, worried by the suddenly broken link.

Dark, whispering words drifted into her mind: *Perhaps the magic did not take your wits. Perhaps the wizard did.*

"That sign," he began slowly, "was a power sink, designed to hold power until the moment of release. When you did not feed it what it was meant to hold, it pulled power from you." He paused. "Were you not what you are, it would have killed you or worse—left you an empty, mindless shell. It might still have done so, had I not intervened."

She caught from him a whiff of turmoil, like blown dust. It disappeared before she could identify its source.

He studied her, then said at last, "What shall I do with you?"

The question sounded rhetorical. Jen did not take it as such. "Set me free, lord," she whispered.

"No."

"Then let me earn my freedom!"

He made an abrupt gesture, a gesture of impatience or frustration or anger. "I do. Every day, I let you earn your freedom—or your bondage."

He made it sound so simple. So simple, and yet so untrue. She stood and spun away from the table, away from him.

"What am I to you?" She didn't want the answer to that question. "What good am I to you?" she demanded instead, a far safer question.

But he did not answer either question, and his silence was answer in itself. No matter what freedom or what bondage she earned, he would not let her go. He knew what she'd attempted, and why. He would keep her from the Otherworlds.

Jen crossed to the tall, many-paned windows, pressed her palms against the glass. Under her fingers, the mullions felt like the bars of a cage. As her hand had crept across the table and into her master's, it now stole to the window latch and turned it. The casement swung open, and she fled out into the garden, escaping to the brief, slight extent she could.

Chapter 9

"Something's wrong, Burn," Jen whispered, smoothing salve on the dog's red and blistered skin, letting healing magic trickle through her fingertips.

She glanced up at the ceiling and corners of her room, a habit she'd developed long ago when she'd first realized the house was more than a simple construction of stone and wood and plaster. Today, as then, she saw only the moldings of stylized leaves, the pickled oak paneling. Yet still she whispered as if the house—and her master— might hear.

"Something's wrong, and I don't know what it is."

It had been three days since the disaster in the alley, when she'd tried to conjure the sign. Not once had her master called her to his presence. The first day, she'd considered it a grace, yet another he'd bestowed. But the first day's relief had turned by the second to a certain suspicious uneasiness, which had by now grown into something nearer a desperate impatience. If her actions were to carry consequences, she wished to face them and have them over with.

Jen shoved to her feet and crossed the room to the window. Flinging the casement wide, she took breath after breath until she was dizzy. At last, she folded her arms and scowled. She'd have to meet her master. There was no way around it.

She'd almost reached the stairway that led up to his study when one of the pages, a boy named Bran, came bounding down. At the sight of Jen, he checked himself, slowing to a pace more respectful of the armful of books he carried.

Jen's eyes went narrow. "What are you doing with those?"

Bran's adam's apple bobbed. She realized how sharp the question must have sounded, but could think of nothing to soften it.

"Master told me, take them to the Prince's wizard," the boy answered in a small voice.

The Prince's wizard. Palimur. Who had the *Malmidion*. A fierce hope leapt.

She put on a more encouraging face. "I can take them," she said. "I'll go ask the master."

The boy wouldn't—couldn't—refuse. He didn't dare show resentment, but he did look crestfallen.

"Of course, l-lady." He stumbled over the gender of address the way the younger servants often did, speaking in a smaller voice than before.

Jen felt sorry for him and offered a grin. "Thank you!" She whisked the books from his arms.

He only blinked as if amazed at the speed at which he'd been robbed of his grand adventure.

She gave him a solemn wink. "If you ever need a favor, come to me and I'll see what I can do." And she darted past, up the curving stairway.

She had to concoct a pretext to offer her master. The door opened, revealing the study, and her master within.

"Come in, Jen" he said, not turning from where he perused titles on the shelves. He took down a book, studied it, replaced it.

Her heart, which had lurched into a gallop at the mere sight of him, now slowed again with his apparent distraction. Jen swallowed even as poor Bran had. "Bran said you wanted these books taken to Lord Palimur. Isn't that something I should do?"

Open book in hand, he turned and raised a brow. She faced him with all the calm she could muster.

"Indeed you should," he finally said, closing the book and turning back to the shelves once more.

She let the merest trickle of breath spill through her lips.

He went on, "Perin should have the trap waiting by the front door."

Perin was the stablehand and, as occasion required, the driver. Her master didn't have a large stable, only two horses, but no man of his position would resort to hired transportation.

"Yes, lord." Jen's thoughts immediately ran ahead toward what lay between her and the *Malmidion*: the wizard Palimur.

Yes, he *looked* at her. He was smug and snide. So what? She could bear both for the sake of getting hold of the *Malmidion*.

The books growing heavy in her arms, she turned to leave.

"Jen," her master said.

She froze, then turned. His gaze upon her held that new keenness that raised the fine hairs on the back of her neck.

"Remember, you are my apprentice."

Jen's brows twitched in the beginnings of a frown. Her chest swelled with a sudden question. Repressing both, she only said again, "Yes, lord," and hurried out.

As she ran down the coiling flight of stairs, suspicion and uneasiness circled her.

お

Riding along beside Perin in the trap, Jen plied the precious books in her lap with seeking spells. Without long preparation and great expenditures of power, objects could only be transferred by magic across short distances. Far simpler to have someone carry the books, so they were hers as long as it took to travel from her master's house to Palimur's. She intended to take advantage of every moment.

Perin cast her an occasional glance as he maneuvered the trap through the traffic of Grand Avenue. He would wonder what she was doing and if she should be doing it, but would keep his own counsel.

The sun flashed gold on the cover of the book she added to the growing stack on the seat between her and Perin. He twitched the reins to ease around a slow-moving dray hauling bricks and lumber. Jen leaned an elbow on the top of the stack to keep the books from sliding.

Too soon, they arrived at a gate taller and far more ornate than that in her master's wall. Jen gusted a sigh and stacked the books once more into her lap. It wouldn't do to be seen riffling through pages at the Prince's doorstep.

The two red-liveried guards with their polished cuirasses and silver-bound pikes must have been merely for show, for both the gate and the walls surrounding the grounds of the palace shimmered with spells. Ordinary mortals would be oblivious to the layers of protection, though the particularly sensitive might notice a slight uneasiness within the field of those spells, or perhaps a tingling or a subaudible hum.

With wizard's senses, Jen saw and heard and felt them: singing spells of protection refracting the summer light like cut glass; guard spells growling softly, prickly as burrs; spells of entrapment that dangled thin, hook-lined tentacles across the gateway, snagging at her skin.

Distracted, she scarcely heard the guards' questions. When the gates swung noiselessly open, she hunched her shoulders and raised her own wards.

Then they were through, rolling along a wide, cobbled drive that followed the contours of three low hills. A great house of pale grey stone commanded the highest hill: the palace.

Perin was a quiet man with a hard, lined face who only seemed wholly comfortable with the horses. He talked to Jen though, treating her with much the same patience and quiet.

"Here's the wizard's house," he drawled, jerking his chin at a many-winged structure at the base of another hill. It was single-storied with plentiful large windows, and sprawled within the precincts of a low stone wall. "The Prince had it built special for him, so they say."

The wheels of the trap rattled across pavers as they rounded the shoulder of the right-hand hill. For a moment, she lost sight of the wizard's house. The drive curved more sharply, and they came to an open gateway.

The horse snorted explosively and reared in the traces, rocking the trap on its two large wheels.

"Ho there, Cloud, ho!" Perin called to the horse, managing to shout and soothe at once.

Jen saw the problem instantly. "Back up!" she cried.

While the horse continued to jerk back and forth in her harness, oblivious to Perin's hands on the reins, Jen hung onto the side of the trap and sent a calming spell. At once, the mare quieted, dipped her head twice and blew. Perin, reins gripped in both vein-laced, big-knuckled hands, dropped into his seat again, exhaling through pursed lips much as the horse had.

"Fear spell," Jen said in disgust. "Couldn't Palimur just have a gate like anyone else?"

Certainly her master's was no ordinary gate. It could thwart any intruder (or would-be escapee), but it didn't do so by assaulting innocent visitors. Angry for the sake of the horse, and with the metallic taste of alarm still in her mouth, Jen swung down from the trap.

Immediately, she encountered the fear spell. It built around her stone walls, darkness, a man's shadow against dull red light. Even knowing what it was, she had to fight being sucked down into terror and pain and memory. She pushed back, using her own power to recreate the graceful archway, the smooth green flanks of the hill, the glimpse of the low house surrounded by its gardens. The spell pushed back too as Palimur's house shifted its attention to this annoying upstart of an apprentice girl.

"Lord Palimur," she called to the air, "We're here with the books Lord Barras sent. May we come in?"

She supposed it would be bad manners to attempt to break the house's defenses, though the spell itself was bad-mannered.

An awareness swept down upon them. The horse spooked and snorted yet again. The fear spell fluttered, then winked out. Jen gave a twist of her lips and climbed back into the trap. Perin said nothing, but his thinned, downturned mouth spoke clearly enough of his disapproval. He clucked and flicked the reins. Cloud tucked her head and drew the trap through the gateway.

Perin brought the horse to a clattering stop before the house. Men came out, saw to the horse and trap and carried the books inside. Jen, Perin in tow, followed a footman through a carved gate and into a courtyard.

While Jen couldn't say she much cared for Palimur, she admitted that his house pleased her a great deal. The courtyard was a pretty place full of potted lemon trees and rosebushes and vivid with flowers. A wind chime's bronze plates bonged in the breeze.

Perin showed no awe of either house or grounds. Once in the entry foyer, he took off his cap. "I'll be waiting for you," he said, clearly swallowing the 'Miss' he usually appended to his statements.

Jen thanked him and followed the footman to a comfortable room with a coffered ceiling, a room that seemed to be a combination of study and parlor. On shelves lining the walls, books alternated with small oddities, gyroscopes and colored spheres of blown glass. An enameled globe stood on a stand. Stacked on a low table were her master's books, which the servants must've brought in before her. She headed toward Palimur's bookshelves, but discovered little more than the *Malmidion's* absence before footsteps sounded in the hall outside. She crossed the room to tall casements that looked out into another walled garden and donned the guise of perfectly composed visitor.

The door opened and Palimur strode in. She eyed his puffed sleeves, his ribbons, the short cape slung artfully over one shoulder. He, in turn, looked at her just as frankly as always.

Jen bowed her head, not a servant but her master's emissary, to the eye a well-dressed youth.

"Lord Palimur. My master asked that these books be brought to you," she said in her most careful accents, gesturing at the tidy stack of books.

Palimur crossed to the table and picked one up. "Excellent. Convey my thanks."

Again, she bowed her head. "I will, lord." This would be the appropriate moment to take her leave, but she badly wanted another look at that page in the *Malmidion*. She had to learn what had gone wrong in conjuring the sign. She hesitated, holding herself from fidgeting, trying to think of how to phrase the request.

At last, she said in an attempt at grace, "Your house and gardens are very beautiful, lord."

Palimur looked up from the book in his hand. Something—perhaps calculation or amusement—flashed in his eyes.

Replacing the book on the stack, he sketched a bow and smiled. "Yes. The Prince has been most generous." He cocked his head as if considering, then asked, "Would you care to see them?"

Taking a breath, she answered, "Please, lord."

He came to her, and she fell back a step in confusion. He swept an arm toward the door, curving the other behind her in the way gentlemen guided ladies. "Come."

All Jen knew of how ladies behaved, and of how gentlemen behaved with ladies, was through her observations in shops, at market, alighting from carriages. Outside the Wall, in the slums, boys grinned and groped at girls; men shoved and slapped their women. At her master's house, Marin had made cautious attempts to teach her ladies' manners, but Jen had made a mockery of them.

Palimur seemed to believe that ladies allowed themselves to be handled a great deal more than a young man would, for from time to time, he'd take her elbow or put his hand lightly on the small of her back. But her acute consciousness of these—gallantries? familiarities?—faded as he guided her through the lovely rooms with their large casement doors, their fine furniture, rugs and hangings.

Each room seemed to have its own private garden nestled between wings of the house, and each garden was an emerald, a delightful jewel of the gardener's art.

"Thank you, lord," she said, "for showing me."

He gave his slight and courtly bow again. "I'm glad my home pleases you. I'm quite pleased with it as well, as you may have guessed," he said, strolling beside her along the sheltered, winding path. River-smoothed stones crackled under their feet. "The Prince's patronage has been a great boon, for which I'm grateful. Barras would, I think, discover similar advantages if only he would accept the Prince's petitions. The Prince would do him great honor, you know."

Not knowing any such thing, Jen only nodded politely.

"If you have any influence with Barras at all," Palimur added, "you may wish to suggest he reconsider. He's far too fine a wizard to waste his powers as he does. He's a man made for much bigger things."

"I'm only his apprentice, lord," she apologized. Why should Palimur even suggest such a thing? Influence her master, indeed!

The wizard made a deprecating noise. "Barras isn't the sort to take on *only* an apprentice."

Her brother's puzzled voice came to her: *But Jen, why'd he pay all that jingle for you?* Something in her middle gave an unsettling twitch.

They came to a wooden bench scattered with cushions. Palimur paused there, took her hand and bowed. She stood trying to understand the meaning of the bow and the gesture. After a moment, it occurred to her that she was being invited to sit. Embarrassed, she hastily did so. The wizard seated himself beside her.

Jen sat rigid, hands upon knees. Palimur's knee rested no more than a hand's breadth from her own. She could think of no way to extricate herself that would not appear ill-mannered.

"Be easy, lady," Palimur said.

He was smiling, as aware of her as her master always was. "I'm only an apprentice, lord," she insisted.

"Not for long, I think."

She bit back a blunt, *What do you mean?* Wetting her lips, she said instead, "Why should you say that, lord?"

"Call it instinct." He leaned back and extended an arm along the back of the bench behind her.

Jen held very still.

"You're no longer a child," he continued. "Only the apprentice-binding must constrain your powers now."

She made no answer.

Palimur went on, "It should be near time for you to study under other masters."

"Other masters?" she blurted out, then added, "Lord."

"Oh, yes. Didn't Barras explain? After apprenticeship, most young men will work under the supervision of other masters. This way the young fellow can learn new knowledge, different methods."

Her thoughts were already skipping ahead, first from the conviction that she did not want *another* master, next to the realization that here was an opening for the very request she'd come to make.

"My master and I already discussed my masterwork."

Palimur's brows went up. "Indeed. That surprises me."

"In fact, I hoped you might be done with the *Mulmidi on*. For my masterwork, you understand, lord."

"I see. And what will that be?"

"I plan to travel to the Otherworlds," she told him, there being no reason not to.

He smiled, a sudden, somewhat conspiratorial smile. "And Barras agreed to that?"

Her mouth was dry. "He wasn't pleased, but didn't forbid it."

"Yet he lent me the book you need."

"I don't think he knew I needed it," Jen parried. Was she being maneuvered?

"You didn't want me to take it. That much I saw. Barras must have seen as clearly as I did."

"It's his book." She shrugged with a nonchalance she did not feel. "He'll do with it as he pleases."

"As he will with you?"

Her breath caught, then she stammered, "I—I beg your pardon, lord?"

He shifted, and his knee settled within a finger width of hers. "Oh, come," he chided gently. "You're an intelligent young woman. You've danced this dance of truth and omission cleverly enough. Barras hasn't sanctioned your masterwork, has he?"

Resisting the urge to edge away, Jen said nothing, for she could not deny what he said. Any feint she made would only confirm his suspicions.

"You see, in spite of Barras' opinion, a keen sense of politics has its uses. There is a great deal you could learn on the subject, but..." He pulled a regretful face and spread his hands. "Barras, of course, will never let you go."

Why not? she wanted to ask. But she wouldn't show vulnerability to the wizard. Instead, she said, "Perhaps, lord. But I don't know any reason my master would want to keep me."

Palimur's look suggested embarrassment. "Why, lady, don't you?"

Jen shook her head, knowing she'd do better to get to her feet and walk off.

"Wizard-women are rare as hen's teeth," he said as if regretting the necessity of an explanation. "He's raised you to be his mate."

The words struck like fists to the gut, sharp, breathtaking. It was as if she'd been struggling for five years to hold a door closed, barring from the daylight of her mind a dark and slavering beast. For five years, it had been growling, shouldering that door. And now, it burst the door asunder and bounded into her consciousness.

She said nothing; could say nothing. Gripping her knees, she only held herself still, held calmness around her like a spell of illusion.

Palimur put his large square hand on hers, covering hand and knee both. "Forgive me, lady. You've been with Barras since you were nearly a child. It must be as repellent as it would be to discover that your own father had designs on you."

She pushed to her feet, dislodging the wizard's hand. "My master is not my father." She closed her fists.

"Yet you dress as a boy—"

"Why are you telling me this?" she said, shedding courtesy like soiled clothing.

"Clearly, Barras has not. Is it not something you should know?"

"From you? You play the gentleman with me, lord, but these aren't the sort of things a gentleman would say. What do you really want?"

Palimur's lips quirked in his square, smug smile. He turned the question back on her. "What do you want? A book, a spell? A passage to freedom?"

Jen knew it was useless, but she had learned long ago that one got only what one fought for. Or bought, or stole. "I want the *Malmidion*."

"But I could give you so much more."

This was ground she knew. She'd seen the slum boys tread it often enough, tempting girls with trinkets or sweets. Somehow, it gave her courage. She laughed. "No doubt. But at what price?"

Palimur affected a wounded look. "Price? Is it base barter to offer opportunity? Come, sit down. Let us talk."

"I think we're doing fine as we are."

As it had in the parlor, something flickered in the wizard's amber gaze. A spell slipped into being. The foliage of the garden seemed to move and thicken, submerging them in green twilight.

"You misread the situation," Palimur said. "If there is to be bargaining, all the strength is on your side. Don't you understand that you possess an unmatchable treasure? Yourself! Your very rarity. What can I offer that doesn't pale before that gem?"

The ribbonlike leaves of willow, the hard, shiny leaves of bay dissolved into a fragrant green mist.

"Flattery!" She made herself laugh again. "You wooed my master the same."

"Yes," Palimur said, "the Prince has one wizard already, but nowadays finds he needs another. Why shouldn't it be you? You're ambitious, as I am. And I would allow you so much that Barras never will."

Somehow, she was standing before Palimur now, attending to words more reasonable and appealing than any she'd heard in a long time. She shook her head, confused, and whispered, "I'm bound."

His blunt fingers enclosed hers. His thumbs brushed her knuckles. "What will that signify when I speak to the Prince on your behalf? Barrras will then be induced to release you. Should the terms prove sufficiently compelling."

The stone had said much the same, when she'd known that the binding broken would only be replaced by a new one. A voice within whispered, *D'you think it'll be any different now?*

Jen plunged back into herself. Like the rush and roar of a furnace, her power erupted, searing the green illusion. She tore her hands from Palimur's grasp. "I won't be bound to anyone. Least of all a man who tries to beguile me with wizardry."

Across his face, anger chased surprise. "How did you do that?"

Breathing hard, she wondered herself, for she knew he was stronger than she.

He seemed to struggle a moment, then smiling, mastered himself. "Excellent! Barras chose well—a woman who'll get him wizard brats as strong as he is. No sorceress or witch or, gods forbid, common mortal bitch for him, eh? None of those will breed true. But he'd best bar his gates and set dragons to guard his treasure."

"I'm no man's possession!"

His eyes narrowed. "No? It seems to me you are." She opened her mouth for another retort, but he overrode her. "I'll tell you the truth, my lady. You can choose your master, or be possessed by the man strong enough to take you. Or the one clever enough."

"Think you're the one who can take me?" She spoke as softly as he had. "Try your spells on me again, lord."

Power leapt like lightning through her now, prickling at her fingertips. He might be a wizard to rival her master, but she didn't care. She wanted to pit herself against him, show him she was no prize, but something a great deal more dangerous.

"I'd be delighted, did I have the leisure to. I'd like to explore that magic you used against me just now." He smiled again. "Another time."

She cursed him succinctly.

He stretched out his legs, draped his arms across the back of the bench and looked her up and down in a thoroughly insulting manner. "Oh, you'll tame down fine," he said in the accents of the street.

Jen spat, the appropriate response on the street to such a remark. Turning on her heel, she strode off, longing to peel off her skin, to change this body for that of a man, even as she wore men's clothes.

Chapter 10

Jen's throat was so tight she could scarcely breathe. But still, she walked the tall, wainscoted corridors of her master's house with their sconces of etched glass, steering herself downstairs where she sensed her master in his basement workshop.

The stone walls gave off their soft, directionless glow. The usual clutter of the workbench, however, was gone, replaced by a great map weighted at the corners with half-spheres of metal, the metals of the four directions: brass at the south, copper at the west, silver at the east, iron at the north. He bent over the map, upon which rested a small, six-pointed star of gold, like a child's jack. The star stood quivering on one point, then rolled jerkily onto another point.

Jen recognized a finding spell. The map depicted the far eastern deserts. He might be seeking a lost caravan, or a lost treasure. She forced herself to stand quietly. The little star shivered, then skipped across the surface of the map toward her.

Her master looked up.

She knew she should apologize for disrupting his spell, but words suddenly deserted her.

"Yes, Jen?" he said with patience real or feigned.

At last, words came again. "Forgive me, lord. Lord Palimur asked me to convey his thanks for the books."

He made a slight, irritable gesture. "He conveyed them himself some time ago."

A wizard could simply write a message in letters that would glow in the air before the recipient, or speak words to a bird that would fly to its destination and repeat them.

Her face burned with the thought of what else Palimur might have communicated. All she could say was, "Oh."

"He was concerned that you returned safely."

Jen could not tell if she heard irony in his voice.

"Threading amongst plots and intrigues," he went on, "makes him fretful and suspicious."

And you should be suspicious of him! she thought, but could not say. Oh, no, she couldn't say that. "He— Lord Palimur also asked me to tell you again how much the Prince desires your services. He said the Prince will do you honor. And that you shouldn't waste your powers."

"Did he indeed?" her master said. "And asked my apprentice to carry the message?"

At once, she saw her blunder and where it could lead, but only said, "Yes, lord."

He considered her a long, uncomfortable moment. "And did he show you courtesy?" he asked. "I expect he should."

Did he wish to protect her? Then it occurred to her to ask, *Why? Simply because I'm yours?* She kept her face expressionless. "He showed me his home. It's very beautiful, full of gardens."

"But did he show you courtesy?"

A nauseous thought rushed over her, that he knew what Palimur had attempted. Her face burned. "If you were worried, why did you let me go?"

"Why did you wish to go to him?"

Jen couldn't move or speak but that she stepped into a trap, and today she had been game enough and had enough of games.

"Why shouldn't I have gone?"

And she thought, wild and reckless and driven beyond prudence, *Let him say, if he's man enough to say it to my face! Let him tell what he wants with me!*

With maddening calm, her master asked, "Why do you suppose?"

She could not bear—any more. The world seemed to narrow to her master alone. She saw him in sharp relief: his grey-threaded hair, his stern-lined face, eyes lit with the lightnings of his power.

She clenched her fists. "You bought me and bound me. Do you have to shame me more than that?"

"What are you talking about?" he demanded in— irritation? Confusion? Disquiet?

"Can't you say it?" Her voice sounded thin and queer. "Or is that something else you'll compel of me?"

He moved, a flash of expression across his face, a shift as if to go to her. "Jen, I would never—" he began, but she flung a spell of silence and stillness that in that first, stunned instant, held.

Her whole body shook, with rage, with degradation, with revulsion. "I won't—" *be any man's possession.* "I won't—" *be your mate, bought and raised for the purpose.* She could not speak those words. At last, she found some she could speak. "How far are you willing to tighten your grip on me, lord, to hold me?"

He was far stronger than she; he had brushed aside her spell before she finished speaking. He took a slow step toward her. "You're talking foolishness. Tell me what—"

"No," she said with a savage, cutting gesture, only interrupting this time. "*Leave me be.*" The light in the room pulsed with her heartbeat, brighter then dimmer. Her mouth tasted of dust and rusty metal. "Just leave me be!"

The stairs reeled into view as she turned. Her foot struck the lowest step and she stumbled, caught herself painfully on one knee, then struggled up again. Lurching blindly upward, she fled. If her master called out, his voice was lost in the thunder of blood in her ears.

Jen ran down carpeted corridors, heading for the door. Once through, it would be like long ago, before her master had come and taken her away. She'd once again have to find places to sleep where no one would come upon her. She'd have to evade the street predators who'd circle like wolves around a lame deer.

Not this time. This time, she was no barefoot young girl in a too-small patched shift with no place to go and no place to be.

Cool reason made her slow, turn toward the stairs and climb to her room. Burn lay in his basket, quiet in his binding. Purple twilight showed through the uncovered windows. Lights from nearby houses glimmered through the small seedy panes, tinted red or blue through the stained glass border.

She needed money, or something that passed for it. She crossed the room and scrabbled jewelry from her dressing table drawers. Gold brooches and pearl earrings and emerald necklaces spilled to the floor.

She pulled open the next drawer, started to empty it as well, then realized she could hardly run through the City streets trailing gems from her hands. She gathered up what already lay on the floor, tugged open her belt pouch and stuffed it all inside. On her knees, she thrust an arm under the bed and felt for her treasure box. She pulled it out and hugged it a moment as if it held her courage.

Touching the dog in his basket, she murmured, "Come on, Burn. Let's go."

The dog stood and came to her. Jen flung her arms around him, held him tight and transferred herself, him and the treasure box as far as her power would send them.

お

Slumping houses and rickety shops crowded too close. Beggars' cries hounded behind and raucous singing sprawled through tavern doors ahead. Jen ran blind, unthinking as an animal.

She found herself before the gate of the stone's garden. Burn, who had trotted anxiously beside her, sank down on the slimy stones, his black lips pulled back in a fearful smile. Heedless of her fine clothes, Jen knelt and wrapped him in a hug. She hated leaving him outside, but Burn would no more willingly enter this enchanted place than he would her master's. She gritted her teeth, tucked a spell of protection around the dog and went in alone.

The old house loomed over the garden. The stone's consciousness enfolded her like darkness, not the darkness that threatens, but that which conceals. Jen sank down in the long grass, hugged her knees and bowed her head. The stone did not speak.

"What will I do, stone?" she said at last, unable to bear the silence any longer. "I can't go back. If he drags me back like last time, I'll—"

No. She wouldn't die after all, would she? Not unless she sought her own end. She'd survived too much already for that.

The stone's voice drifted into her mind. *You asked me of the Otherworlds. Did you ask what you most desire?*

Jen snapped her head up. "What are you saying?" But something within her leapt up as if it already knew.

I am very old, the stone replied. *I am very strong.*

"And what can you do for me?" she asked, half-hopeful, half-jeering.

Much.

"Can you protect me?" Once more, she meant to jeer, but tears pushed into her eyes. She'd spent all she could remember of her life yearning for safety, for the knowledge that no one could bully or beat her or—

She shut off the rest.

I can, the stone replied.

She took a breath, like a swimmer about to plunge into deep water. "Then will you?"

You must remain with me. I am a spirit of the earth and where I am, there my power is also.

The seed of hope that had so eagerly rushed forth now withered. Jen burst out, "Protection! That's imprisonment!"

What fortress stands without walls?

"I don't want walls!" she said with a shudder. "I want wings, to fly wherever I wish. I want power enough that no one will ever threaten me, or what I care about."

I have that power, the stone said in its subterranean whisper. *None will threaten you.*

She hesitated, struggling. But the stone could not touch her. Not as Palimur had, as her master could.

And she would never, ever choose to let it bind her.

"I can stand to stay here. For a while," she muttered to herself. Until she opened her gateway to the Otherworlds.

She crushed her knees to her as if she could fold herself small enough to disappear. "Just don't let my master reach me."

A tear spilled over, stitched a cold thread down her cheek. Since the day he'd ceased calling her only *girl*, since he had first called her by her name, something had begun changing. No longer could there be any pretense of that equilibrium that had sometimes seemed, almost, to be peace.

Jen squeezed her eyes shut—and felt, tugging at the roots of her mind, her master's Call.

Her eyes flew open. "No," she whispered, then lunged to her feet. "No!"

She reached down into the hot core of her, molded the magic there into the strongest ward she could form.

Something wrenched as she heaved it up, flung it out; a cracking of soul or will that tore from her a cry and dropped her to her knees. Breathless, she hunched, the strength of the Call gnawing its way like a parasite to the center of her mind.

She pushed out words: "Help me."

Be still, a voice whispered, deep and dark and dispassionate. *You are weary. Rest. I shall keep you, and keep you well.*

At once, the tidal pull of the Call ceased, swallowed by a silence so vast that her senses, her very thoughts seemed only bright motes adrift in infinity. Jen sailed free, cut loose, incredibly, from the Call. Raising her head to gaze past the twisted branches above to the stars beyond, she gave a single laugh of amazement. Relief swarmed over her in a warm rush, then drew her down into darkness, welcoming, and just as warm.

Chapter 11

"Jen," a voice said.

With the voice, thoughts congealed out of darkness. Her master had been Calling her...

Something touched her forehead, brushed her cheek.

With a snarl, she wrenched up and opened her eyes.

Moonlight poured over the world. A face, pale, framed with moon-silvered curls, stared wide-eyed at her. She dragged in a breath and said, "Col."

She sagged back again on one elbow, sprawling half in the grass, half on the flagstones of the walk. Just a few paces beyond, the great gate stood ajar, opening onto a wedge of darkness.

"You all right?" Col asked.

"What are you doing here? How'd you find me?"

He hitched forward and hunkered beside her. "I been worried about you. After that magic you tried. I been waiting and looking for you, but then I saw your dog. He wouldn't let me catch 'im, but I followed him here. What happened to you? You laid there like a sack somebody dropped."

"Oh, Col." A headache was building behind her eyes. Her stomach roiled threateningly. "Everything's gone wrong." She rubbed her face. Her hand was cold, and it shook. "I ran again last night. My master Called me—"

At once, the cloud of exhaustion that muddled her thoughts and damped her powers evaporated. She made a lurch for her feet, but only managed to topple into her brother. He gripped her, holding her steady. Slumping against him, she gazed wildly around at the garden.

"It's real, isn't it?" she pleaded, her heart shriveling. Would her master lock her in a deep binding, as he had Burn? The kind that created its own reality for the one bound? But Col's clothes reeked of smoke and the more pungent odor of unwashed body. Surely *that* wouldn't be part of a deep binding.

The stone's voice came whispering into her mind, unbidden. *I said I shall keep you.*

Still leaning on her brother, Jen turned slowly toward it. "What did you do, stone?"

"What stone?" Col asked. "Jen, who you talking to?"

The stone answered her, *I protect you.*

She remembered the void that had swallowed the Call and searched herself, but found nothing more—or less—than her master's binding upon her, unchanged. But between her and that binding lay a vast stretch of blankness that separated them as surely as if she had crossed the boundary between worlds. She gave a single, giddy laugh of incredulity. "He can't reach me," she whispered. "I'm free."

Here, with me, you are free, the stone said.

Col's eyes darted. He tugged at her. "C'mon, Jen. Let's get outta here."

If you leave, the stone whispered, *the wizard will have you.*

Her breath stuck in her throat. "I can't."

"You can't stay *here*," her brother insisted, hauling her to her feet. "This is a bad place."

This place can be yours, the stone said. *Even as it is mine.*

Jen pulled away, but her legs buckled, dumping her. "I can't leave, Col," she cried. "Don't you understand? This is the only place I'm safe!"

The night's abuses rolled over her. Red light webbed her vision, a hollow ringing filled her ears, became a voice: "Jen. Jen. Here. C'mon. Sit up. All right. It ain't so bad here. Better'n where me and Rik stayed. Hear? You hear, Jen?"

Her brother's face, frightened, worried, loomed over her, rimmed with pulsing indigo, the painful glitter of stars. The ringing in her ears turned to the roar of the sea, the rush and thunder of blood through her veins.

"What's wrong? What can I do?"

"I used too much power," she said, or hoped she said. "I have to eat. To rest." She felt her lips moving. She didn't have the strength to put her voice into his mind.

Col moved her, somehow. The gnarled branches and glossy leaves of the live oak spread between her and the throbbing sky. Her brother lifted her head, held a cupped hand to her lips. The water that trickled over her tongue tasted as if it might give her the trots, but she did not have the power to make it pure.

"I'll nab us some eats," he said. "Rest. You don't look too good."

Yes. Thank you. Did she speak the words?

Then Col no longer held her, but the stone was there, close enough to touch, could she only raise her hand.

Yes, rest, the stone said, whispering in the deep lightless places of her mind. *You are weak now, but I will show you how to turn weakness to strength, and helplessness to power.*

お

"I can't pawn 'em, Jen," Col said and pushed Jen's jewels back to her. "What'd a slum kid be doing with a lady's sparkles?"

Jen touched the jewels: a pair of emerald earrings, a brooch spangled with stars of garnet and sapphire and topaz. Beautiful things, things she'd never worn, only taken out of her dressing table drawers sometimes to admire.

Morning sunlight angled the house's shadow long across the garden. The growing warmth hadn't yet penetrated here, where they sat on the dressed granite of the portico, but she still lacked the energy—or the will—to move into the sunlight.

She bent her head to her knees. The headache was better than last night, but her skull still felt like an egg about to hatch. And the food her brother had brought— hard, moldy, rat-gnawed bread, five shriveled apples and a stiffened mold of porridge rescued from a pig trough, judging from its coating of dirt and slime—wasn't near enough after the power she'd used yesterday.

"Can't you magic us up anything to eat?" Col said. "Or maybe jingle?"

"You can't eat magic," Jen said. Her mind worked so slowly. "I could transfer things here, but if anyone finds out I'm stealing from them—" She bent her head and rubbed her temples.

There were stories—whispers—of wizards or sorcerers gone bad, using their powers for wicked ends. Marin had told her those wronged by such rogues sought the aid of other wizards, and how those wizards descended on the evildoer and stripped him of his powers. Jen had tried to imagine living dark and powerless, earthbound, and could understand why those so dispossessed had gone mad or killed themselves.

"What about the hinx you done when we was kids, remember?" Col said. "Just made the shopkeepers look the other way when we stoled stuff."

Jen jerked her head up. "It might work," she murmured, half to herself, half to him. She'd been thinking like a wizard, not like a street kid who would use anything that came to hand.

"Stand up," she said. Using the splintery post she leaned against, she hauled herself to her feet. Her head swam.

Col reached out to steady her. "What?"

When she was twelve, she'd worked a trick on the women who came to watch her at market. She'd done the same once or twice on her mother, and had been rewarded with a rare laugh of pleasure. This time, she'd do the trick on Col.

Jen drew a long breath, steadied herself and reached for her power. She tried once, again, then the magic finally came: an illusion that turned his ragged breeches and jerkin into of one of the dresses in her wardrobe at her master's house—midnight blue silk with a black bodice and overdress, both stitched along the edges with silver thread. She'd admired that dress in spite of herself, fingering the whispering, slippery silk.

She let out the breath and staggered backward. If she'd had the strength, she would've laughed at the way he looked, a scruffy, gangly boy dressed in a debutante's gown, but she only completed the illusion, transforming his appearance into that of a tall young girl. His untidy curls became glossy ringlets. She sagged, appalled at her exhaustion after such trifling magic.

"Jen, what did—" He stopped, clapped a hand over his mouth, for his voice had come out high and clear and sweet. He looked down at himself and cried out, scrambling backward as if he could escape what he saw there. "What'd you do?"

A weak laugh did come then. "It's only illusion, Col. You're still you. But now you can pawn that jewelry."

Col stood panting, his fists clenched, looking somewhere between outraged and horrified. He slowly relaxed. "Well," he said at last, "You dressed like a boy to take care of us. Guess I can be a girl for a bit for you."

She sensed determination and the same caring she'd always sensed from Marin. And realized then what it must have been for Marin to care for a powerful wizard-child, to know what sorts of things she, Jen, was capable of and yet not flinch from her. It suddenly amazed and humbled her, that ordinary, powerless folk could care for such a perilous creature as herself. Did they know that, if she wished, she could mold them to her will? Annihilate them on a whim? Col had seen what she did to their brother, Rik. Even then Col had taken her in his ragged, skinny arms and held her.

She touched him lightly. "Thanks, Col." Her fingers fell to the liquid links of a gold necklace, then, before she could change her mind, she quickly bundled the jewels into her belt pouch and thrust it at him. "I'll put a ward on you so no one bothers you. And so you don't get cheated."

He tucked the parcel away, gave her a searching look and left her.

お

Col had returned the belt pouch heavy with coin—as well as a sack full of food: fresh-baked bread, cheese, a cold roast chicken. Between them, they'd devoured it all. Now he was gone again, this time for wood and oil and blankets, a pot or two to cook in.

Bleakness swept over Jen, so strong and sudden it felt like a spell. She found herself at the gate and the archway, but dared not cross. She peered through. Burn lay on the slimy cobbles outside, head on paws. His tail thumped a greeting when he saw her.

She crouched down. "Come on, Burn. This place is mine. It's safe. There's nothing for you to be afraid of."

The dog smiled submissively, still wagging his tail but making no move to rise.

Like a cold draft, doubt stole into her heart.

"Won't you come in, Burn?" she pleaded.

Wagging apologetically, Burn turned his head, refusing to look at her. *Please*, that language told her. *Don't make me come.*

Doubt urged her away from this dim, dreary, derelict place. She set her jaw and pushed to her feet. Tucking a spell of protection around the dog, she returned to the garden.

The stone crouched in shadow like a hunting animal, watching her. Her brain had finally begun to work again. Her steps slowed, and she thought back. She'd transferred herself, fought her master's Call, set spells on Col and Burn—

Her breath came fast. "Stone," she said, "my master will find me here." She turned one way, then the other, as if to flee. "He'll follow my magic, and—"

No, the stone said. *My power fills this place. Where my power moves, yours is hidden.*

She looked back toward the gate. "Are you sure?"

This I cannot mistake.

Jen ran a hand through her hair. The stone wouldn't lie to her in this. After all, it had been trying to get her to stay with it since she first encountered it. Finally, she nodded once and turned toward the house. If indeed she was to stay, she had a formidable task ahead.

She touched open the house's warped front door and prowled the empty, trash-strewn rooms. The entry hall was smaller than that of her master's house, yet still high enough to echo with the soft tap of her footsteps. The walls were stone, solid and stern. The floor, however, retained the beauty of polished marble in patterns of black and white and green, though dusty and strewn with litter and fallen squares of copper ceiling cladding. The dim rooms were empty of furniture, rugs, curtains, lamps; afternoon light filtered in wearily through begrimed windows.

The smell of rotting wood and mildew tangled like cobwebs in her mind, dredging up memories of another bleak day. How, years ago, she'd crept into her brothers' room to take shirt and breeches, then cut off her hair with her mother's kitchen knife. There had been no mirror, and nothing that could serve as one, so she'd only plucked at her short curls, looked down at her slim young girl's body hidden beneath the boy's clothes and thought, *There. Now I'm Jen.*

Jen had been the one who called the wizard's fire that first time. Jen had been the one who'd swaggered out into the market square, thrown back his head, raised his hands and called a Prince's cavalcade out of thin air. People had crowded around the boy she'd become. She left the square that night, not the girl Jenei, lost and afraid, but the boy Jen whose pockets jingled, who carried home a loaf of bread under one arm. By the end of that night, she'd known she need never again depend on anyone else.

She'd been wrong. Now she depended on Col.

She shivered and paced on, along the house's slate-floored corridors, up the creaking stairs of the decaying place that was to be her home. For now.

Jen stopped in the middle of what might once have been a drawing room or parlor and called softly, "House! Are you there?" Her voice whispered away along corridors, up among the dark beams of the ceilings, but no awareness answered. She took another step, sent wizard's senses seeking.

"House!" she called again, for she could discern the old, disused magic in the place, the remnant power that kept out looters and vandals and squatters. For just a moment, something roused, the flickering eyelid of a dying thing, but that flicker faded.

She laid a hand on the splintered wood of a doorframe, sent power into it. Lifting her hand, one palm-sized spot revealed smooth wood, bright paint, unbroken carving. She drew her fingers down it, pleased. An idea fluttered, caught fire. She could restore this tall, dim, narrow old house to the beauty she knew some former owner must have enjoyed. It would take time...

She sighed. But she might have too much of that. She could scarcely spend it pacing, gnawing on frustration and impatience and worry.

She threw back her head and loosed her power.

Magic spilled out like winds through the gates at the ends of the world. The cobwebs festooning the high ceilings fluttered, then tore. The dust and litter on the floor spun up; the tall windows of many small dim panes sprang open with a scream of disused hinges. Clean, fragrant air from the garden came pouring in. Around her, squares of stamped copper whistled through the air. She pointed at them as they flew by.

"You! Up!" she commanded.

Like metallic birds, they banked, swooped up and slapped themselves on the ceiling. Dust wheeled around her in a glittering wall. With a thought, she gathered it up and sent it streaming out the open windows.

A few remaining dust motes danced like sparks in the air. She crossed the room to climb one staircase, then another, narrow and unsteady, to the third story. Magic shouldered open a paneled door, sent it rasping across the crumbled plaster scattered across the floor. She crossed a long room with an angled ceiling, a room she could imagine as workshop and study had it been filled with furniture, instruments, books.

Books. She sagged against the frame of the room's one, narrow window. How would she open a gateway if she couldn't get the books to tell her the proper way to do it?

You call yourself a wizard, she jeered at herself. *And you can't even get a book?*

An image of the wizard Palimur came to her then, sitting with his arms stretched across the back of his garden bench. *Oh,* he'd said, *you'll tame down fine.* She remembered the *Malmidion's* increasing heaviness as it had approached him, showing displeasure in its own, mute way.

An idea unfurled. She smiled. Of course. She didn't have to go out and buy books like a common mortal.

Air whispered into the room, vivid with the smell of roses and jasmine.

"I think there's more to tame than me, Lord Palimur," Jen murmured.

She sent a tenuous whisper across the City to the book that possessed, it was said, the power to choose where it went and where it stayed. "What do you say, Malmidion?" she murmured to the hushed afternoon air. "How would you like to join me?"

お

Jen stood staring at the massive book that rested on the windowsill, washed with moonlight in the very spot she'd leant this afternoon when sending an invitation into the world. She hurried across the room, took up the book and hugged it like a long-lost friend. It felt as heavy as a child in her arms, yet came up easily and never threatened to slip free of her awkward embrace.

"Malmidion!" she said with a laugh. "I knew you'd come! She slid down the wall to sit cross-legged on the floor, cradling the book in her lap. "Will you show me that sign again? Will you let me see the page I found last time, in my master's house?"

The leather-bound cover warmed under her hands, the book's will answering her request. As she had when sitting on her bed that handful of days ago, she riffled pages until she came to the warmest. In red ink, outlined in black, the sign the Fey woman had made, the sign Jen had made almost to her ruin, glared up from the center of the page. Gripping the obsidian knife that still hung around her neck like a talisman of her quest, she frowned down at the crabbed, hand-drawn letters upon the page.

The sigyle of poure was used by the auncien adepts to chanel the poures of erthe and aer and hert unto grete makenings. The adept must therefor harnes those poures first, and plase the poures into the sigyle...

Powers of earth and air, she read again. Elemental magic was the stuff of lore. Old stories contained tales of wizards who worked such magic: the calling of storms, the raising or calming of waters or earthquakes. In the stories, whole fleets had been destroyed, cities razed, lands burned or riven from mountain to sea. Wizards these days did not possess the raw, innate power for such magic—nor the sheer disregard of consequences to attempt it.

The words built like a wall in her mind, towering, unscalable: arcane references, obscure spells perhaps unknown to any living wizard.

Jen hunched over the great book in her lap, turning page after page. "Please, Malmidion," she begged in a strained whisper. "You must be able to show me something. If I can't use that sign, there must be another way to reach the Otherworlds."

Letters on the page moved, scurrying like black, odd-legged bugs. Jen snatched her hands away. The letters continued to writhe, to regroup, huddling together, forming words.

Ply the edge that sunders the fabric of the world.

Jen stared down at the page, blank except for those few words. "What edge?" The same ten words stared back at her, unmoving. Her hands gripped the edges of the book. "Riddles won't help me."

Worry scratched and gnawed at the back of her mind: the money will run out. Col will leave. Your master will find you...

She set the book aside, pushed to her feet and hurried from the room.

The garden, when she reached it, was a puzzle of moonlight and shadow. Jen stopped outside the deepest shadow, where the stone lay. "You said your powers are the powers of the earth," she said.

So they are, the stone replied.

"I wish to know how to summon the earth's elemental powers."

The stone's deep hollow voice spoke in her mind. *I am old,* it said, as it had before. *The magic of earth is my essence. I am made of the blood and brains and passions of men leaching from perished flesh into earth, the faith in seeds planted in the ground, the*

greed and despair of miners tunneling in darkness, the forgotten ritu-
als practiced in the earth's stone womb. I can show you, but I do not
know what time of yours the telling will take. Mortal lives go by in
the blink between sun and sun...

"Wizards don't live ordinary mortal lives," Jen replied, but a sinking coldness clotted in her middle.

I have lived a thousand thousand lives of wizards. How many of
your years can you give for the teaching?

"Years!" she burst out.

Have you asked of me what you most desire? it said, even as it had that first night.

"Yes! I told you. Safety."

No. You asked for protection. And I protect you.

"At the cost of my freedom. At the cost of my power."

You have power. Why should it not serve you? Why should it not bring you all you wish?

"Because if I send my magic out into the world, my master will find me," she replied. "What good is it then?"

Wizards' power is of man's strength.

She barked a bitter laugh. "Well, that's the problem. I don't have a man's strength."

But you have woman's.

Clenching her fists, she spun away. "What good is that?"

There are old magicks, subtle as the rising of the moon, powerful
as tide, that men do not know. Power that bends the fall of chance
like water bends around a root. Power that sways minds like wind in
grass. Why wield magic not made for you, when you might command
that which belongs to you by right?

Jen hesitated, staring across the shapes of tree and bush and grass etched in shadow. Such magic could bring what she needed. She faced the dark, impervious form that housed an entity of unguessable age and power. Suspicion prickled along her neck. "I've never heard of anything like that."

You would not. The dark, whispering voice held no irony.

"Why not?"

My Sisters once knew, but now have forgotten. Long ago was I bound in the well, beneath the cold, still waters, and could not teach them.

"But you'll teach me? Why?"

Once my Sisters brought me power, and I gave power in return. Even kings came, bearing gifts that they might be allowed to kneel before me in the sacred grove. Long and long was I bound in stillness. The waters fell away, and I could touch the world once more, but yet, there was silence. Then you came, and lifted me, carried me into the world once more. As you gave me that gift, can I not gift you?

The house, so imprisoning a moment ago, turned in her imagination to a stronghold, a citadel in which she might repose with every comfort while she searched for her gateway to the Otherworlds.

"Can you teach me?"

Come, the stone said. *I will show you.*

Like a prisoner groping into darkness toward freedom, Jen crept nearer. The stone's ox-sized bulk blotted the moon, enfolding her entirely in its shadow.

Chapter 12

Magic seethed around her like a fiery sea. In a dim, silent room high in a tall house, Jen swam in it, rode its crests and troughs like she'd been born to it. She *had* been born to it, magic her master could never have taught her, for no wizard knew such lore. Only the stone. And now Jen, after a week lost in the stone's whispered teachings.

With the stone's instruction, she reached toward the river with power silent and delicate as night, brushed docks with their stacks of crates and barrels and blocky warehouses; prodded shuttered shops and slumbering markets.. *I'm hungry,* she told them all. *My house is cold and empty.*

The magic crept and coiled, answering her, touching minds. Rumors, snatches of gossip people remembered hearing, somewhere, from someone, just can't remember who. Such a whisper had brought the furniture dealer who wanted his competitor's business. Such had sent him customers sure that the other fellow down at the Arches sold shoddy goods. A simple trade, magic for a spindle-legged table, a rug, lamp, and four tall, thronelike chairs of dark wood with embroidered cushions.

Yes, the stone whispered. *Just so.*

"I could have used spells like these in the slums," Jen said. "They would've filled the cupboard and saved me a few thrashings."

Men have forgotten all powers but their own. The force of arm. The strength of command. They must learn to honor others not so blunt.

"I'm not worried about teaching them, only about surviving."

Beasts survive. Do you not aspire to more?

"Freedom," she said. "The Otherworlds."

To use great power, one must gain great power.

"I'm trying, but…" Jen opened her eyes to an empty room bounded by grim stone walls, patterned floors in black and grey slate, high ceilings clad patchily with squares of blackened copper.

Last night, she'd dreamt of a great, eyeless beast, snuffling. The night before that, a bright sword slashing through layer after layer of muffling cloth, and the night yet before, she'd dreamt of a knot slowly unraveled by unseen fingers. She shuddered. Six nights of such dreams of the eight she'd been here.

"My master's seeking me. I'm afraid he'll find me before I'm strong enough."

If none betray you, this magic will not.

She jerked a frowning glance toward the window as if she could glimpse the stone, though all she could see outside was a swatch of night sky, rooftops and chimney-pots. "What are you saying?"

There is one who might speak of your presence.

"No."

She scrambled to her feet, chilled by more than the stone floor upon which she sat. Hurrying along echoing hallways, down shadowed stairs, she searched the house with wizard's senses, found her brother outside on the front steps.

With someone else.

She froze, pressed to the wall as if she could disappear into it. The memory of the dreams swept down on her, throbbing with her heartbeat.

Col appeared at the far end of the hallway. The lamp in his hand sent shadows rearing.

"Jen," he said. "There's a man outside. Says he wants to see the sorcerer."

Panic choked her. If it was her master—

No. He'd just fetch her and be done with it. She let go a breath and closed her eyes.

"What d'you want me to do, Jen?"

Still, word could get back to him of where she was. She held up a hand. "Wait. Let me think."

Memory stirred. A day long ago, when she'd still been the girl Jenei. Jenei, fleeing her home in pain and fear, had dissolved herself into the boy Jen, who was strong, who would protect her. But Jen had not been proof against the wizard, her master.

Now Jen must grow into a man. No one would trifle with a man and a wizard.

"A seeming," she whispered, swept by a sudden, defiant hope, an inspiration so simple and so obvious, she was astounded she hadn't thought of it before.

A seeming gave weight and texture, scent and sound and sight true to the form created. It was a spell that could be spun only by a wizard or a strong sorcerer, truer than simple, mind-fooling illusion.

A current of rising excitement bore her along. "Watch."

Raising her hands on either side of her head, Jen closed her eyes and called up power.

From head to hips, her hands slid down through the air beside her, building around her the image she wished to be true, the image of what she must become. She made herself taller, though not so tall as Rik or Col, with a man's hands and broad shoulders and heavier muscles, the strong bones of a man's face, her own brown eyes beneath a man's brow.

Col gave a cry and stumbled back.

"You see?" Her voice was a husky tenor a little lower than his. "It's still me. But only another wizard, one stronger than me, can tell different."

Col hung on the door frame. "God's balls!" He looked her up and down. "Why you want to do something like that to yourself? Whassamatter with you?"

Jen clenched a fist. The stone's hints of betrayal echoed in her mind. "Do you want me to be found, Col?" she said softly.

"No! But—"

"How many wizard-women do you think this city holds?"

Col shut his mouth. "I didn't think of that. You want me to tell him he got the wrong squat?"

She paced a step up, one back, held out her hands—a man's, strong and sinewy. "What's he look like?"

Col shrugged. "Shorter than me, or maybe it just seems like that—he slouches. Skinny. Black hair. Scarred cheeks. Scruffy-dressed, too."

In spite of herself, Jen suppressed a smile. Col was one to talk about dressing well. As far as she knew, his first decent set of clothes these, that her jewels had bought.

She considered the visitor again. This man must be another drawn by her spells.

"Well, let's see him," she said.

Col looked unhappy, though about what, she didn't know. "Want me to put 'im in the room with the furniture?" he said. "Don't think nowhere else'll do."

"The drawing room." Thinking of the new furniture, she crooked a small, pleased smile. "That's good. Thanks."

"Want me to stay after I bring 'im?"

Did she? "No." If there was danger, no point in including Col. Especially when he couldn't do anything to help. "I'll be fine."

Turning, she started back down the hallway, toward the single furnished room. Jen shut the door, lit a lamp and arranged herself in her imposing chair.

Footsteps and voices approached. The voices fell silent and the door opened to admit a man fitting the description her brother had given. Jen beheld him with wizard's senses, touching and finding only a sorcerer's power.

"Welcome to my home," Jen said. "I am Arjen." She relished the sound of the name.

She watched the sorcerer for any hint that her youngman's seeming might be anything other than perfect, but his gaze only met that of the seeming, a handspan above her own eyes.

He bowed. "I'm Kerr. I knew someone had taken over the old Erran house, and came to see who it was."

"I'm afraid I get busy and rarely go out."

Still waiting at the door, Col shifted from foot to foot.

Jen had a sudden fear the man would see her equivocation for what it was. But no, she reminded herself, this slightly stooped, slightly seedy man was only a sorcerer and possessed no mind-magic. Nevertheless, she let a ward slip into being between her mind and his.

"Come," she said with a gesture of invitation. "Share a glass of wine with me. I've been working hard today and would welcome the respite."

Col took the cue and hurried out, quickly returning with wine and two glasses. Jen took them and gave him a nod and an encouraging smile to send him on his way. She shut the door again.

Kerr the sorcerer, first eying the dark, antiquated furniture, sat. "Thank you," he said.

Jen lifted her own glass and sipped. "What brings you here?"

"Curiosity." He touched his wine but didn't drink. "And dismay, when I discovered a man of power had settled here. Especially when you never emerged to introduce yourself."

Back in her street-magician days, the custom had been to ensure one wasn't infringing on another's territory. Sorcerers' battles over turf were colorful common lore. But Jen was no sorcerer. She was a wizard, more powerful than any number of sorcerers with their chants and wands and words of power.

She forced a rueful laugh. "Preoccupation with my studies, I'm afraid. I didn't mean to worry anyone."

"Then you aren't practicing?"

"Not now," she said, a truth that would not bind her actions as a simple *no* would. "At the moment, I'm seeking the means to open a gateway to the Otherworlds."

"No gate to the Otherworlds has been opened since the days of Evaud the Silver," Kerr said.

She nodded. "Eight hundred years ago. And they say Fey blood ran through Evaud's veins." She cocked her head. "Where did you learn that?" She'd read the tale in one of her master's books.

"From an old sorceress," he said. Then added, smugly, "My grandmother."

"Indeed! Do you know more?"

Kerr gave a slight, mocking smile. "You, a wizard, ask for mere sorcerer's learning?"

She leaned back in her chair. "I'm no lordling's pet. I learned from witches and sorcerers as a boy, and found even then that witches and sorcerers possess odd bits of knowledge that often fails to make its way into wizardry."

"Those witches and sorcerers must have been trying to win you as apprentice. Knowledge," Kerr said, "has value."

The sorcerer was no spy, no secret enemy, only a man scraping for his next coin. Jen almost laughed with relief. "True enough. But in my experience, knowledge grows if shared freely."

His thin fingers moved over the wine glass. "I ply my trade for a living. As far as I'm concerned, it's no different than if you asked for a spell."

"Ah," Jen said, smiling. "But what will you do with knowledge of the Otherworlds?" She let the smile thin to a hard line. "What power will you use to open a gateway?"

"What power will *you* use?" the sorcerer said, giving her an answer without meaning to. "There's a reason a gateway hasn't been opened in eight hundred years—wizards don't have the power they once did."

"Perhaps not," Jen replied. "But I've learned of forgotten magicks. Old spells long unused."

Kerr made a disparaging noise. "All the old stories say even the Fey used the portals in the stone rings and sacred places."

Jen squelched the impulse to sit up straight. Portals! She'd never considered that there might be existing gateways in the world. Perhaps the sign she'd made to her disaster had only failed because she hadn't used it in the right place. But what place?

She considered. She could simply take what she wanted from his mind—

A jolt of sick cold went through her. How could she even think such a thing? She stood, breathing hard, turned away from the sorcerer. She could feel his surprise, his sudden wariness. She swallowed once, again, trying to still the quiver that shook her.

"Perhaps we can speak again later," she said. The seeming she'd cast also muffled the quaver of her voice. "When I can offer more than wine for your knowledge."

His chair scraped across the stones of the floor. "Perhaps," he said.

She turned back. "May I ask where to find you? In case I encounter anyone seeking a sorcerer's services, you understand." She gestured him toward the door.

He hesitated, then said, "Just tell them, ask for Kerr. They'll find me. If I want to be found."

Jen gave a slight smile and bowed her head. The man was afraid of her. She should be pleased. Shouldn't she?

She chatted as she guided him downstairs, through the front hall and out into the garden. The stone squatted by its dark-shaded pool. She hoped Kerr couldn't sense its cold appraisal as she could.

The sorcerer glanced at the stone, then away again. "I'm surprised you can live here. There are evil tales about this place. It's always had a shadow about it."

With a hand between his shoulders, she hurried him toward the gate. "Yes, but it is a place of rare power."

She bowed. He stepped through the gate and wended his way down the street.

Jen sagged against the stones of the archway. The sticky dampness of the breeze up from the river brushed cold over her sweaty face. A dull, queasy pain thumped in her head. The dim monotones of the street, sickly grey and dreary black, seemed overbright.

Abruptly, she wanted no more of spells or stones or sorcerers, no more of the darkness that forever lapped at the edges of her thoughts.

"Burn!" she called and sent her mind out seeking the dog.

The last time she'd seen him, two or three days ago, he wouldn't even come as she crouched, coaxing, just inside the gate. She hadn't used power on him, though. She'd never do that to the dog.

But Burn had not come then, and did not come now. She couldn't bury her face in his fur, letting his simple trust and pleasure in her company wash over her.

Footsteps and voices roused her: three girls in shabby homespun shifts walking all in a knot up the street. They shushed one another and moved to the far side of the street, which, narrow as it was, wasn't very far. With a slight, cool bow to them, Jen stepped back inside the gate, sent it swinging shut behind her.

She folded her arms and stood chewing her lip. Her stomach still churned—with anger, with upset, she didn't know. At last, she crossed to the stone.

"He told me of gateways," she said. "Portals to the Otherwords in the old sacred places. You told me you know of such things. Why didn't you tell me this?"

What I have seen, you know.

Do I? Jen thought. The place from which she'd taken the stone *was* a sacred place. Was it her own fault that she'd thought only of the magic, and not where it must have been worked?

"You said the Fey spoke to you. Did they ever speak of this?"

The Fey came to seek my knowledge. What need have I of theirs?

She wanted to curse and stamp her feet. If she'd only known when she met the stone in its sacred well, she could've opened her gateway there!

"If I carry you back to your well—"

No, the stone's voice rumbled in her mind.

Of course not. It would no more return there than she would to her master.

"But there must be other holy places. If I find them, I could take you with me. You could have a place of your own, where people might come and speak to you again. And I could open my gateway."

The stone remained silent for a time. *The fearful flee*, it said at last. *The weak seek escape. You have begun to find your strength here. Will you so quickly abandon it?*

She tucked her chin. "What strength?"

See what is becoming. Yet more can unfold, if you so choose.

"What?"

Continue, and see, the stone said.

"Maybe," Jen said.

But she'd still search for those gateways. How, she didn't yet know, but if her magic could bring her a sorcerer who just *happened* to have knowledge of gateways to the Otherworlds, surely it could bring her those with knowledge of where those gateways might be found.

Chapter 13

"There's a girl I wish to marry, lord."

The young man sitting opposite had introduced himself as Gere. A little taller than Jen's young-man's seeming, with light hair and a pleasant face short of handsome, he was dressed in a tunic, short jacket and hose. His callused, ink-stained fingers and earnest eyes peering through small round lenses marked him as a scribe or bookkeeper.

Or a mapmaker.

"You'd best go to a witch for a love charm then," she said, smiling at the fidgeting young man. "I could make one, but you'd be paying more than you ought."

Gere fidgeted more than before, then locked his fingers together. "The love's in no short supply, lord. She wants to marry me just as much as I want to marry her. She's a bond-servant and I don't have the money to buy her from her master." He slouched. "Nor do I hope to for some long while."

The fine hairs at Jen's nape prickled like hackles rising. "Ah," she said and smoothed the back of her neck, the sudden surge of anger. "And what would you have me do? Compel her master to part with her for a sum within your means? I could do that, but he'd realize soon enough what had happened. Neither you and your lady, nor I, would be pleased with the consequences."

Gere pushed his spectacles up his nose. "I don't know about these things, lord, but I thought surely there must be something..."

"Certainly, but the problem is cost. My fees won't be any bargain compared to just buying the girl's contract."

"Oh." His lips only shaped the word. He sat still in his chair a moment, downcast, then climbed to his feet. "I'm sorry to have taken your time, Lord Arjen."

Jen waved him back to his seat. "Wait a moment."

He hesitated, then lowered himself back into the chair.

"I'm willing to barter, if you have anything I need," she said. "What do you do? Who is your master?"

"I work for Master Trellan, the head archivist in the Prince's library. I'm a copyist."

Jen almost choked on exultation. The spells the stone had shown her would indeed bring all she needed.

She managed to say, calmly, "Indeed." She tapped her lips with a forefinger, feigning thought while she regained her composure. "As a wizard," she said at last, "I'm ever in need of books. And maps. Can you help me with either?"

Behind the small lenses of his spectacles, his eyes widened. "I—they aren't my books, lord."

"You're a copyist."

"But, lord," he stammered, "Do you know how long it takes to copy a book?"

"What about maps, then? Could you copy one?"

He shook his head. "The Mapmaker's Guild puts spells on its maps. The ink will fade as they're copied, or the copyist will go blind. I've heard that some men have hired sorcerers to copy maps. The sorcerer wouldn't go blind, and he could hold the map whole while he worked, but somehow the copies came out missing reefs or ravines that were on the original. And then the original— something always happened to it, later."

Jen had heard such stories. All her master's maps had been commissioned from the Mapmaker's Guild—at great expense, from what she'd gathered from Alannan's mutters. Indeed, that Guild was one of the more secretive, dealing as it did with ship pilots and caravan guides who guarded their own secrets just as jealously. Selective in its clientele, the Guild was as likely to turn down a commission as grant it, should that client's credentials be deemed insufficient. The illusions, compulsions and bindings she'd have to spin to assure the sufficiency of her credentials would leave a trail broad and plain.

"Well." Jen stood. "It seems we won't be able to reach an agreement. I'm sorry."

This time it was Gere who said, "Wait!"

Jen had half-turned, and now turned back. "Yes?"

"It isn't easy to get things out of the library," he said, half defiant, half apologetic. "Even if I cared to steal something, it would cost me my livelihood. And my hands. I wouldn't be able to support a family then."

Nodding, Jen waited.

"But I've heard wizards can see across long distances and into locked rooms and such. I could leave a map out where you could look at it."

"True," she agreed. "But for my purposes, I need it in my hands. And besides," she added, "that isn't barter enough to free your lady. Let me think." She tapped her lips again. "Would a map be missed if you were to, say, borrow it for me?"

Gere went pale. "It could be, if the Prince were to ask for it."

"Of course. But things are misplaced occasionally, surely. I'd think it would take time to realize something was truly missing."

"I won't steal," The young man said again. "Not even for my Ela."

"I spoke of borrowing, not stealing."

"Borrowing," Gere said doubtfully, as if it amounted to the same thing.

Jen leaned forward. She wanted those maps, and this young fellow was her best chance to get them.

"Borrowing," she repeated. "I keep the map awhile, then return it to you." Leaning back again, she spread her hands. "Surely a not an extraordinary thing to manage in return for the spells I'll forge to free your lady."

"Yes." He wet his lips. "But how will I—"

"*How*, is your business," she said. As were the consequences. "That is," she added, "if you care to pursue such a bargain." Her spells may have brought him here, but his choices must be his own.

Still, a spell of compulsion sparkled like a tempting bauble, teasing her. She locked the thought away in a high cupboard of her mind.

Gere nodded at last.

"Good. How long can I keep a map?"

"Two days," Gere said quickly.

"A week," she countered.

"Four days."

"All right," Jen said. "But two maps."

"Two?" The spectacles slid down the young man's nose. With shaking fingers, he pushed them back up.

"One of the City. The other of the surrounding countryside for…" How far? Ten leagues? Twenty? In all her life, she'd never been farther outside the City Wall than the slums. The countryside was a misty fantasyland from Marin's tales. "Ten leagues around," she decided, having no clear idea how long it would take to travel that distance, but thinking ten was more achievable than twenty, should she find a gateway somewhere nearby.

"Maps of the City?" Gere said, looking less worried than he had. "That's not too bad. How will you get my Ela free?"

"That's my concern," Jen said with wizardly obscurity.

"And you'll return the maps. Unharmed." It wasn't quite a question.

"After four days." She decided to be amused rather than insulted.

Gere expelled a breath. "All right. Pray God it won't get me caught. There's no point in going through any of this if I'm caught."

"I assure you," Jen said, "Neither do I have any wish for you to be caught. However…" She paused, thinking, then held out her hand. "Give me your spectacles."

After a moment's hesitation, the young man unhooked the spectacles from behind his ears and handed them over.

They were a good subject upon which to work. Glass held certain properties of focus and magnification and metal was a good conductor of magic. And he wore the item almost constantly—the metal frames glowed with his aura and the glass lenses shimmered and swam with the echoes of his thoughts. Jen slipped the spectacles over one hose-clad knee. Stroking them gently, she eased magic into the interstices of Gere's own aura.

"There." She handed them back.

The young man eyed his spectacles, unchanged to the mortal eye, but did not put them on. "What did you do?"

"I've put a ward on them—a spell to protect you from mischance and ill intention."

A general, benign spell that would arouse no undue suspicion should it be noticed, a spell as passive and un-traceable as that of an amulet. Yet it would serve its purpose in protecting *her* purposes.

At last, he replaced the spectacles, blinking through them as if he expected the spell to have some effect on their utility. "Thank you, lord. Do I—that is, will I—" He plunged ahead. "What do I owe you for this spell?"

Jen waved a hand. "That's to ensure you're able to uphold your end of the bargain. No charge."

Gere expelled a breath. "I'll get your maps."

"I have every faith in you."

But she eased a spell of silence upon him so that if he were questioned about the maps, he could never say who had wanted them.

Col came to escort the young man out when the business was concluded. Jen rose in their wake, paced out into the hallway.

The house no longer seemed quite the prison it had. Feet now walked its marble halls, dispelling its emptiness. Perhaps the noise and the movement, the life, were waking the house out of its long slumber. She sensed magic moving, felt a glimmer of awareness. But it was a dark glimmer, one that reminded her of the stone.

Jen walked through the front door and into a splash of hot noon sunlight. Today a marbling of cloud painted the sky above the garden walls; bees droned among the pink faces of the roses; the rich sweet scent of roses mingled with that of sun-heated grass. The stone's shady pool was an island of coolness in a brassy summer sea.

"Did you hear what that man wanted?" she asked, deciding to find out just how far the stone's awareness reached.

I did, it replied in a voice of night and darkness and ancient hollow places.

Jen's heart gave a little squeeze of dismay, but she only said, "It's a good job."

You are well suited to right such a wrong.

"What do you mean?"

Were you not bought? Were you not held against your will? Have you not been wronged?

"Not that you know."

But I do. The wrongs done you brought you to me.

Jen drew breath to ask what wrongs it meant, but clamped her jaw. "Maybe," she said. "Or maybe I just felt sorry for you, trapped at the bottom of that well."

Sympathy, O yes! There is much we share. Much strength we can give, one to the other.

It had said much the same in one of their first conversations. The words stirred in her now, as they had then, a certain uneasiness. Thus, on that night that seemed so long ago, she had extracted from the stone the promise that it leave her free to follow her own will.

"Be careful, stone. I'm a wizard and this is my house. Don't be too forward."

Do you not trust me? Do you not trust your own power?

"Trust won't bring me what I want."

Power will.

The words warmed her like wine. "Yes," she whispered, turning back to the house. Power had brought her knowledge. It would bring her freedom, as well. Freedom from the darkness that haunted her, freedom from fear.

Power burned within, warming her as the sunlight did. She looked up to see Col on the porch, watching her.

Had she not been able to sense his doubt, his uncertainty, it was clear enough on his face.

"What's wrong, Col?" she asked, putting her foot on the bottommost step of dressed granite.

He looked over her shoulder, toward the stone. "You talk to that thing."

"That I do."

He eyed her. "It talk back? I don't hear nothing."

She tapped her temple. "Here. In my mind."

"What's it tell?"

"Oh, all kinds of things."

"What things?"

She wondered where this quizzing would lead. "What are you worried about?"

"I ain't worried." He twisted a shirt button.

Jen had to resist the impulse to reach out and still his hand. "You are. You think I can't feel it?"

"It—it ain't you. It's this place. I'm always dreaming there's somebody whispering at me. When I'm awake, I feel somebody watching me, but I look and there's nobody there."

"It's only the stone," she said. "The monks were just as afraid of it when I took it from the temple. It won't do anything. It's glad to have us here."

Col shuddered. "Maybe it's glad to have us here, but it ain't glad for the same reason as me or you."

Chapter 14

Thin moonlight trickled through the study window, picking out every old nick and scar on the spindly-legged table, sheening like white satin on its much-rubbed surface. An owl swept from the attic above, casting its broad-winged shadow across the moon, across the table.

Jen reached out magic. Light flared to life in the green-shaded lamp on the table, illuminating the two scrolls tied with red ribbon that lay upon the table. She took one up and slid off the ribbon. It snagged a little on the deckled edges of the paper. Carefully, reverently, Jen unrolled the map and held it flat.

This map was of the City within its Wall, and of the portion of the river that ran through. It depicted the towers guarding the river entrances on right bank and left, upstream and down. Every house and shop, well and square was marked in blocks of black or red or blue.

The second map showed only the major landmarks within the City. The Prince's palace. The temples of the monk's god, that of the Moon, and that of the hero-god Fiora, who was said to have destroyed the invading fleet of the murdering Sciorri by swamping their boats with a great wave. It showed the Basilica where the great gatherings of merchants and nobles were held. Cormilone's Fortress, whose dungeons and catacombs brooded over secrets.

This map showed a longer stretch of the river and outlying villages—a whole world she'd never seen and scarcely guessed at. She hungered to travel those roads, to climb those hills.

She had no spiky gold star shaped like a child's jack, like the one her master used in his finding spells, but she had a small white pebble, almost round. Weighting the maps' corners with stones, she found the black-inked square she calculated was her house, and placed the pebble there. She cupped her hands, one on either side of the maps, and closed her eyes.

A gateway, she wished. *Find me a gateway to the Otherworlds.* The magic fixed like a burning-glass on the round pebble, leaping from facet to facet of milky crystal within it, finally bursting forth to scatter across the map in pale rainbow sparks.

Behind her closed lids, it was as if she hovered above the City. The river was a black satin ribbon dropped into the glittering jewelbox that was the City, a ribbon gemmed here and there with the lanterns of barges or fishing boats. Smudges of smoke veiled the warm gold of house lights; smithies glowed like garnets and the kilns of glassworks and potters burned hot amber. The sun-shape of the god's temple flickered with the citrine of a thousand lamps radiating outward from the central altar fire. The Prince's palace glittered like rings on a rich man's hand.

All this Jen saw through her mind's eye, through her wizard's power as she worked the finding spell that would locate her gateway. At last, a tug came. Full of the City, ponderous with City, she let that tug hook her, draw her forward. On she rushed, ethereal wind streaming through the wings of her mind.

Straight down she plummeted, toward a jumble of tile roofs, into the haze of smoke hanging over them. Through the smoke and out again, those roofs grew larger until she could see chimneys, tiles, then the tangle of bird's nests in stray angles. One roof became all she could see.

She tensed, but her disembodied sight only knifed through the roof and into the dark mustiness of an attic, plunged through dusty floorboards, heedless of oaken rafters, into a room scantily lit by a single lamp. Foreshortened from above, she saw a table spread with maps, a figure bent over them, a head of dark brown curls...

Jen shook her head and straightened, blinking the room into focus. The white pebble remained where she'd placed it on the map, on the square representing her house. She picked it up, replaced it, then looked up at the ceiling, half-expecting to find her disembodied self floating somewhere in the air overhead. Obviously, something had gone wrong with the spell. Taking a breath, she reached for her power and tried again, directing her thoughts outward, away from the currents of power in the house, away from the stone, from herself.

This time, she sped along the river. Docks with their stacks of crates and barrels and bales flew by, warehouses dark and blocky and anonymous. Narrow, crooked streets gave way to farmland, to orchards, a patchwork of black and grey and silver in the moonlight. Even as her mind quested outward, she was aware of her body in her silent, narrow study, aware of the slither of the little pebble across the surface of the paper between her hands.

Her disembodied sight descended toward the wild woods that lined the river. The river shone lighter than those woods, a dark glimmer between billows of blackness. But in that blackness sparked a gleam like an open eye. As if caught in a whirlpool, Jen was sucked down until her awareness stopped with a jolt.

She seemed to stand at the verge of a pool, perfectly

round. Oaks, ancient and twisted, stood guard in a circle all around, more sentient than any standing stone. In this state, she possessed only sight and wizard's senses. Sight showed the unnatural regularity of the place, but wizard-sense hummed with an awareness of power long-unused and buried, but so concentrated that, had she been there in the flesh, her skin would have tingled with it. *Here*, then. Here was the place she'd find her gateway to the Other-worlds.

Her concentration unraveled. The world seemed to fray in a blur of monochromatic threads, tangling, snarling, until they at last rewove themselves into the marble floor and stone walls of her study; and before her the map, lying between her hands in a pool of yellow light.

Jen blinked her surroundings into focus once more. The white pebble lay at the edge of the map, a little distance from the wavy blue lines that represented the river. Her fingertip brushed the paper as she traced a line from the City to that spot beside the river.

No symbol marked that spot. Just an anonymous stretch of river somewhere between one village and the next in wild lands claimed by neither. She walked her fingers across the distance.

It's so far, she thought. The gateway was there, yet it might as well be beyond the edges of the world. Even if she had Col bundle her into a carriage or tie her to a horse, her master's Call awaited beyond the garden walls. It would swaddle her wits, leave her helpless to locate or open the gate itself. Helpless do anything but obey the command of the Call.

The shifting lamplight made the river's wavy lines appear to flow like real water; the crosshatching that marked the City Wall looked like the shadow of massive stones. If only she could somehow put herself into the map, travel its inked roads instead of risking the world's roads!

That was magic dreamed of by assassins, spies and the leaders of armies, that could turn whole kingdoms in their courses. Another magic of old tales, requiring great power. Another magic to seek out and learn, if she could. Another magic…and more time.

Jen shoved away from the maps. Lamplight threw her shadow across floor and wall, a distorted blot of darkness larger than she. For an instant, she fancied that the shadow would consume her, if it could.

She shifted away from the light. The darkness dwindled, once again only a shadow near her own size and shape. She approached it where it awaited by the room's single tall window. Leaning shoulder to shoulder with it, she gazed out into a night jeweled here and there with the same kind of lights that must show from her house.

More time. Everything came down to that. Yet every day she spent here cost her. Each day meant food and fuel to buy. A great many days meant even more things: clothes, bedding, soap— The list went on.

Her head came up. Gere had come as a client. She'd only settled on barter with him because he was as poor as she was. If he'd had money…

He would've paid her. As her master's clients paid him. Jen was a wizard, too. Men would come here, to her house, and pay her to work magic for them.

"I'm Arjen," she whispered, picturing again the seeming of the short young man, the seeming only a wizard stronger than she could see through. The sorcerer who'd come had seen nothing but a young man. So had Gere. The wizard Arjen could ply his trade like any other wizard.

Lamplight played over bare stone walls, bare marble

floor, but in her imagination she saw fine rugs, shelves filled with books, carved chairs, tables, a desk, a marble worktable. Everything a wizard's study should be—

Jen shook away the image. No, she'd remain here only until she found her way to that gateway by the river. That long, and no more.

お

The last bloody light of sunset spilled through the drawing room windows. Jen did not glance up from her pretended deep thought when Col ushered the day's client into her presence. Instead, she let her gaze rest on the man's shadow, splayed long across the rug.

At her continued silence and lack of welcome, the undercurrent of nervousness she'd sensed in the visitor grew, became a rumble of uneasiness almost audible to wizard's ears.

"Master," Col said. By now, the stutter with which he'd at first addressed her was entirely absent. "This is Master Verin."

At last, Jen, in her guise as Arjen, looked up. Col took the man's hat, then met her eyes with a disapproving frown. He disliked her wizardly theatrics, particularly when the visitor was nervous and uncomfortable, as this one clearly was. In reply to her brother's displeasure, she only lifted one shoulder with the hint of a shrug. Behind Master Verin's broad, beefy shoulder, Col turned quickly for the door. Too quickly. Unease breathed on her neck, but she pushed it away.

The man stood mopping his forehead and thinly-covered pate. Bowing, she gestured at the chairs. "I am Arjen. Please, Master Verin, won't you sit?"

Returning his handkerchief to his pocket, he bobbed his head. "Thank you, lord." Seating himself, he twiddled the buttons of his coat.

Jen settled into her chair. "What brings you to me?"

"I've been thinking of coming for a while, but I—" He produced the handkerchief again, dabbed his forehead and fell to crushing the cloth in his big hands. "It never seemed the right time, if you know what I mean." His accents weren't cultured, they weren't in the patois of the street, either. The man would be middle-class, maybe a small merchant.

Jen nodded encouragingly.

"But finally, I told myself, 'What are you waiting for, Verin? Take care of the business! You planning on just letting it go?' Gossip in the market has it your lad's a sorcerer's servant, so when he was pointed out, I followed him a ways to be sure I had him right, then asked him to present me, as it were."

Entering quietly with a tray, Col brought two glasses of rich red wine. Two bottles had left her little change from a silver piece, but she couldn't be serving common man's swill to clients.

Verin took his glass and sipped. His brows went up and he held out his glass to study it. Jen felt the leap of his surprise and wondered if she should've set her standards in wine somewhat lower.

Beneath the man's nervousness and surprise, though, she sensed something else. "What has made you angry, Master Verin?"

He spluttered on his wine. He put down the glass, then clenched his fist and set it on one knee.

"A man's wronged me," he said, the first unapologetic words he'd spoken. "I want him punished."

She raised a brow. "Indeed. Why come to me? Why not take the matter to the justice, or to an assassin?" She was curious, but also, this was the sort of advice her master usually gave such clients.

"I can't." He closed his mouth as if it would take a chisel to open it.

She laced her hands. "Forgive me if I seem to pry, but you must understand that I need to know the particulars before offering my services."

"I've got gold." Verin glared at the floor. "I'll tell you who, and what I want done. Why do you need to know more? Lord," he added.

She shrugged slightly. "Who, then?"

"Lord Annoro." He spat out the name. "The Prince's Minister of Trade."

Jen released a silent breath. Her spells had brought this, a middle-class man with a vendetta against a man so highly placed that neither justice nor assassin would touch it. And neither would a wizard with any sense.

"Lord Annoro," she repeated, thinking as fast as she ever had.

Verin lumbered to his feet, anger now plain on his face. "I knew it. No man'll take the bastard on. Prince's Minister, so he can do as he pleases. Go on to the next girl he finds, do the same as he did to mine—"

Her head snapped up. Verin closed his mouth and took a step back.

"What did this man do to your daughter?" Jen demanded.

The man turned bright red. She felt in him the war of fear and fury and shame. An answering fury ran through her like wizard's fire. She pushed down magic and emotion with an effort.

"You told me *you* had been wronged," she said. "If you're telling me now that your daughter was defiled, she was the one wronged. Now tell me again. And this time, tell me true. I won't be lied to."

"I—I didn't mean to lie, Lord Arjen, but you know how it is. She'll never marry well now. And my reputation, my honor—"

"Gods *damn* your reputation!" Jen snarled suddenly. "What of your daughter? What of the pain she's suffered, and is still suffering! What are your family name and marriage prospects to that?"

"But everyone will think she welcomed it—"

"Be silent!"

It was a spell. Verin could only mouth like a stranded carp. His red face went pale and sweat sheened his brow and lip. He stumbled back. With a flick of a gesture, Jen stilled him.

"Sit down."

He came back and sat; whether of her will or his own didn't matter.

"A woman taken against her will is not the party liable in the matter," she said with false quiet. "Or are you lying to me again? Did the girl go willingly to the man's bed for the sake of ambition?"

Verin mouthed again, and Jen freed him.

Coughing, he touched his throat. "No, lord, no. She's not that kind of girl, she's a shy girl, an honorable girl. She'd never do that. My wife had to hire a healer-witch to see to her afterwards. She was hurt, you understand, more hurt than just a virgin's first bedding."

Jen wanted to close her eyes, but didn't. She knew she'd see a stone room in the darkness. Taking up the wine glass that rested on the table beside her, she squeezed down sips, one, two, three, concentrating on the warmth of the wine trickling down her throat. Her hand shook. She tightened her grip on the glass until the shaking stopped.

"So what will you do with your despoiled daughter?" she said at last in a conversational tone "Disown her? Consign her to a nunnery? Sell her to—" She stopped herself.

"No, lord," Verin stammered, aghast. "How could I? She's my daughter. I love her!"

She narrowed her eyes, probing, finding truth in the words. "Well, then. I begin to see you in a better light. Why didn't you say so straight off?"

He turned red again. "Most men wouldn't understand, lord."

"I'm not most men," she said. "I detest men who use women for amusement. And I detest men who see women as nothing more than property to be bought and sold to best advantage. Tell me what happened."

He wet his lips, braced hands on knees. "I started out on a merchantman sailing the southern routes, but I'm a trader now. I invited Lord Annoro to my home to examine my exotic goods…"

Jen listened, though she only half-heard his words. Most of her attention was on the sparkling undercurrent of emotion, on the occasional flash of a scene. When the image came of a stout woman with overly-elaborate blond curls, when she saw her holding a shuddering, clutching girl while her own face streamed tears, Jen knew there had been no misunderstanding, no mistaking what had happened. And she felt Verin's rage and shame as if they were her own. Through the dark clear current of his hatred, she saw a man's long, pleasant face, well-cut lips, keen eyes. A predator, perfectly camouflaged.

When he'd finished his tale, Verin fished out his handkerchief again, but now he dabbed at his eyes rather than at his forehead.

She studied him a moment, weighing. "What do you want done with him?"

The mingled hope and savage triumph on the man's face, in his heart, was almost painful. "I want him to get the rot on his manhood. The kind that'll give him pain each time he ruts, the kind of pain he gave my girl. Then I want him ruined. But slow. I want him to see it coming. To see him lose his position, his wealth, his noble friends and fine wife. I want to meet him when it's all over, when he's covered with sores and flies and even the beggars spit on him. Then I'll tell him what's happened to him, and why."

Sitting back in her chair, she folded her arms and clasped her chin in thought. If she took the job, she ran the risk of being traced. Lord Annoro would, after all, have access to wizards more powerful than she. And even if they couldn't trace her, it would be a simple enough matter for them to counter her spells. But with the stone's help...

She nibbled a thumbnail and thought of Palimur, Prince's wizard, to whom Annoro might resort did he suspect himself the victim of a curse. That thought made the commission doubly tempting.

A memory of her master's voice intruded on her thoughts. *Do no harm. Don't use your power against the powerless.* She throttled the voice. His kind of scruples had nothing to do with justice for a man who would so rob a woman. Anyway, Lord Annoro was hardly powerless, was he? Quite the contrary.

She glanced at Verin to find him watching her, anxious.

"It'll take time," she finally said. "And it's risky."

Hope and triumph flared anew. "I'll pay whatever you ask."

"What if I ask more than you can pay?"

"Then I'll keep paying."

"You might anyway," she couldn't resist pointing out.

Verin grinned. Not threatening, but with the complicity of a co-conspirator. "I don't think so. You'd be into it as deep or deeper than me."

Jen only smiled in reply. No wizard on earth would allow himself to be blackmailed. A lapse of memory, a sudden death... Far too many methods could be employed to prevent such awkwardness.

Chapter 15

The drawing room door opened not long after Verin had closed it. Col's thin face appeared, peering cautiously around the edge of the door. Jen dropped a bag on the table. It struck with a substantial clink and toppled to the side with a slithering jingle, coin sliding over gold coin.

"Eggs," Jen said. "Flour. More lamps. Real beds, I think. I'm sick of itchy straw mattresses."

Col walked over to the table, picked up the bag and tugged open its drawstring. His jaw dropped. "What'd he hire you for?"

Jen crooked a smile. "A little revenge. That's only the retainer. There'll be more."

He stared, then burst out, "You're damn crazy!"

"Why? The man's daughter was raped. He's justified."

Her brother's pale face flushed. "You don't know—"

"I do know. And I'm glad to have the job. I'd do that kind of job for free."

He looked at her as if she were changing shape before his eyes. "Jen. Let me see you."

She spread her hands. "Here I am."

"No, not that—that lie. You. I want to see *you*."

She sighed and let the seeming of Arjen fall away. Col turned away while she did it.

He took an unsteady breath. "I know what Rik threatened to do when he grabbed you in that alley, but—"

"You know *nothing*," she snapped.

Col shifted his feet. "Rik was a rotten pig. But I don't

think he woulda done—y'know. That. And even if he did," he went on, his voice rising when she opened her mouth for another retort. "Even if he did, it ain't worth hunting trouble now."

Her anger drained away. "I won't get into trouble."

"You will! You're doing everything you can to! First running away, and now you're gonna do some black magic—"

"If you're scared, leave."

He'd endured his brother's abuse out of fear. Unlike Rik, she wouldn't compel or intimidate him to stay with her.

Col shook his head. "I'm scared, yeah. But I ain't gonna go. You're my sister. Think I'd leave you here by yourself? You're scared too, I know. But you shouldn't do this—"

"I'm not scared," she interrupted. "I can take care of myself. And I can stop people who think they can get away with anything."

"If they think that, it's because they can!" he said, flinging up his hands. "And if you try to stop 'em, they'll smash you flat! You know that, Jen. Just like you should know better than to get tangled up in somebody else's revenge."

She shook her head. "Look, I'll give you half of this," she flicked a finger at the moneybag.

He muttered a disgusted string of words that might have been curses. "You ain't gonna bribe me, Jen. But better give me half anyway. I better have payoff for the justice when you get caught."

"If I get caught. Take it. Use it for whatever you want. You deserve something for playing servant." Leaving the money on the table, she started for the door.

"Where you going?"

"Just outside."

He looked sullen, clearly swallowing more angry words. She shrugged and went out.

The evening star gemmed the purple velvet of the sky, and a crescent moon chased the sunken sun. A single cricket sang. Jen's feet hushed in the grass as she made her way toward the stone, and the cricket fell still.

She leaned a shoulder against the pebbled bark of the live oak. "How about the job?"

You must work slowly, the stone replied in its empty, toneless voice.

"I know that. If it looks unnatural, the man will know he's been cursed."

Yes. Use the currents of earth and water as I showed you. Begin with the sickness. Sickness often lives in water. Move that water toward the man you seek to undo.

A simple curse was a much more direct matter: define its terms, set her will to it and let the magic take its course. This magic might be subtler, but it had its own weaknesses.

"Sickness also strikes others who come into contact with it," she said. "I'll give Lord Annoro's whole household the wonky rot that way."

Will this not fulfill the desires of the man who spoke with you?

Jen frowned. "Yes, but—"

This magic is not to be controlled.

True enough, from what she'd seen so far. The net she'd conjured to bring people like Verin to her had been a thing that drifted on the air, not a Calling but a messy sort of sorcery, random and chancy, but one she could practice beneath any wizard's notice, and with a longer reach than she could manage with her power alone.

"All right," she said, but was already thinking of alternatives.

Touch me, the stone said. *I will show you the colors of sickness.*

Jen settled cross-legged in the cool grass, put her hands on the stone's rough surface and leaned her forehead on the backs of her hands. Darkness enfolded her, chill, smelling of still, fetid water. Then that water surged up and over, whirling her away.

お

"This do?" Col asked.

Jen turned from the pot she was stirring. Col stood in the kitchen doorway, bearing a huge and extravagant arrangement of cabbage roses, sweet pea, cosmos, marigold.

She grinned. "Perfect."

He set the flowers on the scarred and battered kitchen table, far from the fire. In the ruddy firelight, they shimmered like flame themselves, tinted red, pink, salmon, orange. Col leaned over Jen, took the spoon from her fingers and tasted the stew.

"Needs something…"

"Maybe pepper," she said, "but all I could find was peppergrass. You'll need to tell me. It's been too long since I had to cook."

"I'll get some stuff tomorrow at market." He stirred the pot and sat on the hearthstones beside Jen. "What're the flowers for?"

"A gift for Lord Annoro," she answered.

Col's face went tense and still. "What you gonna to do with 'em?"

Jen smiled. "Nothing awful, don't worry. But I'll need you to make sure they get to him."

"Leave me out."

She restrained an annoyed sigh. "I'm putting a spell of protection on them. Is that so bad?"

"What? Why? I thought you were gonna do some kind of black revenge spell."

"I'd like to keep the revenge where it belongs."

"You oughta—"

"Keep out of it," she said. "I know. But I won't, so I want to keep the business clean, at least."

She stood and crossed to the table. The flowers spilled from a globe-shaped bowl of cut glass, incongruous on the stained surface crosshatched with years' worth of chopping. Ordinary flowers, of course, wilted and faded in time. These would remain as exquisite as her magic could make them, to be kept as long as their beauty lasted. And they needed to be kept.

Holding her hands on either side of the arrangement, Jen closed her eyes. The magic for the spell rose up glittering, spun crystal that would harden into a thin, invisible shield. She cast the limits of that shield as wide as she could, covering wife, children, servants, tradesmen, every person who might come into the household. But she left one unprotected: the master of the house. Lord Annoro would remain unguarded from the sorcery she and the stone had woven.

She suspected a man like Annoro would have his home protected by spells of ward and guard. Particularly if he made enemies by raping the daughters of business associates. But no ward or guard spell would defend against a beneficial spell. Why should it? And what concern could such a spell generate even if it were discovered? She would do a Seeing to make sure the flowers were accepted and remained in the house.

Jen set the spell and opened her eyes. Col watched, biting his lip. The stew bubbled over into the fire, sending up small, nasty-smelling ribbons of smoke.

"Col, the stew!"

He turned and used the spoon to swing the pot on its hook out of the fire. "Sorry."

"Don't worry about it. Will you have the flowers delivered for me tomorrow?"

"You sure that's a good spell you put on?"

She drew back. "Of course. Do you think I'd lie to you?"

Col dipped in the spoon and stirred. "No, Jen. I don't *think* so."

"Well, I wouldn't."

He glanced up again to search her face. Finally, he nodded, apparently finding what he was looking for.

お

Light swept the darkness of Jen's sleeping mind. Like an animal hidden in its lair, her awareness opened an eye. Another mind, a powerful mind, seeking—what?

Me.

The knowledge rushed over her, flung her out of sleep. Her eyes flared open to the watchful darkness of her bedroom.

Heart slamming at her ribs, she lay still, as if mere stillness could conceal her. Starlight sifted onto the bare floor through the small panes of the uncurtained window. All lay in shadow. At last, she eased wizard's senses out into the night, seeking that which had sought her.

"What're you doing, Jenei?"

Jen thrust herself over in bed, hand raised to fling fire. Another shadow slouched on the edge of the pallet. Something about it, and the voice…

The voice was utterly familiar, one that had whispered to her in the darkness of hundreds of nights, though she hadn't heard it in…what, seven years? Eight? The shadow turned, showing a girl's rounded cheek smoothing into that of womanhood—

But that was wrong. After all these years, she wouldn't be a girl anymore, would she?

"Dee," she said wonderingly. Her next-oldest sister. Silver light flared from Jen's hands, stark and eerie, glimmering on a fall of hair the brown of her own, but lank like their father's. The girl even sat with Dee's slouch, with the same nervous plucking at her skirt. A dream? But Jen felt awake, and remembered waking.

"What are you doing here?" she asked.

"I came to ask you the same thing," Dee said.

Jen lowered herself to one elbow and regarded her sister of dream or memory. "What *I'm* doing? What are *you* doing, sitting on my bed looking fifteen again?"

"Talking to you."

Jen probed the apparition, but her senses touched nothing. Not even the bright rising bubbles of thoughts and emotion she usually sensed from ordinary mortals. Dee was as blank as air.

"I've missed you," Jen said at last. "Worried about you, too. How are you?"

Dee shrugged and plucked at her skirt again. Jen wished that if she had to have a visitation from her sister, it could've been her sister when she was younger. When she'd still teased Jen and laughed with her, and played wild games of hide-and-seek in which Jen was already able to make it look like she'd run one way when she'd actually run another.

Sighing, Jen tried another tack. "Did you know I was bought like you were?"

"How would I know? You were still at home when that—that man took me."

Dee wouldn't raise her face. Jen remembered that mannerism, too, how suddenly one day it seemed Dee would only shuffle about the house with her face hidden by her hair, her once-laughing voice stifled.

"I know why he took you," Jen said. "I knew it then. A man bought me—for almost the same reason."

"Da knew too."

"Hells, yes," Jen said. "But he'd let us go as long as he got gold out of the bargain. We didn't have much worth otherwise."

"You've always had worth, Jenei."

Jen clenched her jaw. "Jenei died when she was thirteen. I'm Arjen now."

Dee glanced up, the peeking of a wounded thing from cover. "Thirteen…"

Jen punched up her pillow with unnecessary savagery. "Let's talk about something else. Are you dead?"

With a shrug, Dee said, "Does it matter?"

"Of course it does! I can buy you free." Jen hesitated. "If you're still alive."

Dee finally looked up. "There are worse things. Hate. Anger. The waste of all you've been given."

"What are you talking about?"

"You're blind. Your heart is filled with old shadows, and you won't step out into the light."

Jen fell silent. The words were the kind a spirit might speak. A spirit, but not her sister. Her heart crumpled.

"I *love* you, Jenei. Ma loves you. Col does too."

"Ma's dead," Jen said heavily. "Da went a little too far one time and killed her. And I haven't been much use to Col, either. What about you?"

"I went free."

"Well, that's what I'm trying to do, too. When I open a gateway to the Otherworlds—"

"Remember what you used to tell us about lying, Jenei? You used to say lying lets bad things in. What about when you lie to yourself?"

"I—don't—lie to myself!" Jen said through her teeth.

"Do you wear the necklace?" Dee asked suddenly.

Jen blinked at the sudden change of subject. "Which necklace?" She thought of the little ivory face with its closed eyes, that had opened to guard her when she slept, then remembered she'd taken to wearing that necklace after Dee had gone. Her hand strayed toward the knife on its chain, set aside for the night on the upended crate that served as a nightstand.

"It's the key, you know," Dee said.

Jen picked up the knife. "This one, or—"

Dee was gone. Jen reached out, touched the depression in the mattress where her sister had sat. Neither spirit nor dream could leave such an impression. But there it was. Atop the second-hand blanket, she felt the warmth of a living body, gradually cooling beneath her touch.

She flattened her palms on the place where her sister had sat, eight years younger than she should have been. Wizard's senses met no residue of magic, no lingering human aura. Nothing but the solitude of night and the wards she'd raised to ensure the privacy of her bedroom.

お

"Burn," Jen called again. Her voice echoed from walls and tenement fronts, a little hoarse. She bit her lip, wishing, *If only he'd come.* How long had it been since she'd seen him? A week? Two? Not since a pouchful of Verin's gold had bought Lord Annoro's strange and sudden misfortunes. She set down the bowl of scraps for the dog and drew another breath. "Bur—"

She sensed movement just out of sight, swivelling ears, a twitching, sensitive nose. Reluctance hung in the air like smoke, avoidance of something once known and loved, but now very different. Something dark. Fearsome.

"No, Burn," she whispered. "It's only me. Please come. Please. I miss you."

The dog came to a sudden decision. A moment later, the clicking of claws on cobbles came. She caught a quick, swelling breath. Daring a few steps out the gate, into the street, she crouched down and waited.

A yellow head and shoulders appeared around the corner, then a body with a fuzz of new-grown coat. The dog's ears perked at her, then he looked back over his shoulder. Jen cast out her senses again, wondering who or what he saw, but felt nothing.

But someone stepped around the corner.

Jen scrambled to her feet and fell back a step, seeing with mortal eyes what wizard's perception said wasn't there: a girl with a pale face and patched skirt, one she'd seen days ago and had thought never to see again.

Dee dropped her hand on Burn's head. Wagging his tail, the dog smiled up at her.

"Come on, Jenei," she called. Between the walls, her voice drifted light as a forgotten scent. "Come see the kittens I found. Come to the square and see the acrobats there. Aren't you lonely? Aren't you tired of walls and whispers and weaving hate and harm on the winds?"

Jen fell back another step. Her foot struck the bowl, sent it spinning. "No…"

Dee's hand caressed Burn. "Once you healed, instead. His burns are all better. Don't you want to come see?"

"I can't," she whispered.

Patting the dog's side, Dee sighed. "Oh, well." She turned. Burn turned as well, following.

"Wait!" Jen ran a few steps along the street. The sense of the stone faded, and with it, she knew, its protection. She stopped. "Come back!"

"Come away," Dee replied and stepped around the corner.

"Dee! Burn!"

In the gloom of the street, in the shadow of caked and spalling walls, Jen hesitated, straining ears and senses. The stone waited behind her, a shadow so wide and dark she could lose herself in it. Burn trotted ever farther away, a dwindling flicker of light. She found herself running, feet slipping on the rounded, slimy heads of the cobbles.

"Wait!" she called again.

Wait, the echoes mocked her, but she didn't heed them. She'd nearly reached the corner.

"Burn, come back—"

She ran headlong into someone coming around the corner, someone tall, whose strong hands gripped her arms.

"Jen!"

She reeled, tried to pull away. The hands gripped her harder.

"You all right? What's happened? Jen!"

She looked up into Col's alarmed face. "Did you see them?"

"Who?" He turned her. "What're you doing out here? C'mon. You gonna get caught."

"Burn," she said, panting. "And Dee. They—"

"*Dee?*" Col stopped, looked back. "Our sister Dee?"

"Yes, I was talking to her—"

"The dog ran right past me." He cast her a troubled glance. "Wasn't nobody with 'im."

Jen tensed. "She couldn't have just—" *Disappeared.*

She closed her mouth, wet her lips. The open gate loomed before her, a portal that would sever her from Burn. She set her feet. Then something seemed to reach out, soothing the painful loneliness and yearning.

The stone's presence enfolded her once more, pervasive as cold, seeping water. She stepped through the gate, away from her brother.

"Why are you here?" It really didn't matter; it was only something to say. "Weren't you going to market?"

Col drew a breath then let it go, unused. "Yeah," he said slowly. "But I heard something while I was there."

"What?"

He glanced toward the shadows where the stone lay. "Let's go inside."

She shrugged and led the way.

Col stalked behind her. Closing the drawing room door behind them, he said in a rush, "They say Lord Annoro's got the wonky rot."

Jen clapped her hands once and laughed. Already! She'd dipped her fingers in the stone's still, black pool, had dropped sickness there that would travel the City's waters to find its mark. Subtle, silent magic that would never give her away.

"It ain't funny!" Col said, shocked. "They say his favorite mopsy's scared she's got it now, and his wife, too."

Jen's grin went slack. "No…"

"They say ain't nobody'll go to his house no more," Col said. "Not the milkman, not the slopsman, not nobody but monks and wizards."

She turned a glance on the dark fireplace. Fire sprang into being there, in the absence of fuel. The silver flames provided a screen for what she wished to see: Lord Annoro's manor amid the nobleman's houses that clustered near the Prince's palace. She flicked past scenes of servants shoving one another, a cook raging over a haunch of meat boiling with maggots, a woman, straight and still, her lovely, impassive face streaked with tears and turned away from a locked door. And Lord Annoro himself, thin and haggard, shouting and pleading outside that door.

"Where are they?" she muttered, Seeing faster and faster, into room after room. She wove a finding into the Seeing, careless of the power she'd already expended. "Where *are* they?"

Scenes flashed through the pale flames so quickly she could no longer recognize all she Saw. At last an image caught and held: the flowers, bent and bedraggled, half-buried in a trash heap.

The flames collapsed like silver tissue, crumpling as silently as they had burned. Her stomach rolled over and she cursed.

"Whassamatter?" Col demanded.

Still facing the dark fireplace, Jen closed her eyes. "Someone threw them out. Those flowers. The ones I put the protective spell on."

"You gotta do another spell, then," he said, unexpectedly stern.

"Yes," Jen said, then, "No. No." She straightened, flung away from the fireplace. "This wasn't supposed to happen!" she railed. "Why did they throw them out?"

The lord's house was too far for her cast a spell of protection directly. What, then? Mind-magic had a much longer reach. A Call? A compulsion for everyone to flee the house? Yes, and when an entire noble household responded blindly to a spell? Not a thing to go unnoticed. Nor something to be dismissed.

"Wait," she told Col. "There might be something else I can do."

She brushed past him and hurried out.

The stone was silent when she reached it. She took a breath, then another, struggling for calm. "Show me how to remove the curse we placed on Lord Annoro. It's too...undiscriminating."

Are wizardly curses so easily removed? the stone asked.

"Of course," Jen said. "That is, a curse is no more difficult to remove than to place."

The magic I have shown you rolls forward like the ocean, like ripples spreading across the surface of a pool, small happenings building ever larger to shape what you have willed. Can you turn such momentum aside?

Cold settled in her belly. "You're telling me it can't be removed?"

Can the pain the man inflicted be eased? Can his cruelty be erased?

"No, but—" She rubbed her forehead. "Others are suffering. I never wanted that."

She left the stone as hastily as she'd left her brother. Fleeing to the kitchen, she braced her hands and stared down at the scarred and battered kitchen table, willing her fluttering thoughts to settle.

Col came in, filling the kitchen door as if barring it. "What you gonna do?"

"I'm thinking!" she flared. She cast an eye over the worn hearthstones, the smoky, flickering fire, the soot streaking into the shadows above, as if to find an answer there.

Only one answer came. "I have to go there," she muttered.

"No."

She'd forgotten her brother. She turned, surprised. "What?"

"I'll go."

"No, Col—"

"I said I'll do it. You'll just get caught. I'll get the flowers. I'll put 'em back. Will that fix things?"

"You can't—"

"Yeah, I can. But take the curse *off*, Jen. This ain't worth it. I don't care how much gold that merchant's paying you."

She opened her mouth for a retort, then hesitated, seeing her brother afresh. Was he taller than he had been? Certainly he'd filled out, put on muscle. No longer was this the timid, starveling boy she'd taken from the slums. This was—

This was a man.

Col frowned. "What's wrong?"

Jen found herself backed into the table. "Nothing," she said. Knowing the lie, appalled she'd spoken it.

He took a step toward her. "Tell me what to do."

She struggled to slow her breathing. "Yes. All right." She steadied herself. "The spell is like a shield. But since I bound it to the flowers, they must have contact with the thing they're supposed to protect. Even if they only touch the outside of the house. If you could just, say, put them against the foundation stones. Or stick them in a drain-pipe."

He nodded once, grim. "And then you'll do what I said? 'Cuz I ain't doing nothing like this again."

She swallowed, then nodded. "I'll do my best."

Chapter 16

A drizzling rain had slunk in, deepening the chill of the stone house. Shivering, Jen drew her coat close and pinched the bridge of her nose. A dull headache clamped her skull and queasiness slithered through her gut. Whether it was the magic she'd been working to counteract the curse or the realization that nothing she did seemed to work, she couldn't say.

At least the flowers' protection had been returned to the house. Col had seen to that three days ago. Slum-rat that he was, he'd found the trash heap with a scavenger's unerring instinct, retrieved the flowers and tucked them in a hidden spot behind a hedge against the house's foundation stones. But the damage done for however long they'd been gone—

Was done.

Jen rubbed her arms and made her way to the drawing room, the echo of her footsteps following like the tappings of a restless spirit.

Firelight spangled the darkened, rain-spattered windows with rubies and garnets, deepening the gold of the lamp she lit. She stood halfway between bright fire and darkened windows, smelling the scent of rain-wet stone and gardens, listening to the fire's silky murmur in the quiet of the house. None of it calmed her, or eased the black mood that gripped her.

She let her senses range down the hallway, outside into the dripping garden. There the stone rested like a great spider in the center of its web. Jen suffered the infiltration of its strands into her house, though in some places, like her bedroom, her study, she forbade it. Otherwise, the stone remained unobtrusive, never entering her thoughts unless she went outside to speak with it; never indicating its knowledge of her doings unless asked.

She felt movement. Through the entry hall, along the corridor, Col was coming her way. Agitated. Jen concentrated on him. He was speaking—arguing? Pleading? With whom? She called the seeming of Arjen. Her mortal ears heard footsteps now, two sets. Two sets, when she could only sense one mind, her brother's.

She turned toward the door. It opened, and the satin gloss and carving of the wood receded to reveal Col's face poised halfway between uncertainty and outrage.

"Master," he only had time to say before the door was pushed open, out of his hands.

A man's voice said, "No need to stand on formalities, boy. I'll introduce myself."

A man pushed past him. The wizard Palimur.

Cold shot through her. She called power to transfer herself elsewhere, anywhere…

But she had nowhere to go. Nowhere at all.

Palimur's eyes flared wide, then narrowed. He smiled that smug, square smile, just as she remembered it, and gave an overly elaborate bow. "Lord Arjen. So pleased to meet you." His voice dripped with mockery.

Jen stood frozen. Her thoughts jumped. Of course he could see through her seeming, see the thin, curly-haired young woman beneath. She wouldn't deceive herself about that.

He strutted into the room, resplendent as a phoenix in a crimson doublet slashed with claret. A gold necklace set with rubies and dragon's-blood amber flashed.

Col scrambled in behind the wizard, but only hovered.

She said to her brother, "It's all right." It absolutely, positively was not all right, but Col could do nothing to improve the situation.

Still smiling, Palimur looked from Jen to Col. "Kin?" he asked. "Brother, or cousin?" His gaze settled on Col, who swallowed visibly.

"He's my brother," Jen said sharply.

Palimur turned to her again. "Indeed. You're a kind sister to put your poor relations to honest work."

Col started at the word 'sister.'

The insult was a clear warning. Nevertheless, the threats weren't open yet, and she'd keep control of this situation as long as she could. "Excuse me." She stepped past the wizard to speak with her brother.

"Jen, what—" Col began in a strangled whisper.

She put a hand on his arm to quiet him. "Take the money from Verin," she whispered, "and get out of here."

"But—"

"Do like I say. Don't argue with me now."

For a moment, she was afraid he'd refuse. But the streets made one ever practical. He took a step back, then turned and ran.

Palimur took the door from her hand and shut it, then stood gazing at her with folded arms, an appraising look in his eye. Her heartbeat shook her.

"Excellent seeming," Palimur said at last, nodding. "If I hadn't wondered why a wizard felt the need to cloak himself in a seeming, I would never have made the effort to look through it. And the house! Why, it fairly broods with awareness. You've managed to make a true wizard's domain in an astonishingly short time."

It was the stone's awareness insinuated throughout the house and grounds that he'd sensed, not hers. If only she *had* worked to make it a true wizard's house, the house itself would work her will.

Breath came short. Spells whispered through her mind. *Not yet*, she told herself. *Wait.*

"I have tea," she said. "Here's an extra cup…"

She touched heat through the plain teapot and poured, using both hands to keep from spilling. Turning to offer him the cup, she found him *there*, behind her. Jen stumbled backward, bumped the table, sending the tea things rattling.

Palimur reached to steady her, but she stepped away.

"I've had a sorcerer come visit me here," she said, "but you're the first wizard."

Palimur's brows went up. "Indeed?" He took a polite sip of tea. "Barras hasn't come to see how his old apprentice is settling in?"

Jen shrugged, cautious as ever of lies.

"I'm surprised, especially since you seem to have gained your freedom so soon after you and I last spoke. It must have been very sudden."

He knows, Jen thought, but said, "Yes. It was."

"As sudden as the disappearance of the Malmidion from my library," he said with a small, knowing smile. "I must have misjudged Barras. I'd never have expected him to let go so easily. I certainly wouldn't have."

"It was time," she said.

"I agree," the wizard said. "Though it must be irksome to go disguised as a man."

She sensed the threat coming, hot breath on her neck in the darkness. Nevertheless, she spread her arms. "What disguise? I am Arjen."

"And yet I look and see the woman Jen, hiding behind the seeming of a man."

"Jen was a boy. He's all grown up. There's only me now."

Palimur's smile thinned. "Don't trifle with me, lady. You know who you are quite as well as I do. You're Barras' apprentice girl, gone rogue."

"I'm a wizard, plying my trade as I see fit," she retorted.

His grin told her she'd said the wrong thing. "Even accepting a commission involving an astonishingly slippery curse on Lord Annoro?"

Through sheer force of will, Jen kept her face calm. She turned and paced toward the windows. "I've heard his luck's turned bad," she said. "But what does that have to do with me?"

"I couldn't be sure for some time, of course," he admitted. "Though I was asked to find the spells responsible and neutralize them. And their caster."

He'd called her a rogue. Like the rogue sorcerers of Marin's bogey-tales, stripped of their powers, left mad and helpless by greater wizards. She reached the window, set down the cup and braced her hands on the stone sill. The raindrops jeweling the small panes glowed pale with moonlight.

"However," he went on behind her, "I could find nothing more than an unseemly amount of bad luck. Rather embarrassing, I must say. Then, from an anonymous source, a gift of a flower arrangement arrived, one that served as a vehicle for spells of protection—a spell placed by an unfamiliar hand. I had the servants remove the arrangement from the house on the off chance that I may have missed something. But the flowers and their attendant spell assumed rather more significance when someone stole onto the grounds to replace them by the house."

She felt walls closing around her. Jen fumbled at the casement latch, opened the window.

"My master said your life at the palace made you suspicious." Cool air slipped inside, chill on her face. She turned and found the wizard had closed the distance between them again. "Seems he was right," she continued. "You're worried about a spell of protection?"

Palimur laughed. "You're very good, do you know that? What a delight. No, my dear, but you must allow me to finish my story. For you see, I sensed the same hand when I visited the Prince's library just yesterday. A spell with precisely the same aroma I'd inhaled from Lord Annoro's flower arrangement. But this time on the person of a lowly copyist in the library."

She'd bound the copyist so he couldn't say who wanted the maps. She hadn't taken the same precaution for the inoffensive ward she'd placed on his spectacles.

Jen assumed an expression of polite interest and leaned back on the windowsill. "And?"

"The poor fellow was quite terrified when I questioned him. That in itself seemed odd. But I was more interested in who had woven the ward he wore. He told me it was a wizard named Arjen. And then, who should I find at Arjen's house but Jen, Barras' young apprentice?"

Jen snorted. "So you're calling me rogue because I placed a spell of protection on Lord Annoro's house, and a ward on a copyist in the Prince's library?"

Palimur came and leaned against the window frame opposite. "What need has a copyist for wards?" he said. "And it is I who have always served Lord Annoro."

"Maybe your spells weren't giving satisfaction."

Reaching out, he ran a fingertip from her temple to jaw. "Jen, my dear. Bravado can take you only so far."

She struck his hand away. "Did you come here to insult me with your presumptuousness and insinuations? This is my house, and I'm tired of you. You'll leave. Now."

He folded his arms. "You're being rash. I think you'd much rather keep me here, talking to you. You are, after all, in an extremely awkward position."

He stood too close, but Jen stayed put. "And what position is that?"

"You're a runaway. I needn't ask Barras to know that."

"Are you threatening to go tattling to him that you've found me?" She snorted again and paced a step away. "I'm afraid the threat doesn't have much leverage with me, since I presume the alternative is to submit to you."

"I assure you, I don't require your submission."

"Try," she challenged softly, for if he did attempt to bind or compel her, he'd have to tamper with the bindings her master had placed. She felt a queer, queasy shock to realize that she was willing to accept any benefit from her master's binding.

He laughed.

"I guess you'll tell me what's so amusing," she said.

"This, my dear, is where Barras' scorned politics comes in. You see, he's currently in no good odor with the Prince, having refused the Prince's repeated overtures. Now, Barras somehow manages to lose his apprentice, who can be connected, however tenuously, to some rather unsavory affairs involving one of the Prince's ministers. Perhaps Barras is simply an inept master. Or perhaps it's more sinister. Perhaps that apprentice is Barras' cat's-paw, doing his will unwittingly—or not."

Her mind churned. "What do Barras' bad relations with the Prince have to do with me?" With her master's downfall would come freedom. Yet with that realization came, not glee, but something that felt strangely like dismay.

"Very little," he answered. "But as Barras is dealt with, someone will have to deal with his wayward apprentice."

Cold slapped her, shot tingling through every limb. She dropped the seeming of Arjen, hurled a fending at Palimur, then plunged into a spell of transference.

The fending collided with a greater fending in a silent clash that rocked her. The transference was simply whisked away like some forbidden trinket from a child's fingers.

Jen spewed forth a magma of wizard's fire. But mere sparks crawled across her hands, then spluttered, quenched as effectively as she would grind an ember beneath her heel.

Palimur no longer smiled, and his eyes flashed with the uncanny lights of his wizardry.

"Don't," he said. "You surprised me once. Did you really think you'd succeed a second time?"

His power swaddled her. She floundered after the magic the stone had been teaching her, something fast, something strong—

No, a low, whispering voice said in her mind. *Bring him to me.*

Jen froze. *Is it the stone?* she wondered, disoriented by the sudden intrusion.

Yes, the stone replied. And again, *Bring him to me.*

How? she thought back, but it made no reply.

She swallowed. The sharp tang of metal lay on the back of her tongue. Palimur's power smothered her. Her lungs seemed to snatch at nothing. It was hard, hard, but she settled her weight back, took a shaking breath.

"All right," she said, and her voice shook, too. "All right. Tell me—" What he wanted? No. She didn't want to hear that. She wet her lips and tried again. "Let's talk. Outside. I can't breathe in here."

He studied her a long moment. She would not think of the stone. At last, Palimur relaxed, assumed a gentle expression, stepped near and took her hand. Jen did not restrain the impulse to snatch it away, but he held fast.

"Why not." Circling her waist with an arm, he said, "Be easy, lady." Mockery tainted his voice. "The storm has cleared, the moon and stars shine, and I would delight to linger in the garden with you."

Jen shuddered. The impulse to turn on him with nails and feet and teeth nearly drowned her. She gasped once, scarcely feeling her feet on the floor for the horror of his body pressed close to hers, the imprisonment of his arm. The drawing room door tilted at a dizzy angle, then yawned open. The hallway passed in blinks of light and shadow. Suddenly they were in the entry hall. She wasn't sure if he had transferred them; she couldn't remember walking there. The door opened onto night.

Cool, rain-scented air touched her face and she returned to herself, inhabiting her own body once more. Palimur was a source of heat at her side. She clenched her jaw to keep from screaming. The world spun in her vision, a reeling of leering moon and mocking stars bordered by a ragged edge of cloud.

The wizard said, "This is a pleasant spot, don't you think?"

Grass swept her feet. Shadow swallowed the moon, leaving them in darkness. Bark and foliage were sketched in black and grey. Just there, in the deepest shadow, waited the stone.

Palimur's hands gripped her. His breath touched her face, lips brushed her neck and he thrust her backwards and down.

Her back struck something hard and cold. She exploded, striking with fists and elbows and knees. His grip tightened and he pinioned her arms. Cold of stone behind her, heat of a man before her. Her mind went blank, black—

Be still, a voice whispered in her mind, sinuous as dark water through blind earth. *Be still.*

She ceased struggling and panted. The stone's presence wound around her like a clinging fog. The world reformed around her in moonlight and shadow. Palimur loomed over her, his hot weight pinning her to the stone's bulk behind. She turned her face away, shrank back against the stone's cold, rough surface.

"Are you through?" he asked.

Clamping her jaw, Jen nodded. His excitement rippled over her like fetid swamp water.

The wizard's hands wandered over the woman's body beneath the man's clothes she wore. Her stomach heaved. She jerked to lunge away, but he trapped her, hands between her and the stone.

"Enough foolishness," he snapped.

Her voice wouldn't come. At last, it did. "Take your hands off, or I'll take 'em off for you."

"You still have that street fire," he said with renewed humor. "Perhaps there's something to be said for an upbringing in the slums. Did Barras also find that attractive?"

Stone! she cried silently.

Palimur eased his weight upon her. "Now. Let's discuss the terms of our association." His hands moved down her back, between her and the stone, half embrace, half imprisonment. "I see you already understand the situation. I'll leave you to decide how it progresses. What do you say?"

She stood rigid in his arms. "I'll kill you first."

He chuckled softly. "Oh, come now. Such drama. And in any case, you don't have the wherewithal—"

He broke off and stiffened.

"Stop it," he said with perfect calm. Once more, his power enwrapped her. "I said, *stop it.*" This time strain colored his voice, a tinge of what might be alarm.

The stone's patient malice oozed forth. Its presence seethed with power she'd felt only once before, when it had crushed her to the coping of the well in which it had been imprisoned.

Palimur first jerked one hand, then the other, but something held them fast. "What have you done?" he demanded, struggling in earnest now.

In silence, the stone poured forth alien power, power as surreptitious as deadly gas at the bottom of a mine, as irresistible as the grinding of stone on stone. She remembered how, there in the cell beneath the monks' temple, it had drained her own, leaving her dark as a snuffed lantern.

And she understood.

She tried to slither from between wizard and stone. Palimur's magic seized her, locked her in place, so strong she struggled to breathe.

"Release me," he demanded, crushing her with some spell of force.

Black spots jiggled across her view of the night, flaring to red as he tightened his hold. Pressure squeezed the air from her lungs. Her ears rang and throbbed; her teeth and eyeballs ached. Vision diminished to a small, round window surrounded by glittering darkness, and she lost all sense of hands and feet, then legs and arms. Darkness, no longer glittering, but velvety, swallowed what remained of her sight, leaving only a feeling of suffocation, of coldness, of terrible helplessness.

At once, her senses exploded into being again. Jen heaved a whooping gasp of moist night air and shoved at Palimur. He thrashed, and his heavy body slammed her back against the stone. With another gasp, this time of pain, she writhed free, found herself sprawled on the ground at his feet.

Palimur shrieked. He seemed to embrace the stone. His body pressed to it, his arms encircled it—

Her stomach did a slow, sickening twist. No, he wasn't embracing it. The stone had engulfed—*consumed*—the wizard's arms. As she watched, stunned, Palimur's knee, braced against the stone, sank beneath the surface as if into a lump of black clay. He screamed again, and his voice cracked.

"Let me go," he shouted. "Make it let me go!"

Jen stumbled to her feet, took an uncertain step toward him.

Be still, the stone commanded.

"Stone," she pleaded, hovering, unable to move forward, unable to flee. Palimur's legs disappeared to the hips. "Don't—"

"Make it stop!" the wizard begged. Spittle hung in strings from his chin, flecked the black surface near his face. "*Make it stop!*"

He gave another agonized scream. Jen clapped her hands to her head, ground her palms against her ears. But the scream went on and on, a nightmare of mindless terror. She wanted to scream as well, wanted to beg the wizard to stop, wished him to die so he would. Squeezing her eyes shut, she spun, turning her back on horror.

Turn! the stone commanded. *Watch!*

She turned as if dragged by unseen hands. Her eyes opened as if pried by irresistible fingers. The stone had consumed all but the wizard's chest and head. His cheek was pressed like a lover's to its face, his mouth and eyes stretched wide. Wizard's fire crawled luminous across the stone's surface. The stone remained oblivious. Palimur's face subsided into the black surface: ear and cheek. An eye. Stone crept into his mouth. The wizard's screams shredded into blind, splintering terror—

And stopped.

A serpentine sparkling of gold slid down the face of the stone. Falling with a liquid clash into the grass, it lay glinting in moonlight: Palimur's necklace.

The stone whispered into Jen's mind, as cold as ever, *It is done.*

Chapter 17

Jen stumbled backward. Her vision narrowed, the world pitched and heaved. Her knees gave way and she flung out an arm to catch herself.

The world settled once more. Damp chill seeped through her clothes. Breathing hard, she blinked a shivering greyness from her vision, put her hand out to lever herself up. And realized what she leaned on.

She thrust away, shuddering. "What—what did you do to him?"

He threatened you. I stopped him.

"You—you swallowed him."

His power is now mine.

"You didn't tell me! I didn't know you were going to murder him!"

You could not withstand him. Did you not say you wished to kill him?

She nodded, but backed a step.

Do you fear me? the stone asked.

"Fear you?" Jen whispered, shivering. "You—"

Have I not done as you wished? its hollow voice echoed, insistent. *Have I not protected you?*

She whispered, "Yes." The night air ran cold fingers beneath her tunic.

Will you then flee me? Where will you flee?

"Anywhere!"

I will do you no harm, but there are others who have. Others who will do you harm again if you flee. Come, and I will show you.

"Do you think I don't know who's done me harm?" she raged. "Do you think I need you to show me that?"

You do not remember. But I have seen.

Jen hesitated, wishing to know what the stone spoke of but having no wish whatsoever to come near it.

Come, it said again. *I have kept my promises, and I promise to do you no harm.*

Palimur's face, stretched with terror, leapt into her mind. The sound of his pleas and screams—

She stumbled backward. The stone's presence abruptly surrounded her as it had beneath the temple of the monks' god, surrounded her like air, like water, then turned solid, inescapable. Jen stopped, held.

"Let me go," she said, as Palimur had.

No, it replied, implacable. *I will show what you have forgotten.*

Her feet moved toward the stone, step by unwilling step. She struggled to keep her hand by her side, but it slowly rose, slowly. Terror clawed at her. A whimper escaped as she strained muscle against magic, but the stone's will dragged at hers, inexorable as the earth's pull upon her body.

Her hand reached out, lighted upon the stone's dark, rain-damp surface. Her flesh cringed from the contact.

The nightbound garden disappeared.

Another dim scene replaced it, an alley at twilight, dawn stars glimmering in a strip of sky above, the power-sign of the Fey blazing upon the air before her. The scene replayed itself, the sign growing, devouring, then shrinking again when her master severed the link between it and her. All this she remembered.

But where her memories failed, the vision the stone gave continued with merciless clarity. The dim stone room to which her master had transferred them. His shadow looming over her. The grip of his hands upon her. The fire that had erupted from her—

"Don't touch me, filthy bastard!" she screamed.

Jen shoved backward, hurling fire, wrenching out of the memory. Flame splashed the stone, spattered grass and leaves, crisping greenery to black crepe. Blazing, rain-wet foliage spat and sputtered, smoke curled from a blackened branch. She stood shivering.

Fire had saved her once, but could not prevail against her master, just as it hadn't prevailed against Palimur. She did not need to relive the rest of the memory to know what would have come next. To know what her master had done, what all her strength and wizardry couldn't stop.

"No," someone whispered. It was her voice. The breath came from her lungs. Her lips shaped the word. "No. He couldn't have. Not my master."

The darkness that lay at the bottom of her soul, waiting, always present, whispered like the stone, reminding her: Of course he did. Wasn't that the fear you lived with every day for five years? Didn't you strive to escape him for that very fear?

Her master had done it, what had been done once before, long ago, when she was little more than a child. He had done that thing, that terrible thing, to her.

Jen staggered away and vomited.

Heat and chill coursed over her in turns. She spat out sour bitterness, spat again, then finally crawled away from the mess.

She whispered to the stone, "That's what happened?" Her voice sounded like a child's, pleading. "What I couldn't remember after I conjured the Fey woman's sign?"

I saw it in your mind when you touched me, after you left the wizard who holds you bound.

With a shaking hand, she wiped her forehead, her mouth. The stone had told her that it wasn't the spell that had taken her wits, but her master.

"How could he?" Something warm ran down her cheek, leaving behind a cold trail.

She crouched trembling in the wet grass, head bowed to knees, gasping for breath.

"Why do I hurt? What's hurting me?"

Betrayal, the stone whispered.

The pain was like a dull blade carving from throat to belly, disemboweling her. She clapped both hands over her mouth.

Tears slid down her face, fire and ice. "I never trusted him." Her voice broke and another sob escaped. She ground her teeth. "I never trusted him! How could he betray me if I never trusted him?" She hugged herself as if clutching a wound. "Why now? After all these years, I thought—" She closed her mouth. "No. I never thought that," she muttered. "I never thought I might be safe with him."

He robbed you of one memory, the stone whispered.

Jen jerked her head up.

Perhaps he robbed you of more.

The chill of her wet cheeks stalked down her arms, her back, congealed in her gut. The darkness within her rose.

The stone said, *What do you feel for the wrong done you?*

"Rage."

What do you feel for the man who has wronged you?

"Hate," she whispered.

Anger gives strength. Hate gives purpose.

The two had long been like arrowheads lodged in her

flesh, points that pained her with every breath. Those bitter shards worked inward, deeper, to her heart.

You are a wizard, the stone said. *Let none threaten you.*

She straightened, rose to her knees in the wet grass. "Yes," she whispered, speaking to herself now. She had sought the Otherworlds these weeks as the only escape. There was another solution to her imprisonment. One so simple, and yet so unlikely, it had never occurred to her.

Eliminate the one who threatened.

Palimur had come seeking a rogue wizard and found instead an enemy far more formidable. He'd been an example of what was possible, what she had never so much as whispered to herself in the darkest corners of her mind.

She surged to her feet, brushing at the mud and damp and leaves on her clothes. "My master betrayed me," she said.

The stone said, *I can show you how to revenge yourself and be free.*

"Free." A dizzy rush of longing rolled over her. "He'll never touch me again. None of them will. I'll be safe."

Safe, O yes, the stone said. *And powerful. Invulnerable. No need ever to flee.*

She took the few steps to the stone. Where Palimur had stood, holding her helpless with wizardry and man's strength, there remained nothing but a trampled space in the wet grass. Stooping, she sifted the grass with her fingers until she felt cold metal. Gold blazed, gems caught fire. She rose and headed for the house, dangling Palimur's necklace from her hand.

Chapter 18

A sense of someone lurking at the gate plucked at Jen's consciousness, insisting she wake. She cried out and shot upright in bed.

A level shaft of sunlight painted the grey stone a soft rose. Darkness welled within her, trying to drag her down. Jen took a breath, held it, straining to remain in the light of the new morning. The terror of the night receded.

She sent out wizard's senses, probing the damp, narrow, shadowed street for the mind that held her name...

And found Col.

Jen sent the gate swinging open and whispered into her brother's mind, *All's well. Come in.*

She sensed his unease as he peered through the open gate. She sensed him come creeping in along the flagstone path to the tall, forbidding front of the house, knowing disaster had struck and not knowing how to account for the unexpected calm.

She pushed the coverlet aside, rose from bed, quickly pulled on her clothes—Arjen's clothes—and made her way down the narrow, uncarpeted stairs.

Earlier, in the cold night hours, she'd had to face her woman's body when she stripped off her wet, muddy things before the kitchen fire and bathed from a bucket. The alternative would've been not to bathe. But with Palimur's scent clinging to her, the very thought sickened her.

Now she wore a knee-length coat over a long, trim tunic and hose. Once more master of her house.

Jen met her brother in the front hall. Morning sunlight slanted his shadow long across the floor, sent it rearing up against one grey wall.

"Jen," he said, then ran and crushed her in a hug.

She stiffened in an instant of white panic and pushed away. He looked shocked, hurt.

She busied herself with smoothing her clothes and called up a smile. "I'm fine, Col. Don't worry."

Brows crooked with worry, he looked her up and down. "Where's that man at?"

She turned, led the way down the hallway. "Gone."

"Gone where?"

She didn't answer until they reached the drawing room. "Just gone." At the table, she lifted Palimur's necklace and dangled it from a negligent finger. "He won't bother us anymore."

"How—" Col took a step, staring at the necklace. "What happened to him, Jen? How'd you get that?"

Seating herself, she admired the necklace a moment, then lowered it to her lap where it glittered red and gold, like a pile of dragon's scales. "Don't worry about it, Col."

"Don't tell me that," he flared. "You think I'm stupid? I seen how scared you was when that pelf came. And now he's gone and you got his necklace. He's dead, ain't he?"

She shrugged. "I didn't kill him."

Col drew his hand down his face. "Jen. Let's jig off. I got the jingle hid. There's enough to get out of the City— who knows?—maybe go a long way. I won't let nobody get you. But—"

"But what?"

"But you gotta get outta here. You gotta see what that—that *thing*—" He jerked his chin in the direction of the garden. "—is doing to you. There's a man dead and you ain't bothered one bit. Are you?"

"Should I tell you what he would've done if he'd lived?"

Col glanced away. "I know he didn't have nothing good in mind. But have some sense. People may know he come. What'll you do if soldiers show up?"

"They'll discover I'm no one to be meddled with."

"You been hiding like a rat in a hole the last month, remember? When'd you get so brave?"

"When I realized that even the Prince's wizard can't touch me," she shot back. "I'm not hiding anymore, brother. *Or* running."

"*Prince's wizard?*" He shut eyes and mouth. When he opened them again, both look and voice were hard. "So's that mean you'll go to market now?"

She smiled her cold wizard's smile. "Why should I go to market? You don't seem to understand the favor Palimur did me, Col. He showed me that all my weakness was here." She tapped her chest. "He showed me power takes what it wants. I don't have to be afraid of soldiers, Prince, or wizards. They'll learn to tread with respect around me."

Her brother stared at her. "Da used to say twat like that. And Rik. *They* wanted to make sure everybody knew how strong they was, too."

She gasped, struck speechless, then shouted, "I'm nothing like Da! *Nothing!*"

"No?" Col set his feet and clenched his fists. "So tell me. What you gonna do if somebody don't want to do what you say? When people start whispering about the bad wizard in Red Quay, the one everybody's scared of, the one what stomps over anybody what gets in his way."

She glared at him.

"What you gonna do when your master comes? 'Cuz you know he will."

She broke from his gaze and toyed with the necklace again.

His disappointment and grief rolled over her. "Yeah," he sighed. "That's what I thought." He crossed the room and knelt beside her chair. "Jen, please, you gotta listen. If you do all that, you ain't gonna find what you're looking for at the end of it. Whatever you find, it ain't gonna be nothing right."

Her fingers clenched in the links of gold. "But it'll be better than what I've lived with half my life."

His lips pressed together and he shook his head hard. She almost reached out to take his hand and promise him that it wasn't as bad as he thought, that she wouldn't do anything terrible. She couldn't. To say it would make it so, and then she'd have to become weak again. Weak, and afraid.

He pushed to his feet. "If I'd'a knowed you'd end up plotting to twitch a man, I never woulda done a thing for you."

Col strode across the room, banged the door behind him. Jen didn't move to follow as the last echo of his departing footsteps fell into silence.

お

Jen sat and stared unseeing at the walls, a book open on her knee. Silence, unbroken in the last hours by voice or footstep, spread around her. She never knew emptiness could so painfully fill a soul, yet leave it so hungry and echoing.

"Jenei," a voice said behind her. "Where's Col?"

She whirled in the chair, but saw nothing but the play of dust motes in sunlight. "Dee?"

"Did he see what Burn sees? Did he leave you?"

She tossed out an unveiling spell that revealed nothing. "Let me see you, Dee. Did you make them leave?"

"You drove them away." Dee's voice came from everywhere and nowhere, inescapable.

"How? By taking control of my life? By putting an end to my fear?"

"Fear will put an end to *you*."

Jen turned back to her book. "Go away, Dee. I don't need you yammering nonsense at me."

"Love, Jenei. Trust. Are they nonsense? Can you live on hate and pain?"

"Don't," Jen snarled. "*Don't* you talk to me about that. You're dead. What do you know about pain?"

"I'm not dead, Jenei. You haven't killed me yet." A hand touched Jen's face. "And what I know is that love will save you."

Jen started, flinching away from empty air.

The touch came again, on her hair, her arm, gentle as her sister's voice. "Trust will hold you back from the last step into darkness."

"Shut up!" Jen bolted to her feet, slapping at the air as if pursued by hornets.

This time, silence answered her, the same eddying emptiness that had oppressed her before. Her book lay face down at her feet, precious pages crumpled against the floor. She swept it up, dropped it on the table and fled the room.

She stormed outside and paced inside the wall enclosing the garden, reaching outward with wizard's senses.

Beyond the protective spells that imbued the walls, life pulsed all around her. The few joys, the many sorrows; lust, envy, anger, fear. But she did not sense her name in another mind, nor did she sense any mind searching for hers. The binding her master had placed upon her did not stir.

Her hands clenched and unclenched. "This has to end."

Yes, the stone said. *You must call the one who binds you.*

She paced a step up, one back. "Palimur came upon me without my sensing him. What if my master does the same? What if he comes while I'm asleep——"

Stone walls and a man's hard, grasping hands stirred in the depths of her memory. She fought those memories back into the recesses of her mind, away from *now*, down into the stinking well that was *then*. She gasped a breath, then another, until the sensation of choking diminished.

Do you fear the wizard? the stone asked.

"Yes!" She had always feared him, from the moment she'd realized how completely and irresistibly he held her. Now that she knew what he'd done to her, she feared him more.

He will not touch you again while I am by, the stone said.

"How could he have done it?" She gritted her teeth, feeling anew the pain of that knowledge.

You will be free, the stone whispered. *Secure. None will dare your power.*

"None had better! Not my master, not the Prince. Not any of them!"

The ruler will honor you for conquering the wizard who thwarts him. But you will give the ruler what you choose. You will show your strength by this, that you are a powerful wizard, and he will approach you with care and respect.

Jen crossed to the stone. "Care and respect," she repeated. "What if instead he decides I'm too great a threat to abide? What if he sends wizards to deal with me?"

The ruler, the stone said with its usual passionless chill, *will then learn his error.*

Relief shot though her. The stone, dark, impervious, invulnerable, crouched before her. She hungered for that sort of invulnerability.

"No one will be able to hurt me," she whispered.

Palimur, screaming, intruded upon her consciousness. In her mind's eye, his face became her master's. Something under her breastbone shrank at the idea. She crushed that quiver.

For a month and more, she'd used the stone's magic for her purposes. She'd placed spells on objects—Lord Annoro's flowers, the young copyist's spectacles—spells that could be traced to the objects, but to her only if one knew her magic. Always avoiding the greater spells, avoiding touching the elements of the outside world. She need no longer avoid anything.

Closing her eyes, Jen opened her soul to the fire that burned within her. It rushed up, eager, too long banked, tingled along her nerves, finally spilling forth in a joy as fierce and free as flying. Jen spiraled up, carried on a flame that seared away darkness, that scorched away fear, tossing wizardry like bright baubles out into the world for all to see.

"If this doesn't bring my master," she said, "nothing will."

Chapter 19

It was hard, hard to wait. Jen felt like a sheet handled by the washerwoman: rasped across the washboard, twisted in the mangle. But it was done. Her master must know now where to find her. Nothing could change that.

Late sunlight spilled like blood across the floor. Jen's shadow stretched long before her. Silence spread around her.

The stone, which generally spoke to her only when she went down to the garden to speak with it, whispered into her mind:

He comes.

She snatched a breath. The blood shot cold through her veins. "My master?"

The wizard who holds you bound, the stone replied.

"Why?" She clenched a fist. "Why did he have to bind me?"

Yes, the stone said. *Anger is strength. Remember the wrong done you.*

"He never should have—have—done that."

He shall not again, the stone promised, its hollow voice whispering through the shadowed corridors of her mind. *Come, let us end this.*

Jen came, hurrying, not least because she had no wish to meet her master far from the stone. Even now, she feared sleep, lest nightmares come of that long walk with Palimur from drawing room to garden, the wizard's arm imprisoning her.

The stairs, dimly lit by the narrow window at their head and squeaking as always beneath her weight, took her down to the second story. She hastened along the short length of the hallway. The stairs leading to the ground floor yawned to her right, treads of polished oak and balusters carved in fancy swirls. At the landing, she paused.

Only a small square of the entry hall was visible from where she stood. But her wizard's ears heard the faint whisper of clothing, the rhythm of breath. Even fainter, a smoky, herbal scent, one she knew well.

Finding her hand locked on the banister as if to keep her from going further, she clenched her jaw. No more waiting. She straightened, tugged the sleeves of her coat, smoothed her tunic and descended the stairs.

Her master stood in the entry hall, gazing up the stairs as if awaiting her. Looking down on him from above, he looked smaller than she remembered—what, was it only a little over a month ago? Her heart gave a queer, painful squeeze, as if it had taken a dagger yet continued to beat. She found herself standing still, six steps up from the floor.

She bowed slightly, mockingly. "Lord Barras," she said in Arjen's husky tenor. "Welcome to my home. I didn't realize I'd left the front door open."

His storm-colored eyes met her own, true eyes, a handspan below Arjen's.

"Jen," he said, ignoring the rebuke. "I've been looking for you."

She took the remaining steps with the hint of a slow swagger, stopped before him. "Indeed." Her fingers prickled with fire barely restrained. She spread her arms, a reckless thing to do while power pulsed so close beneath her skin. "I've been right here."

He looked up at the ceiling, around at the walls. "This place has a taint of ill. You don't belong here."

She smiled her cold wizard's smile. "What, should I return with you?"

"Yes," he said, inclining his head in agreement. "That would be best."

"Are you *asking* me now?" Hands behind her back, she paced a slow arc in front of him.

He hesitated. At last, he said, "I'd rather you came of your own will, yes."

Jen made a thoughtful noise. "Interesting. You might've given me that choice five years ago."

"Were you capable of making a choice then? What did you know but squalor and cruelty? Could you even have believed in kindness?"

"Kindness," she spat. "O yes. The kindness, the *care* a man shows any valuable purchase. You bound me, lord. Did you think because I was slum-born, I have no pride? Because I was a woman, I have no wishes of my own?"

"You *are* a woman, Jen," he said quietly.

She stiffened. "I am Arjen! A wizard, with powers *you* never taught me."

"You are Arajenei, a wizard, with your own powers, yes. And a woman."

"D'you think I don't know what that means?" Her voice shook. "Think I'd never find out?"

"It means..." He let go a breath. "It means a great deal, I know."

She was trembling all over now, fists clenched. "It means," she said, "that you never would have set me free. I'm too *valuable* to be free."

His dark brows twitched together. "Where did you get an idea like that?"

"Palimur told me," she said, spitting the words like a curse.

His frown deepened. Jen felt a flash of emotion escape his control: anger.

"Palimur," he repeated. "Palimur is a schemer. I thought you'd realized that. You should know better than to believe all he says."

She so wanted to correct Barras, to suggest the past tense when speaking of Palimur. Instead, she said, "Are you saying Palimur lied? That wizard-women aren't rarities, not some precious gem to be coveted and locked away?"

Again, that flash of anger came from him, brief and bright as a lightning strike. "I'll tell you that Palimur colored the truth with his own inclinations. But not all men are like him. Not all are what you learned of them in the slums."

The memory the stone had recently returned to her reared up: the dark, and her master's hands upon her. She thrust away the image. He'd been willing to do that when she was weak and confused, vulnerable. Palimur had found her here and also thought her vulnerable.

She resisted the impulse to reach out her awareness to the stone, to reassure herself of the security it offered. It had been quiet since her master's arrival. Perhaps the stone knew or sensed, should it speak, that the binding between master and apprentice might allow him to hear.

She stepped past him to the door, opened it, and invited him outside with a bow and a gesture.

"You know nothing of what I've learned," she said at last.

His gaze flicked to the open door. "Jen—"

She exited ahead of him, confident he would follow to prevent another escape. Within its stone walls, the garden was a well filled with blue twilight while the sky yet glowed above. The pool at the garden's center mirrored the brass and copper of the sky, the hunched black limbs of the live oak beside it—and the stone. Clasping her hands behind her with false calm, she descended the front steps, her master following.

She kept her attention on the flagstones beneath her feet, on each crack and irregularity so that her master would not sense the boil of her emotions. Golden moss, crisping beneath her steps, carpeted the joints between paving stones. Her master's longer stride brought him near, then he slowed his steps to match hers. Once more, she smelled the scents of smoke and herbs. He did not try to touch her, as Palimur had. Nevertheless, it took all her will to avoid shrinking away.

"Jen, you can't stay here."

"Is that for you to say?" she said. "Do you think because you've found me, you can resume control?"

"You're my apprentice."

"I *was* your apprentice. But no longer. Believe me, lord, you didn't find me because of my own carelessness."

He sighed. "Don't make this more difficult."

"What?" She opened her eyes wide in feigned surprise. "You'll still try to reason with me? You're more powerful than I. Why not just force me?"

His hand came up to pinch the bridge of his nose. "I used my power over you as little as possible."

"As little as possible," she mocked. "And what of my memories? How infrequently did you find it necessary to tamper with them?"

He stopped. "What are you talking about?"

"Please, lord," she said with excruciating politeness, the sort of manners she had never learned in the slums.

"Must I be indelicate?" She stepped off the path and onto the grass, gold-green with the end of summer. She waded through it, broken stems pricking through her hose, and finally entered the gloom in which the stone lay. "There are certain things I forgot, which I have since had the—well, 'good fortune' doesn't seem quite the term. At any rate, I've remembered things you might prefer I didn't."

He touched her arm. "Jen, you—"

She whirled and struck his hand away. "Don't touch me," she snarled. "You've done so before, but I promise you, lord, you'll never touch me again."

She caught a glimpse of sudden comprehension on his face, then the expression vanished.

"I've never harmed you," he said. "And I've never tampered with your mind—though the gods know, had I done so when you first came to me, so much would have been easier."

She heard that, appalled. He admitted, *admitted* such a terrible thing. How could she have ever doubted, ever flinched from what she planned to do now?

The stone lay near, black, silent, waiting, only a few steps away. She backed a step toward it, then another. Her master followed. She darted around the stone, putting it between them. Amazing that he allowed it, that he did not seize her with magic as Palimur had. Maybe he thought to lull her with his restraint and so snare her when she least expected, in her weakness, in her sleep—

Jen shook away the rest.

"Listen to me, Jen," he said quite, quite calmly. "You need to understand what happened."

The stone came only as high as her breast. She put her hands upon it, felt its coldness, its forbidding will, mantled, hidden, still.

"But I do understand, lord. Shall I tell you what you didn't want me to remember?"

Oh, yes, he knew exactly what she was talking about.

"You were confused." He took a step nearer and spoke in that same, ridiculously calm voice, when he should be growing very worried indeed. "I told you that. I was relieved you'd lost the memory, because of what you'd already gone through."

She drew her hands back a little, curled the fingers against the stone's black, iridescent surface. "Yet that didn't stop you from putting me through it again," she said in a voice of false cheerfulness.

He drew breath to speak, hand outstretched, pleading.

She lashed out and caught her master's wrist, thrust his hand down upon the stone's surface. "Stone, this is my master, who I've told you so much about."

Her master's eyes went wide. For once, she felt the pure, clear leap of his fear. He tried to snatch his hand away, but the stone already held him fast.

Strong, the stone commented even as its magic poured around them in a dark, irresistible current.

"What are you doing, Jen?" Her master's eyes roiled with shock, horror…and sorrow?

Her heart briefly quaked, then turned flinty again. Sorrow at his own predicament, no doubt. Sorrow that he was about to succumb to his lowly apprentice.

"Stronger than Palimur, I'll wager," she answered the stone. "Though I'm by no means certain." To her master, she explained, "Palimur came to visit me yesterday. He thought, to use an expression from the streets, he'd caught me with my breeches down. He also thought he could extort certain favors."

Her master closed his eyes.

"He underestimated me," Jen went on. "And the strength and lore I have to draw on."

He opened his eyes again. Desperation tattered the edges of his calm. "You must realize," he said, low and intense, "that if the Prince thinks you've done his wizard harm, you'll be in great danger. You'll be branded a rogue. Then it won't be an apprentice-binding you'll suffer, but the annihilation of your powers."

She leaned a casual elbow on the stone. "I hope the Prince does know. What will he do, send more wizards? That'll please the stone."

"Stop this now, Jen. This spirit, the thing in this stone is more danger to you than is any man."

He seeks to frighten you, the stone said.

Currents of magic churned the air, raising sparks that crackled when she moved, lifting the hair on her head. In the deepening twilight, Jen thought she saw a sheen of sweat on her master's face.

"Ah, yes," she said, nodding. "Such spirits are dire and perilous things, I seem to remember you telling me. Yet this spirit, this stone has done me nothing but good. It has never compelled me. It taught me the kind of magic I should have been using all along. It gave me freedom from you. It rescued me from Palimur when he would've forced upon me what you did."

Her master's hand had disappeared to the wrist beneath the stone's surface, yet he met her gaze as if he could still reason with her. "Only one man has ever forced himself upon you, Jen." He said in a voice like a hand smoothed down an anguished child's cheek. "I am not he. I am not your father."

With those words, he might have struck her. Her face stung with the leap of blood and shock and shame.

"Shut up!" she screamed. "You don't know! You don't know anything about my father!"

"I've known from the first day I brought you to my house. And I've never harmed you. I've never hurt you as he did."

She saw her father's lank blond hair; his eyes, small and mean as a boar's; his hard, thin lips that had opened so often to speak words of cruelty.

Jen lurched into a pace, up and down, blind to everything but memory. "I should've killed him. For Dee. For Ma. For Jenei. I shoulda killed him, but I only burned 'im an' run away."

Her master's voice came, maddening in its persistent gentleness. "You wouldn't have killed him. You had the power to do so even then, yet you didn't."

"And I had t' go back again," she went on, locked in the old nightmare. "Jenei was only a kid, only a girl. Where else'd she go that wasn't the same—or worse? I had t' go back to take care of her."

"I took you away from there."

She rounded on him. "You took my freedom, you made me helpless again! What else did I have, but knowing I was stronger than him?"

"I took you from a place where your power would have grown twisted," he said. "Once I'd found you, I didn't have a choice. You must understand that."

He lies, the stone whispered. Its voice echoed chill as hatred.

She cocked her head. "The stone says you lie, lord. I'm inclined to believe it."

"How does it know whether I lie or tell the truth?" Her master was panting now, his arm consumed to the elbow. He took a breath and his next words came steadier.

"That spirit can't enter my mind. If it could, it would speak its words through me. Words to isolate you. As it's doing now. Who is here with you now, Jen, besides this spirit?"

She thought of Burn's desertion, of her brother's. Of Col's accusations and Dee's. She frowned. "I don't need anyone else."

"You don't trust anyone else. And while this spirit trickles poison into your mind, you never will."

For a moment, Jen couldn't gain air enough to form words.

"Trust!" she finally gasped. "I remember! *I remember* what happened. You'll talk to me of trust when you—you *raped* me—"

"Not I." He shook his head hard. "*Never*. But this spirit with which you have allied yourself will rape you far more thoroughly than any man ever could. It will rape you of your soul. Look at what it's doing to you now. Can you feel anything but rage and hate? Do you want to spend the centuries of your wizard's lifetime in the thrall of this stone, consumed by the evil done you as a young girl? See what I see when I look at you. Look!"

Before she could resist or appeal to the stone, her mind was sucked into her master's, just as it had been that first night. But this time, instead of the flickering magic-lantern images of her own thoughts and memories, she lived his thoughts, saw through his eyes.

Through him, she saw a young woman bright with potential, testing, growing into power like a young dragon spreading wings to flash and soar against the sun. She felt his pride and pleasure, disappointment and frustration and despair. Jen struggled, not wanting to know what he felt, not wanting that terrible intimacy. Felt a warmth—

She flung herself out of the link. Her face was wet.

He intrudes, the stone said. *He invades.*

And he had bound her. Taken her freedom.

Robbed you, the stone whispered. *Violated you.*

That truth lived in her mind, in her heart. There, there, seething in the pit of her soul: terror, rage, disgust, shame—

Jen ground the heels of her palms against her eyes, blocking out the stone room, erasing the feel of hands upon her.

"You've always cared for others," her master said from somewhere beyond the darkness. "What are you doing now, Jen? Will you follow in your father's footsteps, becoming a rapist as he was?"

"I'm nothing like Da!" she shouted. An echo from yesterday. "*Nothing!*"

He shut his eyes, bared his teeth as against terrible pain, or immense effort. Magic clashed in a subliminal roar, sending tremors through the very ground.

Her master opened his eyes again. "Will you let the evil done you turn you to evil? Will you rape me of my wizardry, of my life, as your father raped you of your trust and peace?"

Voices swirled down upon her like a slashing current, hurling her against memory.

The merchant Verin saying: *I want him never to be able to do again what he did to my girl—*

And the stone, whispering, whispering into her mind: *You are strong. Do as you wish. The wizard cannot resist you.*

"No," Jen whispered as well, spinning, buffeted.

Men hurt you, the stone said, implacable. *Leave them to me, and they will hurt you no more.*

"Don't let this spirit prey on your weakness," her master said.

The wizard will make you helpless again. He relishes your fear.

Jen blinked, aware of a sudden dissonance, feeling a dreadful cold descend upon her. Though she had feared him, her master had never taken notice of that fear, never used it against her. The stone, however...

"*You* relish my fear," she whispered. "You promise freedom, but I can't leave here. If I do, the Prince—"

With abrupt and shattering clarity, she saw then how Palimur's destruction had invited the Prince's wrath. And she wasn't strong enough to stand up to him. Not without the stone. Choice by choice, she'd bound herself to it as tightly as her master had ever bound her—more tightly. In teasing her along with the lure of strength, of safety, the stone had chained her, made her weak, put her in danger.

Seeing that, doubt seized her. Doubt of her own memories, those the stone had returned to her.

Once more, she took herself through those dark, terrible moments after she had conjured the sign of the Fey.

There had been the dimness of the stone room, and her master with her in that dimness. She had thrown fire at him, fire that he had brushed aside as a man would brush aside a child's flailing fists. She had fled him—

Jen ran up hard against realization.

And he hadn't pursued her. He could've snatched her back in that instant. Yet he hadn't. Hadn't Called her until later. In her disgust and horror, she hadn't recognized that single, obvious lapse. And that lapse, that incongruity, called into question every interpretation, every assumption, every dread she had of her master then. Every dread she'd had for five years.

Memory built on memory. Marin feeding her bread and fruit in the orangery. Her master speaking to her there, gently, quietly. Even now, even before the stone had seized him, he had not threatened her as Palimur had.

Jen stared at the stone, then at her master. His arm was consumed almost to the shoulder. She felt the strain of his wizardry against it, felt the stone's dark hunger devouring bit by bit her master's considerable power.

She'd never planned what had happened to Palimur, but she'd deliberately lured her master here. She'd desired his fear, hungered for his pain, craved his weakness. Choice by choice, action by action, she had willingly turned herself into that which she hated most—a man who induced weakness in others, then fed on that weakness. A man who tormented those unable to resist him, unable to escape him.

Jen would not be that man.

She tore off the seeming of Arjen. Ripping away wards and guards, fendings and protections, abandoning every shred of magic she'd gathered to defend herself, she collected her magic, clenched it, readied it like a fist drawn back for a swing. Instinct told her to hurl the fiercest fire she possessed at the stone. But Palimur, with his greater power, had done so to no avail. Palimur, however, had not known what she knew. He hadn't known of a hunger greater even than the stone's.

She shut out desperation, narrowed the focus of her will and power to a single point as bright and hot as a kiln fire. Her hand rose slowly, tingling, light with her wizardry. Her fingers, curled as if beckoning, sketched a hook, a loop, a sign in the air, a sign that glowed with all the power she could feed it: the sign of the Fey.

The stone's attention fell on her with crushing force. *What do you do?* Its mind-voice rumbled like an earthquake.

"Jen, don't," her master said on a gasped breath.

Once before, by the lip of a well, down in the dark of another stone-walled room, the stone had gripped her with its power, had promised to trap her there in the dark. But Jen had already been trapped in the dark, had been since she was a girl of thirteen. The stone had reveled in the darkness that lived within her. Had fed upon it, cultivated it as a farmer cultivates plump, succulent mushrooms.

And so now she did not fight the stone's grip, that power of earth and darkness, but instead let it swell her own darkness, let it fill her and pour out again into the sign, feeding the sign what it sought. The sign pulsed and swelled in its own turn, blazing with its illusory glare in the air above the stone.

"Let him go," she said, or thought she said; the roar of powers deafened her, the rush of magicks overwhelmed sight and sensation.

He is mine, the stone said, a gathering thunder of landslide. *You brought him to me, strength to feed my strength, magic to fill me.*

"You tricked me!"

You gave yourself to me.

"I belong to myself. Not to you, not to fear."

The wizard will possess you.

"Like you tried to?"

We are kin.

"We are not kin. You're evil and hate. I won't let you turn me into what you are."

You have not the strength to resist.

Jen only cocked a bitter, one-sided smile.

Power poured into her and out again, an ungovernable current. She sensed the blaze of the sign upon her skin—

And something more, something new. Blind and deaf, she reached out wizard's senses, molded, scented. That new force danced an arrhythmic beat against her breast like a second heart, quivering and burning with the magic that seethed all around.

She barricaded the sensation from her awareness and concentrated on the flows around her: her own power, now only a passive channel that received and directed the massive strength with which the stone pummeled her; her master's wizardry, blazing bright against the stone's irresistible pull; and the sign, sucking into itself all her own magic, that of her master, the stone's magic.

You will destroy yourself, the stone said.

"That I may, stone. But not before I banish you."

The stone's power increased to a raging flood, slashing at her wizardry, lapping past the limits of her mind. Suddenly, she was no longer channeling its power, but drowning in a black tide as endless as an ocean.

You are a fool, the stone roared, battering her mind. *You name me hate and evil, but you name me wrong, wizard-woman. I am emptiness. I am destruction. I am born of the night before the beginning of all things, and will birth the night that will be after the end of all things. It is as far beyond your power to banish me as it is for you to banish death and darkness. I was, I am, I always will be.*

Jen, only a bobbing spark against the stone, saw the truth at last and despaired. Her heart struggled against the stone's force, crushed and stilled as surely as if thrust to the roots of a mountain. As if to mock her, that second heart rapped at her breastbone, twitching and straining like a fish on a line. She clutched at that motion as if at a guide-rope in darkness, without thought, without hope.

A voice lanced into her mind like searing light. *Use it!* Not the hollow voice of the stone, but her master's, familiar and suddenly welcome when always before it had been unwelcome.

Heartbeat by heartbeat, she succumbed to the crush of the stone's will. The being that was Jen writhed and twisted, squeezed toward the instant of annihilation.

A word, like a single bubble welling upward through deep water, formed in the dimness of her mind: *Use?* Then another: *What?*

Her master's voice came faint and faraway. *What hangs around your neck—it's resonating to the magic. Take it out! Use it!*

She forced her consciousness outward, a single glowing thread creeping into her flesh. Shadows played against her retinas. Pain cut into the flesh of her hand, her neck, the pain of muscles clenched too tight, the pain of metal cutting skin. Heat. The spitting flare of magic. Only her eyes would move, and they pulled downward, toward the pain in her hand fisted over her chest, closed around—

The obsidian knife.

The words of the magic that enwrapped it screamed suddenly into her mind: *Cut the cloth of mortality, walk the ways of infinity.* Other voices, other memories: her sister Dee saying, *It's the key, you know.* The *Malimidion's* cryptic words: *Ply the edge that sunders the fabric of the world.*

With a flash of hope, she finally understood.

At once, she sent every particle of will blazing along the muscles of her arm and into her hand. She pulled the knife free. Her mortal body, her mortal mind that commanded a wizard's power, struggled for light, for breath, for life. She shut away that mortal like the unruly animal it was. There was only the knife, her hand, and power.

In the heart of seething darkness, otherworldly fire crawled along the knife's fragile, unsheathed blade. From the sign, hoarded energy rushed in a flow of incandescent color, swirling around the blade in an ever-widening vortex. Color pushed back darkness until she seemed to float suspended in a bubble of time.

The shapes of the garden hung in eternal purple twilight, distorted at the edges, drawn to the knife in her upraised hand. Below lay the stone, black, massive, malignant. And arrested in a grimace of pain and effort, her master, his face turned, straining away from the stone. The sign of the Fey blazed, relinquishing the power it had so greedily consumed.

In a single savage thrust, Jen unleashed all will, all wizardry. The knife went plunging down, down, ripped through glowing air and toward the core of blackness that was the stone.

The bubble burst, spewed time and being across the world in a splash of spinning color.

"Use it!" her master was shouting, voice cracked as if he'd been screaming.

With its whirling maelstrom of color, the knife plunged into the stone, all Jen's weight and strength and will behind it.

As if the world were a scene painted on a silk shawl, fragile and rippling on the currents of time, the knife split that fabric, whipped those currents into a maelstrom that widened, widened, until it swallowed the stone...

And pitched Jen, pinwheeling after, into a void shot through with otherworldly light. She screamed and tumbled into a nowhere and nowhen lacking up or down, here or there, now or then. A void in which she would never hit bottom, an endless floating through eternity.

Well, Jen, a detached sliver of her mind said. *Looks like you found your gateway to the Otherworlds.*

But no, she wasn't floating after all, but falling, for the bright flashes and snatches of other realities streaked away, converging on infinity. There came a jolt, a searing pain, then nothingness imploded upon her.

Chapter 20

She smelled lavender. Lavender and balsam. Jen breathed, savoring scents she scarcely would've expected to awaken to at the bottom of her long fall through nothing. Her master…and the stone…

She opened her eyes.

No garden. No master. And no stone. Instead, a rumpled landscape of bedclothes stretched away in rose and periwinkle and dropped over the edge of a bed. The same colors, but in richer tones—flame and midnight—resumed in a backdrop of curtains partially drawn over small-paned windows.

The windows of her own bedroom in her master's house.

Jen's heart gave a squeeze, a mixture of astonishment and relief and dismay. And with it came a seamless recollection of what she had almost done, and to whom.

"Oh, no," she said. Or meant to say, for the words came out as a moan.

Beyond her field of vision came the creak of a chair, the rustle of clothing. She tried to twist to see who shared the room with her, but only managed to roll her head. A hand touched her forehead, her cheek, then gently turned her.

"Marin," Jen said, but once more, the only sound that came out was, "Mmm."

The older woman smiled. "Yes, child." She stroked Jen's hair. Tears slipped down cheeks still rosy as a farm-wife's. "Be still. You're safe, and you'll be well soon enough. Here."

She raised Jen with motherly efficiency, propped her against an angular shoulder. Jen sagged like a tinker's sack.

"Take a sip," Marin said, holding a cup to her lips.

Jen smelled bitter medicine in the wine and made a noise of protest.

"No argument from you. Drink, else you'll be bedridden twice as long than if you'd been a good girl."

Jen could only laugh, the first real laugh in a very long time, though it came out as weak coughing. Marin tilted Jen forward and rapped her on the back, scolding and crying the while.

お

After three days, Jen was able to sit up and feed herself. The bright hot flame of her wizardry burned low and sullen, like a banked fire of dung. Half-dozing in a chair, warm in the sunlight that poured through her bedroom window, that idea grew into a dream of such a fire.

She dreamt she was a child sitting on the dirt floor of her house, playing rock-paper-knife with Dee and winning every game. The room reeked of the smell of burning grass, but it was warm, and the occasional gust of wind across the smoke hole cleared the murky air. Her mother sat on a stool near the fire humming a random, tuneless string of notes as she sewed. Her father sat on the opposite side of the fire, sober for once and showing the three middle boys how to whittle. It was a strange, rare, precious dream, a forgotten moment of peace scavenged from some dusty closet of her memory. She looked up when her mother touched her, caressed her neck…

And woke. Jen blinked and lifted her head. Marin was smoothing ointment on the back of her neck where the chain she'd made for the obsidian knife had cut her. In all that final nightmare of fire and darkness and magic, she could not recall that moment of what must have been considerable pain. The knife, too, seemed to have vanished, and she'd had neither the heart nor the will to ask about it.

But, gathering her courage, she asked about her master.

"He's tired," Marin told her. "Like you, but not as bad. After Master brought you home, Elmanel cleared out half the pantry and had the kitchen staff scurrying to feed him. Being a witch, Elmanel knows all about that sort of thing, I suppose. And I daresay Master slept the clock around that first day, but he seems well enough now. Far be it from me to say what to expect or not expect from wizards after their adventures."

"And…" Jen said. "And…" She twisted her fingers together. "Has he said anything about me?"

Marin left off anointing her neck, folded her arms and studied her with a calculating eye. "Only to ask how you are, same as you're asking how he is."

Jen plucked at the knots of cream-colored thread that tufted the quilt in her lap.

"Shall I tell Master you're asking for him?" Marin asked at last.

"Yes," Jen blurted. Then, "No. Yes."

"Is it yes, or no?" Marin asked with a quirk of a smile.

"Marin, I—" Jen began, then closed her mouth and looked away again.

The older woman waved an impatient hand. "Yes, yes, I know. You ran away and got into some trouble or other, and here Master comes home carrying you in his arms, the two of you looking like you're fresh from under an overturned carriage. You've caused Master a great deal of trouble, child, but I think you've suffered trouble as well. But after a storm, there's no point moaning and carrying on about the mess. You just have to go outside into the new sunshine, rehang the shutters and patch the thatch on the roof."

Jen wasn't moaning or carrying on, but she squeezed her eyes shut against the tears running fast down her face, gulped down sob after silent sob. Not in sorrow for the trouble she'd suffered, but for the suffering she'd caused others, too many others, blind and heartless in her rage and fear.

Marin's arms came around her, cradled her face against a shoulder smelling of pressed linen. "Cry those tears now, Jen, love, then leave them behind. Leave them and go on."

She rocked Jen like a child, murmuring words she'd no doubt murmured to her own children when they'd suffered a broken heart or done something foolish on a dare and been caught.

The wrongs Jen had done were immeasurably greater, but she was content, in her weakness, to rest in Marin's assurances.

The older woman finally righted Jen and rearranged her in the chair. Dabbing at Jen's face with a clean handkerchief, she said, "Now, wait here a moment. There's something I think will make you smile." In a whisper of skirts, Marin rose and bustled from the room.

The door opened again presently. A low yellow shape burst through and came bounding in, nails scrabbling on polished oak floors. A heavy set of forequarters landed in Jen's lap.

"Burn!" she cried, laughing, while he made little dog-sounds of joy and assaulted her face with his tongue while wagging both tail and hindquarters with wild vigor.

Abruptly, she remembered Burn's refusal to enter any wizard's house. With a sinking chill, she reached out to touch his mind. She grabbed his ears with gentle fondness, looked into that bright-eyed, laughing face and said wonderingly, "You're not bound."

"No," her master's voice said. "He's come of his own accord."

Jen started. Except for the night he'd first brought her here, her master had never come into her room. He looked much now as he had then, wearing dark colors and a sober floor-length coat, yet somehow incongruous, like an unsheathed sword on a lady's bed. An old and persistent fear scrabbled at her ribs at seeing him here, in her room, while she sat deserted by both bodily strength and magic. Yet neither the strength nor the magic she possessed had ever been sufficient to resist him.

No, she reminded herself sternly. There had never been a need to resist him.

Her master pulled a chair near hers and gestured at Burn. "The gardener saw him hanging about the gate after I brought you in, and when he opened it, the dog entered, though with tail tucked and belly close to the ground. He's been a fixture at the front door since." He wiggled his fingers and Burn swept the rug with his tail.

Jen smoothed a hand along Burn's head. She swallowed once and said, "Lord, I've wronged you."

"Yes," he agreed quietly. "And I've wronged you, as well. I didn't understand your humiliation over the fact that I paid your father gold to take you. Nor the depth of your resentment of the binding I laid upon you."

Jen only shook her head, unable to tell him what Dee had been sold into, unwilling to speak of her fear of any man who held such power over her.

"Once I understood," he went on, "I couldn't set you free. You're too powerful, and were too consumed by darkness. There resided in you too great a potential for evil. I had a responsibility to minimize the harm you could do—to yourself, and to others."

She could understand that. She had, after all, done harm, done...evil.

Jen risked a glance up at him. The question that had harrowed her for five years struggled to escape even as she dreaded the asking of it. "Then you didn't buy me for—to be your mate?"

He regarded her for a long moment, so long that she at last dropped her gaze again.

"Once," he said, "I loved a woman. We wielded our wizardry together, in joy. Like you, she was rare and precious, a rose cut from brilliant ruby. But I do not buy such things. They come to me...or they do not."

That moment of confrontation in the stone's garden returned, that surfacing from the darkness into which she'd descended, seeing herself as her master saw her, feeling—feeling the—the warmth he felt for her. She reached out to him quickly.

Her hand stopped. A slight move forward and she would touch his sleeve, texture of its embroidery, the warmth of the arm beneath. But her hand hovered there, frozen, held back as if by a scar old and drawn.

Her hand fell.

He bowed his head, and she heard a breath go out of him. After a moment, he rose, clasped his hands behind him, stood looking down upon her. "You are free."

Her fingers knotted in the quilt that draped her lap. Jen tried to read his face, his aura. Both defied her.

"Free?" she repeated.

"You've completed your masterwork—the master-work I set for you. You had allowed your fear and anger to rule you, controlling your actions and tainting your perspective. If you were ever to attain true mastery, you had to learn to rise above both, to see through and beyond them."

It was hard to meet his eyes, but neither could she drop her gaze.

"Under the circumstances," he continued, "I can scarcely expect you to immediately cast off..." His fingers rose, then fell. "...all you've borne. But the fact that you understand now, that you're no longer blindly driven..." He smiled a little. That much emotion peeked through, a wistfulness. "You no longer need me to govern you. You're capable of governing yourself."

She'd spent five years dreaming of freedom. Made countless attempts at escape. Had pursued the flashing, fleeing lure of the Otherworlds as her only hope of freedom, all without recognizing the more profound binding she'd suffered before her master came and took her away. No passage to the Otherworlds, no gathering of power would have allowed her to escape that older, hidden binding, invisible even to her.

"I—I'm free?" she asked again with the stupidity of sheer astonishment.

He nodded once, his expression once more closed, unreadable.

She fumbled though the depths of her mind, seeking the binding that had lain there so long it had chafed furrows in her psyche. But there was no sense of restraint, no sense of the *other* that had always watched, sensing every quiver of her power.

"Free," she whispered. Tears pricked at the corners of her eyes. She stroked Burn again, but he was looking up at her master, head cocked and ears pricked. She followed the dog's gaze.

"Thank you, lord," she said. "Thank you."

He made an impatient gesture, but made no move to go. At last he said, "If you choose to ply your trade in the City, I would counsel you not to do so as Arjen. As far as the Prince is concerned, I destroyed Arjen, the man who murdered Palimur, in our confrontation."

She swallowed a sick knot. "Yes, lord," she said in a strained whisper. "And—and the stone?"

"You'd know what happened to it better than I, since you opened the gateway that swallowed it. Where did it lead?"

"To emptiness," Jen said. "A dark place streaked with lights and colors. I thought I'd be falling forever..." She was afraid to ask how she'd come to awaken in her own room.

He gave a single, short laugh, then answered her unspoken question with his typical insight. "I suppose then you'll find some cause to be glad of my binding over you. That connection allowed me to pull you back."

He left the room then, the hem of his coat belling gently behind him.

Chapter 21

"Why?" Marin demanded. "Why are you leaving?"

Jen looked up from the pile of clothes scattered across her bed—boy's clothes, tunics and hose, shirts and breeches, jackets and caps. She still couldn't abandon them, not now, not when she'd be going out into the world.

Fists on hips, cheeks flushed, Marin faced her across the bed.

"How can I stay?" Jen said.

"Why, you just stay. This is your home, Jen. I love you as much as one of my own daughters. Even that foolish fluffhead, Wynne, was distraught after you left. And can't you see how Master cares—"

Jen closed her eyes and held up a hand. "Marin, you don't know what I did while I was gone." She did not want to think of how she had been the betrayer, when she'd convinced herself that she'd been the one betrayed. She hadn't seen her master again in the two days since he'd freed her, though her thoughts kept turning to him in a roil of confusion she couldn't begin to sort out.

She opened her eyes again to find Marin's gaze gone hard.

"D'you think you're the only one in the world ever to do things she regretted?" Marin demanded. "Or that love flies away when one we love stumbles and falls?"

"If you knew—" Jen stopped, then gritted her teeth and grimly plowed on. "No, I'll tell you. I would've become that spirit's willing tool. I would've allowed it to kill my master and after that, do you think there's anything I *wouldn't* have done? Anything I wouldn't take if I wanted, anyone I wouldn't sweep aside if I were threatened or thwarted? With the power that stone gave me, I would've become a monster."

"Nonsense and twaddle," Marin snapped. "Look here. I know perfectly well what this is all about. Running and hiding." She folded her arms and gave a stiff nod. "Yes, running and hiding. You barricaded yourself under your bed like a wild animal when Master first brought you. You're no better now! Only instead of filling the room with spells to keep us all away, now you're using guilt. Will you go through your whole life jumping up and bolting whenever anyone begins to grow close?"

"Marin, I—"

"Master's tried, and he can't stop you, so one old woman certainly won't." Her lip began to quiver. "You might have yourself convinced you're doing us a favor, but I hope you know you're breaking hearts, girl." Her face crumpled suddenly.

Jen dropped the clothes she still held. "Marin," she said, moving around the bed.

But Marin snatched up her apron to cover her face and hurried to the door, fumbling with the latch before she managed to escape.

Jen, who could've stopped her ten ways with a thought, listened to her footsteps flee down the hallway.

Eventually, she wandered back to the bed and its pile of clothes, stared down at the strewn things, some folded and ready to go into a knapsack, others too gaudy or too fine for a journeyman wizard starting out on an unknown road.

She picked up a sheepskin vest, one of the things she had bought at the clothier's a month ago for this very journey. She stared at it for a moment that seemed to sink into a bog at the center of her heart, then finally stuffed the vest into the knapsack. After it went other things. Soon, she found the knapsack bulging without any real idea of what had gone into it.

Dressed in her traveler's garb of breeches, sturdy boots, short coat and plain cap, Jen looked once more around the room that had been hers for five years: the high bed, the fireplace of pale stone, the diamond-paned windows with their rectangles of red and blue stained glass. Strange that she should be leaving again, fleeing again—

Jen picked up a glove that had fallen to the floor. No. Not fleeing. Marin might think so, but she was only doing exactly what she'd planned, dreamed of, for five years. And her burden of guilt—it might be lighter, if only by a little, when she was gone from those she had wronged.

And Col, too, faithful brother, though she would first have to find him to tell him—

She shut her eyes. To tell him he'd been right. Like Dee.

But she'd never find Dee. Not when she most wanted to offer Dee some repayment, yet was least able to give it. For where would even a wizard look for a ghost, a memory, a pang of conscience?

She sighed, hefted the knapsack and went out.

Wynne stood in the hallway, holding a basket of clean clothes and linens and looking like she'd been caught idling.

"Oh! You aren't leaving already, are you? I was going to put these things away first, but we have to talk before you go." Basket on hip, she trotted by Jen's side.

"So, where'll you go?" Without giving Jen time to answer, she went on, "You know, it can never be as interesting as here. Did I tell you about Bran and Mira? Oh! Everybody's talking about it, and he's, what, only thirteen? Got two or three more years wishing for his first whisker, anyway. You should've seen his face when he left Alannan's workroom. Red as rhubarb, let me tell you! I bet Alannan told him some things he didn't know could happen!"

Jen nodded where appropriate, made appreciative noises and tried to keep from running into Wynne, who somehow kept getting in front of her.

Alannan, the steward, came into view at the bottom of the stairs.

Wynne dipped a flustered curtsey. "Oh...sir...I was just...um..."

"Putting the linens away," Jen suggested.

"Yes," Wynne said and slipped away, snatching a worried glance back over her shoulder.

Jen hoisted her pack and descended the stairs.

Looking down on her from his immaculate height, Alannan said, "All ready to go, are we?"

Jen shrugged. "Ready as I'll ever be."

He eyed the lumpy knapsack. "Forgive me if I suggest you might be just a bit short on planning." He produced a belt pouch, held it out to her. "Even journeyman wizards need money. Lord Barras asked me to be sure you have some."

Her face heated. She reached to take the pouch, but Alannan didn't quite put it in her grasp.

"However," he said with an arched brow, "I will say that if it were up to me, I'd insist that you delay to think this through more thoroughly than you clearly have." He finally relinquished the belt pouch.

Jen took the excuse of fastening it around her waist to avoid his eye. She mumbled, "Yes, well, you're probably right."

"Of course he's right," a scratchy voice said.

She looked up to see Elmanel, the kitchen witch, followed by Kitty and a handful of the scullions. The entry hall suddenly seemed very full of people.

"Here." Elmanel gestured impatiently, and Kitty handed Jen a skin of drink and a larger bag.

Tugging at the drawstring, Jen peered in to see a number of parcels, neatly wrapped and tied with string. Spells teased her senses even as the muted odors of herbs and bread and pepper teased her nose—spells to keep food fresh and tasty, no matter the days and the heat and the abuses of travel.

"Thank you." She looked up at Elmanel, his freckled arms crossed, the witch-knots in his hair bristling. He frowned as if she'd burst into his kitchen and dumped the salt cellar into his most delicate sauce.

"Y' shoulda come to me and got this stuff, and not made me tromp clear out here with half the kitchen staff, leaving things to burn or curdle or any other disaster that can happen while I'm not around to keep an eye on 'em."

The looks on the assorted scullions' faces were those they might have worn had they been responsible for such disasters. Kitty's broad, plain face kept stretching and scrunching, as if she were struggling to hold something in.

Jen felt the same something twist at a painful angle in her chest. "Thank you," she said again, her voice thin and unsteady.

Turning quickly, she headed for the front door. Burn lay outside, head on paws. Perin, the stablehand, stood just beyond.

"You'll need this too," Perin said, holding out a businesslike knife in a worn leather scabbard. "An' I don't want to hear no more pretty words out of you," he said when Jen opened her mouth to thank him, too. "Just take it and welcome."

She set down her bundles to stick the knife in her boot, then awkwardly gathered them up again. The gathering and arranging gave her something practical to think about, an excuse to avoid all those eyes fixed imploringly upon her.

"I think I'll need a horse," she muttered as she draped and burdened herself like a pack animal.

"We got only two," drawled Perin. "And though I like you well enough to give you one, Miss, I won't, 'cos I don't much fancy your leaving like this."

Straightening at last, she found the hall filled with nearly all the servants in the house. Even Wynne had returned, her pretty face unbecomingly blotched with tears. Jen stared, amazed, humbled that these people could care whether she came or went.

Wynne sniffled. "Marin wouldn't come, but I'm sure she sends her love."

"I know she does," Jen whispered. Her chin started trembling. She pressed her lips tight together and clamped her jaw.

No one spoke for a long, awkward moment. A man's cough broke the silence, covering Wynne's sniffles and the sounds of shuffles and uncomfortable shiftings of weight.

Regret and sadness weighed heavier than all the gifts of goodwill she bore, the parcels and bags and pouches under which she could scarcely move.

Yet her master was not there. The knowledge that she had surely wounded him—not once, but perhaps many times—pierced her. Marin might be able to forgive some abstract misdeeds, but Jen could not expect him to, subject as he'd been to the worst of those offenses.

"Well," Jen said. Her voice creaked, and she cleared her throat. "Better go."

She stepped past Perin, head down, avoiding his gaze. Burn rolled his eyes up at her, brown and sad. Only when she passed his place on the porch did he heave himself to his feet with a sigh. Before her stretched the garden with its knee-high hedges of clipped box, its perfect rosebushes, its artful paths and benches, fountain and pool. The surrounding wall shone a benign gold in the early sunlight, the brass ornamentation of the gate flashing brighter.

Behind her came sounds of movement: the rustle of clothing, the tap of feet on a marble floor, the murmur of subdued voices. She knew better than to turn to look, knowing she would only see the people who'd been her family for so long dispersing to resume their workaday tasks.

Jen descended the steps as if wading through quicksand, one step, then the next, slower and slower still. She took the last step down. Gravel crunched under her feet. The bright sweep of the drive curved to the gate: a broad, clear way to the wide world beyond. Like her feet, her innards felt suddenly weighted with wet sand. Her boots remained on that one patch of gravel, refusing to carry her forward. Burn stood beside her, ears pricked.

Dee's voice whispered by her ear, "Look behind you."

At once, she spun to face the house. Alone, framed in the open doorway, her master stood looking down on her.

Dismay squeezed her heart; dismay and some springing, yet painful emotion. Burn's wagging tail swatted her leg.

"I'm still bound!" she cried.

Her master took a step forward, out onto the portico. Morning light fell upon him, firing the silver inlay of his buttons and the stitching of his coat. "It's no binding of mine."

Reaching out with wizard's senses, she touched walls, gate, the very air around her and found upon them nothing more than the same spells of ward and protection they'd always borne. She turned that sight inward where her power shifted and moved, dragonlike, in the corridors of her soul, but again, found her mind unfettered, unhindered.

Once more looking through mortal eyes, she frowned up at him. "I'm supposed to be able to go free."

He inclined his head in agreement. "So you are."

Jen turned away, trying to lift a foot, take a step—just one step!—toward freedom. "But I can't go!"

From behind her, his voice came: "Then stay."

She whirled again to face him, outraged, chagrined, confused.

"Stay," he said again, more gently. He held out his hand, long-fingered, graceful.

From the bottom of the steps, she stood staring at it for a long while, reminded of another day long ago when he had first held it out. She had crouched, terrified, on her cot in her stone room in her father's house. She had reached up then and without so willing it, had taken her master's hand. And now, she found herself climbing the steps she had so laboriously descended, found her hand rising from her side. It hesitated, palm over his palm.

Jen settled her hand in his. She didn't feel terror this time, but dizziness replaced the wet sand in her stomach with flurrying leaves and set her heart to thumping at her ribs.

Her small, thin hand rested in his; the neat, clever fingers curled around hers.

"Lord," she whispered, and a tremor ran through her that reached even her voice.

He reached out, almost, but not quite, touching her lips to still her.

For once, the inclination to flinch away was absent. She wondered at that.

"Barras," he corrected. "I'm no longer your master."

His stern-lined face was soft with a gentleness that made her at once wish to flee and to remain. She said nothing, could say nothing, balanced on the edge of flight, fearful of what words that gentleness might lead him to speak.

So she did not expect him to say, "Journeyman wizard, you've learned a kind of magic I never knew. Will you stay and teach me?"

The almost-terror whirled up and whisked away as if on a spell-wind. Relief rushed in its stead, relief in finding footing, a place to stand, a way to stay. Jen smiled, not her cold wizard's smile, but a smile like an uncovered treasure, a smile she quickly hid away.

"Yes, lord, I'd like that."

"Barras," he corrected her again and relieved her of a couple burdens, slinging the knapsack and drink skin over one shoulder.

Her hand still in his, Jen walked beside him, looking around a house as newly strange as the first time she'd entered it. Then, of course, she had been drawn in bewildered and dreading her fate.

The future still stretched winding and uncertain ahead. But the fear she felt now was a different sort. It was the sort of fear a creature locked half its life in a cellar must

feel when it first creeps out into the light to see spread before it the unfettered spaces and bright colors of the world.

Nails clicking on the marble floor, Burn trotted in behind them as if he knew where he belonged.

お

Also by Kathlena L. Contreras:

FAMILIAR MAGIC

Kathlena L. Contreras writing as K. Lynn Bay:

BLACKTHORNE

CHANCESHAPER

SPRINGTIME IN HADES

ABOUT THE AUTHOR

In other incarnations, Kathlena Contreras has been a small business owner, a copy editor for three nationally distributed magazines, editor of a small literary magazine, an assistant medical librarian and a data manager.

She currently lives with her husband, four dogs and assorted livestock on the edge of the woods above the valley east of Albuquerque, New Mexico, USA, the Land of Enchantment.

Kathlena also writes as K. Lynn Bay.

Visit flyingtigerpress.com